WILD FAE

THE FAE SERIES

JANE ARMOR

CHAPTER 1

Rella led her group of wild fae misfits through the groaning battlefield with a heavy heart. Now that the fighting was over, their work began. They'd save those they could and bring a swift end to those who asked for it.

Skirmishes between Casta and the Dark Emperor had grown fiercer and bloodier in recent weeks. The acrid stench of battle magic lay heavy in the air as they worked their way through the dead and the dying.

Moans of pain reached Rella's acute hearing. Leaving her companions to administer to the dying, she sought out the injured fae. The iron scent of blood and the fizzling blue battle magic of a dying light fae urged her forward. The warrior hid in the undergrowth, his handsome, chiseled features given up to his agony. Glittering prettily in the mud, his silver and blue armor declared him a young lord. He wore three medals, all given for bravery in battle. One such as this would be deeply mourned. The wound to his abdomen gaped open, causing his innards to fall into the dirt. There was little help for him. "Have pity, mistress. I must live!" he cried.

Cases like this were always the most difficult—beyond help, but refusing to acknowledge they were dying.

"He knows you're going to kill him," said Beatty, an ancient mountain elf, short of stature, but with elongated hands and feet. His brown wizened features challenged her to refute his wisdom. "It would be for the best, I'm thinking."

Rella looked into the dying fae's bright blue eyes. She sensed his magic was strong, but he was dying. Soon his magic would desert him in painful spurts until, with a final flash of light, it would leave him and he'd be gone. The fae warrior was young and full of determination. If they had the skills to heal him, such willpower could see him live a long and useful life. Every life saved eased Rella's guilt.

"What is your name?" she asked, kneeling by his side and taking his hand.

"Fedric, mistress, and I want to live. Help me," he said.

Her heart sank. Fedric's wound was beyond her considerable skills. "Do you know who I am?"

"You are the Dark Queen," he said.

This was not the first time she'd heard that name applied to her. Rella glanced at Beatty, who shrugged and turned his face from her. He'd already given his opinion on Fedric's chances, and it wasn't good.

"Ask Gimrir to come."

"He won't like it. Are you sure?" said Beatty, sheathing his sword with a clang.

She whipped around to face Beatty, her speed a warning of danger to the mountain elf. "Just do it," she snarled. Beatty left, muttering to himself. It was a difficult enough decision without him questioning her, but she understood why he did. Gimrir's magic was ancient and only used sparingly. He was a spirit of the sacred oaks, torn from his home by the war she'd started between her brother's kingdom of Casta and that abomination, the Dark Emperor.

Rella put her hand to the young light fae's forehead and felt his will to live. "Do you understand what it means if we heal you?"

His eyes sought hers, and she saw a glimmer of fear wiped away by firm resolve. "Aye, I must go dark. I must join your army."

"Nonsense. Whether you go dark or not will depend on how much dark magic we use to heal you," said Rella, inspecting his wound. "I don't have an army, and if I did, light fae would not be welcome. I don't know where these ideas spring from."

He grimaced. Rella moved her hand over his head, letting her dark green healing magic flow around him, giving him some relief from the pain. She dared not try to heal such a complicated wound on her own.

"I don't care about the price. I want to live."

Just then, Gimrir appeared out of the gathering gloom. Although he was almost seven feet tall, his beard reached to his knees, and he was dressed in homespun linen from head to toe. One glance proclaimed him a spirit-fae, for both he and his clothing were almost transparent. He was a dark fae so rare, few had ever seen his kind, and those who did saw no more than a momentary glimmer of light. Rella left her charge and went to where Gimrir stood under a clutch of rowan trees.

"Why do you want to save the boy, Rella?" Gimrir's deep voice was soft with compassion.

"He wants to live."

"Most creatures want to live, especially the young. That is not enough."

Rella sighed. "He has an attitude, and maybe not a good one, but his will is strong."

Gimrir lifted a questioning eyebrow as Rella struggled with a more satisfactory answer. "I don't know, Gimrir," she said, frustration raising her voice.

The spirit-fae leaned forward and patted her shoulder. "You're tired. It's been a long day for all of us. Very well, let me see him."

"Thank you." The spirit-fae had a reassuring way of making her feel that he always had her back.

Gimrir knelt by the young fae's side. "I don't know what I can do," he said, focusing on the young man's wound.

Rella saw Fedric's hand try to grasp the old man's sleeve. "I need to live," he said. "I will pay the price."

Gimrir looked into his eyes for what seemed like an age before turning to Rella. "We will try. I promise nothing."

Rella nodded and left him to his work while she continued with hers. All wounded fae gradually lost control of their magic energy unless healing took place. It spurted uncontrollably from their hands until they died. To see so many lifeless bodies, their magic lost forever, was a tragedy.

Here and there across the fields and forest floor, shows of magic energy separated the dead from the dying. They managed to save four others that day and send them home. The price was always the same, whether they were dark fae or light fae. They each swore never to fight against Rella or her companions, known to all as the wild fae and made up of dark fae refugees and outlaws. No fae would break that promise for fear of rejection in the afterlife.

Unfortunately, Rella and her crew had to dispatch far more than they saved. It was always thus.

As they worked, Rella kept her guard up. She was sure the Dark Emperor's army had retreated beyond this forest to the untamed lands at the foot of the mountains, but she was ever alert. If one of his scouting parties were to capture her, it would be a great victory for them, and all her plans would come to naught.

Recently, the light fae had not been so diligent at tracking her movements. She suspected they knew where she was, but weren't eager to capture her and hand her over to the Dark Emperor. That would bring an end to the war. Which meant someone at the court of Casta wanted this war to continue. She refused to believe it was her brother, King Calstir, despite his betrayal.

Rella still blamed herself for starting this war. She would end it on her terms. To do so, she must kill the Dark Emperor, and so free the dark fae from his oppressive rule.

Rella and her companions made sure they left the battlefield before relatives of the dead arrived to claim their bodies. Sometimes the wild fae were late leaving. When that happened, they would have to hide and watch the recovery of the dead. That was hard on them. The keening cries of relatives when they discovered a loved one shredded their nerves. Especially if it was someone they had mercifully dispatched to the afterlife. Tonight, however, was a good night. They had saved those they could, brought mercy to those who asked for it, and taken Fedric with them. The healing he required would be too complicated for the battle-field. Perhaps she should have listened to Beatty after all.

Back at their encampment, Rella entered the dim interior of her tent and warmed her bathwater with a wave of her fingers. It had taken some time, but she was no longer reluctant to use her dark magic to its fullest potential. When she stepped into the warm water scented with rose and mint, she thought of Dagstyrr, and the bath they had shared before mating for the first time.

A mating that had bound them together, forever.

Where was he? Had he forgiven her yet for leaving him? She laid her head back, letting the warm water soothe her aching limbs. She imagined him at the prow of the *Knucker*, sailing fast and free with the wind in his hair toward Hedabar with Captain Bernst commanding the *Mermaid* and the *Viper* bringing up the rear. How many more, she wondered, had he managed to recruit in his mission to save the dragon Drago and his family?

"One hundred and sixty-eight dragons, not counting hatchlings or eggs." She quoted the number of dragons in Hedabar's dungeons. To free them all seemed an impossible task for any human, but Dagstyrr of Halfenhaw was no ordinary human. One day she would see the sky darken with the flight of dragons. When that day came, she'd stop whatever she was doing and go to him. For then, his promise to free Drago would be fulfilled, and they could be together. First, however, she must do her part and put an end to this war by putting an end to the Dark Emperor.

Emerging from the water and dressing in a simple tunic of unembellished forest green, she left her tent to walk the camp. In her imagination, Dagstyrr walked with her, and in her mind, she pointed out things of interest to him. She missed him far more than she would have thought possible. His absence was like a void deep within her psyche.

The wild fae camp was growing every day. She no longer had to recruit. Dark fae refugees flocked to her banner. Some were full of impossible hopes, but many were merely sick of living under the cruelty of their self-styled emperor.

Once the Dark Emperor was gone, the dark fae would

return to the benevolent reign of their chosen queen, whoever she might be. With a Dark Queen on the throne of Thingstyrbol once more, peace would descend upon the world. Both light and dark fae would return to their homes and live in tenuous harmony.

The camp Rella walked through was a myriad of fae beings. She had not seen so many different fae since the prison cells in the citadel in Hedabar.

A woman approached. From the look of her, she was a dark fae halfling and worked hard for her living. Her hands were red and callused, her step heavy. "Mistress Rella, might I do your laundry? I do a good job. See here?" The woman lifted her basket to show off the snowy white linen inside.

Rella didn't need a laundress. However, she did want to get to know the dark fae and halflings in her charge. "What is your name?"

"Polly, mistress," she said with a curtsey.

"Very well. What can I give you for your services?"

"My daughter's just birthed her first babe. I'd happily exchange a year of cleaning linen for a good knife. It is for his dedication ceremony."

Rella smiled. She slipped a black knife from her belt. Chased in silver filigree, it was sharp as well as decorative. Perfect for a young dark fae's dedication ceremony. "Will this do?"

Polly's eyes widened. "I should think it will, mistress."

"Very well. It's a fair price. Where is the new babe's father?"

At that, Polly's eyes clouded. "Hedabar, mistress."

"Take the knife, and save me a piece of cake from the dedication," said Rella, walking away and wishing she could do more.

She and Dagstyrr were the only ones to ever successfully

rescue family members from the prison cells of the citadel on the island of Hedabar. Because of that, people looked to her to free their relatives from the vizier, but she had a more urgent task. Besides, once Dagstyrr freed the dragons, the vizier's reign would end, and the citadel would collapse.

Rella, born a light fae princess, had started this war when she broke the only law held sacred by the dark fae: she'd refused to pay the price she'd agreed upon with the Dark Emperor in exchange for her ability to walk unknown among humans. They should shun her. Yet they came in droves and swore allegiance to her. The dark fae were hard to understand, even if she was now one of them.

Startled out of her reverie by the tall figure of Gimrir stalking toward her, Rella watched as he passed silently between the tents and wooden shacks of her followers. He stopped and waved for her to accompany him. Rella caught him up in a trice. "Is it Fedric?"

"There is a decision to be made. Only you can make it," said Gimrir, so solemnly her heart sank.

She followed him back to the base of an enormous tree where dryads occupied the upper branches, and Gimrir made his home at its gnarled base. "What is wrong, Gimrir?"

"The boy has only one wound. Which is strange after such a fierce battle. Nevertheless, that wound is very severe. The boy is strong, just as you predicted. I think his determination will indeed win through as long as I can piece his poor guts back together."

"And can you?"

"Only with your help," he said. "Your ...very special help."

A cold shiver ran down Rella's spine. Gimrir was one of the few beings who knew of her strange magic. Born light fae and having chosen to turn dark, her bright blue flashes of light fae magic had given way to the billowing green magic of the dark fae. Then, an extraordinary thing had happened. The blue returned, and now it worked in concert with the green, a strange phenomenon that Rella wanted to keep quiet. There were enough ridiculous rumors spread about her. "Is there no other way?"

"I've already tried many times and failed. Guts are slippery and confusing to the likes of me. Your clever blue energy can show the way, while your green does the healing. I will keep him sedated. It is the only way."

"I've never attempted this kind of healing. I have no experience."

"I will help you. If we are quick, no one need know."

Loath to risk anyone seeing her using both green and blue magic together, Rella glanced at the young light fae lying within Gimrir's healing circle. His innards still lay exposed to the night air. "You know that with this much dark magic in him, his eyes will change color. He won't be able to return to Casta. We'll probably have to keep him here." Rella struggled with the choice in front of her. If she helped, his life as he knew it was over. If she didn't, he would be dead by morning. "Damn! I should have put him out of his misery on the field."

"But you did not, and this is the consequence."

A breeze whispered through the long grasses where Fedric lay. He was very young and handsome, a prime example of a light fae warrior. Rella sighed. It seemed to her that whenever she attempted a kindness, it went horribly wrong. "Very well, Gimrir."

CHAPTER 2

The next day, word came that the Dark Emperor had broken camp and was heading for his palace at Thingstyrbol. This was not a retreat, merely a tactic he used to rest his forces and keep Calstir guessing where he'd attack next. Calstir dare not follow him too far into dark fae territory where his enemies could ambush him.

After a long night of healing, an exhausted Rella assembled what passed for her guard in her tent. Although her camp was large and diverse, too few were seasoned warriors. Most were creatures of the forests and streams who, though strong, understood nothing of battle or strategy. Many were halflings, like Polly, with diverse and unpredictable amounts of useful magic.

"We march on Thingstyrbol," she said, hiding the shiver that stole down her spine at the memory of the Dark Emperor's palace.

"So soon?" said Beatty.

"It's time I put an end to the Dark Emperor. I am tired of mopping up after him," said Rella.

"You want to confront him at Thingstyrbol?"

Rella turned to face the mountain elf. "It is where he is most vulnerable. Our intelligence tells us that he usually sends his troops home when he's at Thingstyrbol, keeping only a personal guard and some servants to see to his needs. If I defeat him on his own ground, his followers will understand that he is an imposter and rally to our cause. We must show the world he is a creature to be despised, not revered."

"Aye," said Patrice, a dark fae warrior of great renown. She stood tall and slender, short dark hair curling about her oval face. "It is time."

"Your sisters are ready?" said Beatty, standing on a bench that allowed him to look Patrice in the eye.

"Always," said Patrice, "but we are only five. How many of the mountain elves can fight?"

"I can field ten or twelve, but only four are trained for battle. The others are useful, but not in combat."

Rella knew what he meant. She'd come to rely on the mountain elves' stealth and speed when it came to surveillance and intelligence gathering. "Very well. Gimrir will stay behind, but must be ready to come to the front if we need him. The rest of the camp must hide out here. Beatty, we'll use your people as runners between us and the camp."

"Of course," said the mountain elf.

"I'll take Patrice, her four sisters, Beatty, his battle-trained warriors, and myself. That makes eleven."

"Too few," said Beatty.

"I'd rather have too few than too many. Our newer recruits are keen, but until I have the time to drill them, I will not risk taking them into battle. Clearing battlefields is one thing, but this is something entirely different. I'll not take anyone who might hold us back or need rescuing, understood?"

"Rella is correct. Once we are there, we must be able to rely on one another without concern for the weaker ones," said Patrice.

"I'll take two of Beatty's runners as well, but not as warriors. Beatty, you will explain that to them. That makes thirteen in all."

"Fourteen," said a deep male voice from the door of her tent.

Rella looked up and sighed at the beautiful young man standing there. "Fedric, you are too weak. Maybe next time."

"This time. It may be my only chance," he said with the unmistakable accent of a light fae courtier.

"It may be your death. You must stay," said Rella, annoyed that he had slipped away from Gimrir. It was typical light fae arrogance.

The young fae lordling and Patrice looked each other up and down. He was her exact opposite. Male, with blonde fae hair to below his waist, broad of shoulder, slim hipped, even his now-dark eyes were a soft hazel color. He met their stares with a curiosity of his own. Until that moment, he'd probably only ever seen dark fae warriors on the battlefield.

"You'll have to lose that uniform," said Beatty, sneering at his blue-and-white Casta livery.

"Here!" Sophy, one of Patrice's sisters, threw him a shield. "Try this for size."

He hefted the blue-and-green shield with the bright white star in the center. "It fits. I only need to find my sword, and I'm ready," he said, eyeing the magnificent weapon hanging from Patrice's belt as if he expected her to hand it over.

Rella sensed tension growing between the two powerful

fae. She liked to have her warriors deal with quarrels their own way. It was for the best. However, she was wary about Fedric and Patrice going head-to-head. Both of them were battle-trained warriors with powerful magic.

"There are no light fae among us. How do we know we can trust you?" said Patrice, her hand on the hilt of her weapon.

"I guess you don't," said Fedric, leaning casually against one of the tent's posts.

"Enough!" Rella stared him in the eye and advanced on him. He at least had the courtesy to stand upright at her approach. She stood scant inches from him, holding his gaze and assessing him. Had she made a mistake in healing him?

He was much taller than she was, and she had to look up into his face. Even so, her presence was powerful enough to make him cower—just a little. Whatever the latest rumors circling the light fae troops were, they worked in her favor. "You will obey me, or you will leave. Do you understand?"

"Yes, mistress," said Fedric.

"No one here trusts you. There is a reason there are no light fae among us. You must win your place here. For if you return to Casta, you will be killed on sight. You have changed," she said, holding a small mirror up to his face.

The moment he saw his eyes, he faltered, but quickly recovered. Light fae famously hid their emotions. "Is that the price?"

Laughter erupted from deep inside the tent. "No. That is the gift," said Sophy. "The price is your oath never to act, speak, or even think against Rella or any of the wild fae."

Rella paced the dim interior of the tent. "Gimrir will take your oath. You will stay with him at camp. Understand?"

Fedric bowed low, in true courtly light fae style. "Yes, Princess Rella."

She didn't believe him for a moment. This lordling was trouble.

CHAPTER 3

They lay immobile as only fae can. Camouflaged by their brown-and-green uniforms, they blended into the rocks and shrubbery, invisible to watchers. Rella lay flat, breathing in the fresh scents of loamy earth and moss. For the last three days they'd been following the Dark Emperor's army through dark fae territory.

Beatty's runners had brought word from Gimrir that Fedric had absconded. Let him. The last thing they needed now was a light fae outcast striding through the wild fae camp full of arrogance and superiority. He may be wild fae now, but apart from his eye color, he still looked and acted like a light fae. But after the sacred oaths Gimrir had extracted from him as the price of his healing, she knew he wouldn't betray their attack on the Dark Emperor. That was all that mattered.

They were still miles from Thingstyrbol, but from their position high on the mountainside, they could look down into the Dark Emperor's massive camp. Even from here, she could pick him out. His extreme height and strange choice of clothing gave him away. She watched his long legs carry him across the field, his living cloak of leaves, moss, and small insects trailing behind him. His crown of living weeds and spiders accentuated his already considerable height.

At a flick of his finger, his followers prostrated themselves in front of him. "I'll bet they love that," whispered Rella.

Patrice whispered back, "It's not normal or natural. I doubt even the light fae court demands such abject homage."

"You are right," said Rella. "The court at Casta does enjoy very fancy manners, but my father believed having your subjects prostrate themselves is demeaning to both king and commoner. He used to say that a short bow, salute, or curtsey showing respect for the office should suffice."

"I think I might've liked your father," said Patrice.

"I believe you might have," replied Rella, though she hated to think of what her father would make of his daughter now.

"We should rest," said Sophy.

"There is an outcropping I spotted earlier with a little cave behind it. We can spend the night there. All this vegetation will hide our presence, as long as we keep quiet," said Rella. "Tomorrow, we continue to follow him from a distance until he reaches Thingstyrbol and releases most of these troops."

"Aye. Our spies confirmed that he'll dismiss his main army and keep only a small guard with him," Beatty informed her.

"Excellent. That is where we can surprise him," said Rella.

"Aye, where he feels safest," said Sophy, a look of pure

hatred in her eyes as she gazed down on the tall figure of the Emperor.

Rella had no idea what degradations Patrice and her sisters had suffered at the hands of the Dark Emperor, but every so often, she caught a glimpse of revulsion that matched her own. It was none of her business. Every one of the wild fae had secrets. If they wanted her to know, they'd tell her.

Rella signaled for them to fall back. The cave in the mountainside was about twenty paces behind them—excellent shelter for the night.

"No fire tonight," instructed Rella when they arrived. "We're too close, so we'll eat cold rations. No use of magic to heat your dinners or bedrolls either, understand?"

Sophy nodded. "Aye. He will sense any magic that does not spring from his army in a trice, don't forget that. I will take the first watch."

"Thank you, I'll take the middle watch," said Rella. "He has a long way to go. He might make an early start."

"Then again, he might spend half the day preparing for a triumphal procession through the forest," said Patrice, not even trying to hide the contempt in her voice.

"He is holding prisoners," said Clar, another of Patrice and Sophy's sisters.

"Are you sure? He doesn't usually," said Nan, yet another warrior sister. "Where?"

"Come, I'll show you," she said, leading Rella and her sisters a little way along the path. Below, they saw a small camp separated from the rest of the army.

Careful to stay hidden, they watched a sorry line of light fae warriors stagger toward a tent. Unlike any light fae Rella had ever known, they stumbled with heads down, their once-proud bearing gone. Light fae were stunningly beautiful with very long blonde hair, the brightest blue eyes imaginable, and impeccably bearing at all times.

What Rella saw below her was unbelievable. Even in Casta's lowliest quarters, she'd seen nothing like this. Dirty, with matted hair, they'd lost all self-awareness—unheard of for light fae. "Right there. See, the prisoners are walking into that tent inside the bramble enclosure," said Clar.

Rella saw them snarl at each other in attempts to be first inside, and a shiver of primal fear shuddered up her spine. What she was seeing didn't make sense.

"Prisoners. That's new. I wonder what he's up to?" said Jul, the fifth and youngest sister. All Patrice's sisters looked similar with their thick dark hair worn short and dark eyes. Their height set them apart from most dark fae, except for Jul, who was much shorter, closer to Rella's height.

"Whatever it is, you can bet it will be distasteful," whispered a familiar but unwanted voice.

"Fedric," hissed Rella, clenching her fists and turning to find the young man hiding behind a large rock. He was the last thing she needed right now. Rella signaled for everyone to retreat to the cave.

They maintained silence as they made their way back, but their glances told Rella that everyone felt as irritated as she did.

As soon as they were inside, Fedric spoke up. "There was no promise to stay behind, only an order, which I am not obliged to obey. I am free so long as I don't work against you. Besides, I don't want to work against you. I have come to help," he whispered, with an irritating grin as he lolled against the curved wall.

Stunned by his audacity, they all froze in place and stared at him. If ever a silence could echo, it did so now. His presence endangered them all. If the Emperor's scouts had caught him, the dark fae army would scour the hills looking for more spies. Rella was too furious to speak. Yet she noted his perfect appearance, even after the ordeal he'd just experienced. It spoke to her misgivings about the light fae they'd just witnessed. So far in their brief acquaintance, Fedric had always appeared handsomely groomed. Light fae used their magic to make sure they bore no scars or blemishes. Their armor and clothing fit like a second skin, and their impressive hair was always in perfect order. No emotion was allowed to show on their faces—that would be considered very bad manners.

Something terrible was happening to the light fae below them.

Beatty had stayed behind with his men. Now, he was the first to spring into action upon seeing Fedric. "I'll make sure no one followed him." He signaled to his men, and two of them silently disappeared into the undergrowth surrounding the cave's entrance.

Sophy and Patrice held their swords to his neck while Clar and Jul tied his hands securely behind his back. "If you use your magic for anything, fool, even to scratch your arse, we are dead, or worse. So keep your hands still, understand?" said Sophy in his ear, so softly it sounded like a lover's promise. Although they were out of sight, one raised voice would bring the enemy scrambling up to them.

Rella paced the shallow confines of the cave, deep in thought. There had always been something not quite right about Fedric's wound, and suddenly, all the little pieces fell together like a puzzle in her mind. The lack of other injuries, no signs of spent battle magic on him, the way he'd been so well hidden in the gorse, his eagerness to accept the dark magic despite any consequences. He'd deceived her.

But what was worth the risk of so severe an injury? Why was Fedric here?

Now she had to find out his purpose or send him swiftly to the halls of the dead, as she probably should have done in the beginning. It was going to be tricky in the cave. One shout, and they'd have the Dark Emperor's whole army swarming up the mountainside.

Rella waited until Beatty's men returned with the news that Fedric had not been followed. She spent the time going over every meeting she'd had with the young light fae lordling in her mind, looking for a clue to his purpose.

Eventually, she turned to him. "It must have hurt," she said, indicating his belly. "That was a large hole. I might have dispatched you without even asking. It would have saved me from having to do it now."

His mouth twisted in a small smile. "It was a risk I had to take. The wound had to be large enough that it couldn't be healed on the field. I put a lot of thought into it."

He wasn't surprised or embarrassed about being discovered. "I see. What are you? A spy?" Rella lifted her dagger and traced a pattern across his belly.

His soft brown eyes looked straight into hers without flinching. "You have found me out. No matter."

"Ah, not a spy then," said Rella, still able to see through light fae lies. She lifted the dagger to his face and rested it on the corner of his eye. "Whatever your plans, this must have come as a shock." Rella knew well the horror of seeing brown eyes where bright fae blue should be.

"Tell me," she continued in her soft voice, "what could induce a light fae lord to risk his life to infiltrate my camp? What have you come for?" she demanded. The rest of her warriors listened intently.

"Them." He said, suddenly serious. "The light fae prisoners."

"Who are they to you?"

"Personally? Nothing. I don't even know who they are, but I would put a stop to the Dark Emperor imprisoning light fae." Fedric's gaze was forthright and honest. He appeared to be telling the truth for once, but he'd deceived Rella before, and she'd not give him a chance to do it again. Besides, she could hear anger and disgust in his voice, but was it directed at her or the prisoners?

Rella stood and paced in front of him. The blade of her dagger bounced rhythmically on the palm of her hand. Having saved his life once, she was reluctant to kill him now, but she wouldn't allow him to distract her from her goal. The Dark Emperor was her priority.

Aware of Patrice and her sisters, standing arms folded across their chests, just waiting for the order to dispose of him, she knew she must make a decision soon. To say nothing of Beatty's mountain elves sitting around on boulders like so many ancient woodcarvings wanting to help. Trust did not come easy to dark fae.

"I think it better all around if I kill you now," said Rella.

That got his attention. "If you kill me now, mistress, you kill hundreds more," said Fedric, and he sounded sincere.

"And what is that supposed to mean?" said Patrice.

"Another lie from a light fae piece of shit," answered Pordu, Beatty's man.

"No. I do not lie. My only mission is to save those prisoners," said Fedric.

"Who is so important to you, that you risk everything to save them?" said Rella.

Fedric sighed and hung his head. "No one. All of them."

"He's told so many lies, mistress, he's confused himself,"

said Beatty, a grin splitting his leathery face. "Let me deal with him now."

"Let's start at the beginning, shall we?" said Rella, ignoring Beatty. "Who sent you?"

"No one sent me."

"Then why?" said Sophy, her hands open wide.

Rella could see Fedric's frustration. She watched him intently. If anyone could see through his light fae composure, it was Rella.

"Are we supposed to believe you went into battle, gutted yourself, and lay there hoping to be saved so you might rescue a few prisoners of no particular importance?" said Patrice.

"I think his gutting has addled his brains," said Jul.

"If he had any to start with," said Nan.

"Who are they?" Pordu asked Fedric.

"They are light fae warriors taken in battle and destined to a living hell." He ground out the words slowly. "And it is all your fault...*Princess* Rella," he said, venom in his voice at last.

Now Rella might learn some truth.

Patrice's knife was at his throat. "Watch your tongue. If it offends me again, I will cut it out."

Fedric ignored her, keeping his eyes locked on Rella. "What should I call you? 'Rella of the dark fae'? 'Rella of the wild fae'? Perhaps you prefer 'Dark Queen'? Or 'Your Majesty'? Is that it?"

"Oh, Fedric, Fedric, Fedric, if you are going to die, don't let it be your ignorance that gets you killed. At least die with some cause behind your sacrifice," said Beatty, shaking his head at the young man's folly.

"I have a good and honorable cause. I strive to undo

some of the damage Rella Whatever-She-Is, has done," said Fedric, contempt dripping from him.

"Don't forget who put your guts back together," said Patrice.

Jul sped toward him, dagger at the ready, but Rella held out her hand to stall her. "I know this war is my fault. No one knows it better. Tell me, what can you do about it? Really, I want to know," she said, striving to keep her voice gentle.

"I cannot stop the war, but I can stop that," he said, indicating the prisoners below them with a toss of his head.

"Who knows why the Dark Emperor has started taking prisoners?" said Beatty. "If that is your mission, then you must first stop the war."

Fedric's eyes widened. "You don't know. Do you?" he said, gazing stupefied at Rella.

His words brought a stillness to the air that sounded a warning. Rella turned and sat on a stool in front of him. "Tell me," she said.

The young man took a deep breath. "After you rescued Calstir and the Halfenhaw brothers from the citadel, light fae knew not to land in Hedabar. That to do so was death."

"That is a good thing, is it not?" she said, dreading what he was about to say, yet compelled to know.

"You didn't consider that the vizier still needs fae creatures for his cells. They continue to die, and he needs new blood all the time. Or should I say—new magic. Light fae energy is best for his purpose, whatever that is. We are his slaves of choice."

"Then he is out of luck," said Clar.

"You still don't understand," he said, his gaze raking the cave. "He made a deal with the Dark Emperor. Any light fae warriors caught in battle are sold to the vizier as slaves."

All movement in the cave stilled as they listened to
Fedric's voice speak of yet another horror. "The Dark
Emperor keeps the slave pens by the sea shore. Once he has
two hundred or more, he ships them out to Hedabar."

"No," whispered Rella, her voice stolen from her by the
pain his words brought. She remembered well the cells of
the citadel. Her memory brought the stench of dying fae
addicts flooding back—the acrid smell of the walls: the
sweet, cloying reek of the poison; the lingering evil of
dragon-blood addiction.

Fedric was correct. Rella's actions had caused this, right
enough. If she'd kept her promise to the Dark Emperor to
become his consort, then perhaps this war would not be
raging, and no light fae slaves would be bound for Hedabar.

She had to put this right. Now. Before any more innocents entered the citadel.

Fedric's mouth twisted cruelly. "Oh, but yes, *Princess*. We
always thought it strange that so many of our dead were
never recovered, now we know. And not only is the Dark
Emperor no longer content with taking light fae in battle,
but now he has started raiding the outlying villages around
Casta."

"What does the Dark Emperor gain from so dangerous
an enterprise?" said Patrice.

Fedric looked straight into her eyes. "A promise."

"What promise?"

"He wants a dragon."

"Is he insane? No. Don't answer that," said Rella raising
her hands. "What will he gain by chaining a dragon in his
dungeon? He certainly doesn't need to bolster his magic."

"If I told you, you wouldn't believe me," said Fedric.

"Tell me anyway."

"He wants to ride one. He plans to ride over the battle-fields with his dragon spitting fire at his enemies."

"Impossible. No one has ever ridden a dragon!"

"He believes he can do anything."

"How do you know this?"

"King Calstir has spies at Thingstyrbol, how else?" said Fedric, a smile teasing the corners of his arrogant mouth.

Rella's heart had never felt so heavy. Light fae enslaved, penned like animals to satisfy the needs of the vizier, and bolster the ambition of the Dark Emperor. She retreated to the back of the cave. Was there nothing evil men would not do to gain power?

This arrogant little lordling had hoodwinked her, and once more, she was starting to doubt her ability to lead. *Where are you, Dagstyrr?* If ever she needed the comfort of his protective arms, it was now.

CHAPTER 4

Guilt wore heavily on Rella. She'd brought about this travesty. By broadcasting the dangers of landing at Hedabar to the fae, she'd forced the vizier to find other ways to feed his need for the magic of others, and the Dark Emperor had been happy to oblige—for a price.

It must stop.

Her dream of killing the Dark Emperor and freeing the world of his tyranny would have to wait. He wasn't going anywhere. Once he reached Thingstyrbol, he'd stay there for weeks before venturing out again. That was his usual pattern.

According to Fedric, the light fae intelligence stated it was a journey of only twenty miles to the slave pens on the seashore.

After weighing the dangers, Rella and her wild fae warriors agreed. The wild fae would follow the dark fae guards below as they herded their prisoners away from the Dark Emperor's camp and Thingstyrbol.

Once they were far enough away from the main army, they could deal with the guards.

No one wanted to delay the attack on Thingstyrbol, but the fate of these fae was in their hands, and they couldn't ignore the abomination of enslaved fae.

The wild fae would rescue the slaves before going after the Dark Emperor. They all knew the stories of the cells in Hedabar. The captured fae forced to become dragon's-blood addicts, and milked of their magic until eventually, shriveled and insane, they succumbed to a horrible death.

Rella and her companions hid among the brush at the top of the cliffs surrounding a small bay. The smell of the sea brought memories of nights with Dagstyrr flooding back to her.

They had been transporting their rescued brothers aboard the sentient ship the *Mermaid*. Her captain, Bernst, had worked hard to teach Rella and Dagstyrr how to contain the addicted men. He'd warned them what to expect as withdrawal took hold. It was grueling work, but despite the terrible circumstances, love between Dagstyrr and Rella had flourished. Until, she'd taken him, a human male, for her mate.

Then she'd walked out on him, not willing to risk his life in her war until he'd fulfilled his promise to Drago—but it was hard.

Her longing for him grew with every day they were apart.

Pushing him from her mind, she concentrated on the rescue. Below, the light fae prisoners entered an enclosure. It was almost full. Which meant soon they'd be shipped to the vizier at Hedabar. Strangely, there was no coercion going on. Their hands were free to use magic, and Rella could tell that their magic was powerful. Only a few dark fae armed with lightning wands guarded them.

"I don't understand," said Fedric, his frustration like a burr under Rella's leather uniform. "How are they being controlled?"

"Shh." Rella and her warriors had agreed to help Fedric free the slaves on one condition: he understood that she was in charge, not him. They stayed hidden, watching the miserable sight below them. Light fae slaves! Who would have thought such a thing possible?

The light fae warriors were free to move, yet only used their magic for little things like lighting a fire or shaping a piece of wood into a comfortable seat. Otherwise, they lolled around as if they were at home on a feast day. Why did they not free themselves?

Rella and her companions hunkered down to watch. She observed deep tension mar Fedric's perfect face and knew he'd soon give in to his desire to charge down there and free them. He was young and impetuous.

The pens were on the shore below them, close to a makeshift pier. Some prisoners were taking instructions from human sailors on how to use the oars on the longship. They practiced rowing the sleek ship back and forth along the shoreline before returning like sheep to the fold and waiting to have their food brought to them.

"It makes no sense," said Fedric, his tension almost at breaking point. "Where do they think they're going?" The belligerence in his voice was contagious. Other people started to move and shuffle.

"Be still," whispered Rella. "All of you."

"Why? We could easily take those few guards and free

them in no time at all," said Fedric. "We could even have them row themselves home to Casta, now that they have the training," he said, unable to hide the contempt in his voice.

"Your sarcasm only shows your ignorance, lad," whispered Beatty.

"Something is not right with what we see down there. Until we know what it is, we do nothing," said Rella.

"Aye, you're right," Fedric conceded through clenched teeth.

"Of course I am. We wait, and we watch."

Night was falling, and small animals came out of their burrows to see who trespassed on their hunting grounds. Rella sent a soft puff of dark green magic across the fertile earth to spell the space and keep the little creatures hunting in other directions.

"I think I know what's happening," said Rella.

"From the tone of your voice, it doesn't sound good," said Patrice.

"I hope I am wrong. I will know by morning," said Rella, lying back on the prickly heather and pulling a sprig covered in tiny purple bells. The stars were out in force tonight. She lay quietly, letting their magical energy refresh hers.

Fedric also turned his face to the stars. Rella hadn't allowed him to use his magic since his eyes changed color. He hadn't protested. She suspected he wasn't in any hurry to produce the green clouds of dark fae magic that had so horrified her when she first found it spilling from her fingers.

Lying here in the gentle summer night was the perfect way for her to sleep, the stars above and the earth beneath. She saw Patrice take charge of guard duty shifts and closed her eyes.

As morning light stole purple over the horizon, the wild fae lay in the undergrowth and watched the prisoners below line up eagerly for their food, then sit and eat the slops with relish.

It was sickening.

Rella's worst fears were realized. "Dragon's blood," she whispered.

Her companions paled at her words because they understood the stark truth of it. It explained the actions of the captives.

"It is too soon for them to be addicted," said Fedric. "It takes time."

"No. One morsel in food and you crave it more than life itself. The vizier has a good supply of it, and it is the only way to control so many powerful warriors," said Rella, watching Fedric's head drop to hide the despair he must feel at her revelation.

"So, we have a decision to make. Do we rescue the light fae, or leave them to their fate?" said Rella.

"If we rescue them, what can we do with them?" said Sophy. "I would not feed them dragon's blood, even if I had such a thing."

"There must be a supply down there," said Beatty. "Though I suspect only a day's ration at a time. You saw that little skiff that came in yesterday. It is back again today. Pordu can go down and back without being seen. He'll get to the bottom of it."

"Not so fast," said Rella. "What do we do with roughly one hundred and fifty addicted light fae after we rescue them?"

"We'll need Gimrir," said Jul, scrambling up the incline

to join them.

"Aye, and a hundred more like him," said Rella. "I've seen this process before. It takes time and energy, with round-the-clock wards, and supervision by healers who know what they're doing."

"Look. Look there," said Fedric, breaking his silence. "That woman, the tall one whose armor is loose on her."

They watched as the woman in question hungrily grabbed a second bowl of gruel amongst laughter from the guards. Rella and the wild fae watched as she sought a private corner, pretended to eat, then let the slops fall to the ground while she used her boots to cover it with dirt.

"I wonder if there are others?" said Rella.

"Yes, look there," said Sophy, pointing to a young male going through a similar routine.

A flash of hope rose in Rella. "If there are others, we might be able to charge them with supervising and warding the addicts until they can arrange for experienced healers. We don't have the time or manpower to look after them."

They were far enough away from Thingstyrbol and the Dark Emperor after following the slaves yesterday to be reasonably sure of not running into a large contingent of his forces. However, Rella knew that both King Calstir's and the Dark Emperor's scouts roved far and wide, hoping to capture her. Calstir would happily hand her over to the Emperor. Patrice, and her sisters would be a bonus.

"It's going to take a lot of healers to help that lot," said Patrice.

"There are very few dark fae guards," said Rella. "I only mean us to free them. After that, they're on their own."

"It might work," said Beatty. "Let me send Pordu down to gauge the numbers."

"Very well," said Rella.

"We are more than enough to defeat the guards. We might just be able to pull this off, Fedric," said Rella. "Are you not pleased?"

The young fae was on his back, staring up at the morning sky. "I can't come with you. You must do it without me."

"What?" Rella hissed, incredulous.

"Do you see the big male huddled against the tree stump?"

"Aye," said Rella, unable to see the man's face, but noting he looked weakened and lethargic.

"My father," said Fedric, swiping a tear from his eye. "He must never know I've seen him like this."

"Don't be a fool, boy," said Beatty. "He's the reason you're here. We never did believe your vague, altruistic, slave-saving story. Nobody guts themselves like that without a damn good reason."

"Still, he must never know I've seen him addicted to dragon's blood. The shame would kill him."

Rella was watching the farce play out below. "Well, I've good news for you, Fedric," she said. "Your father is one of those refusing to eat. That's why he's so weak. It must be two days at least since the battle, and he was taken before then, for he was already here when the others arrived."

"Really?" said Fedric, scrambling to join Rella on the edge of the precipice. The relief in the young fae's voice was moving. Rella was glad he cared and wasn't afraid to show it. Too many light fae practiced emotional restraint to the point of cruelty.

"It must be at least six days since his patrol went missing. We only found one dead," said Fedric, unable to hide the strange mix of worry and hope rising in his voice.

"We'll wait until Pordu returns and we know the

numbers before we make any plans. Addicts are unpredictable, and those are light fae warriors with all their power intact," said Rella. She nodded to Beatty, who immediately understood he was to watch Fedric. The young fae was likely to stumble down there, ready to fight his way in to rescue his father, risking everyone's life. Rella wanted the advantage of surprise.

She joined Patrice and her sisters for a cold breakfast of stale biscuits and berries. "I never thought I'd feel sorry for those bastards," said Sophy, meaning light fae.

Rella tried not to flinch, for she'd been one of them for most of her life. Then she remembered Sophy's husband had died in the first battle between the Dark Emperor and Rella's brother, King Calstir.

She remembered how she and Dagstyrr had watched the skies darken with green, then flash with blue as battle magic rent the heavens for hours. Unable to do anything other than watch from afar, that was the day Rella knew she must put a stop to the Dark Emperor. She didn't want to think about that idyllic cabin and the memories it contained. To do so weakened her resolve. If she kept at it, she might walk away from here and spend her time looking for her mate.

Many stories of that terrible day had reached her. How the Dark Emperor had proved himself a ruthless and maniacal general, throwing his troops in wave after wave against the bright blue hell of the light fae strikers. The dark fae troops, unable to retreat lest the Dark Emperor finish them off with a wave of his hand, fought to their deaths. Excited by the battle energy all around him, the Dark Emperor sat high on a hill watching the battle below, picking off any he saw running.

Later, both the Dark Emperor and King Calstir declared

themselves victors. It was carnage. Afterward, dark fae warriors abandoned the Dark Emperor in droves, which was how she'd found Patrice and her sisters, and later, Beatty and his friends.

Rella looked up to see Pordu and his comrade, Asti, emerging from the brush. They returned with good news and bad.

CHAPTER 5

"**A**t least a third of them are not addicted, but who knows how long they can continue without eating?" said Asti. "Either starvation will force them to eat, or they'll be found out and force-fed. I reckon their guards won't have to lift a finger. Under threat of receiving no more drug-laced food, the addicts will force-feed the others."

"We must get down there now," said Fedric.

"We do nothing without a plan," said Patrice. "I'm not risking my sisters' lives on a haphazard raid." Silence followed her word as everyone gauged the risks.

Beatty was the first to speak. "The mountain elves can sneak up and disarm those few guards, especially if we wait until the boat bringing supplies leaves. That way, no one outside of here will know what's going on until tomorrow. It should give us some time to sort things out."

"Okay," said Rella, "what then?"

"Then the whole place erupts in chaos. The addicts will fight to defend their supply. The warriors, weakened by hunger, will throw themselves into the fray trying to subdue them," said Sophy.

"But they'll be in no fit state to fight the addicts who are well fed and fueled by their addiction," said Patrice.

"The addicts are not as strong as they appear," said Rella.

"What do you mean?"

"You won't have had time to notice, but as the time draws near for their next meal, they become twitchy, unstable. That is when we should strike."

"I agree," said Beatty.

"So, when is their next meal?" said Fedric, bouncing on his toes as if ready to take flight.

Patrice put her hand gently on his shoulder. "You need to relax. You didn't want your father to know you'd seen him addicted. Luckily, he isn't, but don't forget he hasn't seen your eyes either. I understand the light fae don't take well to those who turn dark. He'll probably take one look and fell you before you can call him Papa."

Rella watched the truth of his situation dawn on Fedric. The young man's pain stole across his face with every word Patrice uttered and reflected in his eyes. "I can never go home," he said, with proud resolve. "But I can make sure that my father does."

"A noble sacrifice," said Rella. "Tell me, how will your brave warrior father live with himself after he kills you?"

She watched Fedric's shoulders slump. He'd gone from a defiant warrior about to save the day, to a confused boy. His eyes sought hers. Rella knew it was essential to give him some hope. "After his experience here and knowing what awaited him in Hedabar, your father may understand your sacrifice, and thank you for it," said Rella.

"You are trying to console me," said Fedric. "If any of that were true, you would still be a princess in Casta."

Rella's serrated knife was at his throat. "Don't ever presume to remind me of my brother's treachery. I live with it every day," she said, her voice a dangerous growl.

Fedric looked away. "I apologize, Princess. I meant no harm."

Rella slowly removed the knife, her eyes never leaving his face.

"Then keep your mouth shut," said Patrice. "And don't call anyone here Princess. It is not a designation we recognize."

"No. My apologies," said Fedric. "We are trained to kill on sight any light fae who turns dark. I never imagined I'd be one of them."

Fedric remained subdued as they discussed their plans. They quickly decided on tactics. Though what on earth she would do with all those addicts immediately afterward, Rella couldn't think. Hopefully, those who had resisted the dragon's blood would be able to help the addicts once they were free. Rella had bigger plans to follow. "Beatty, did you send for Gimrir?"

"Yes, he should have your message by now. And we all know how quickly he can move through the forest," said Beatty.

"I know the tree spirit can move quickly to get here. However, I'm not sure Gimrir will be willing to take on that lot," she said, indicating the camp of addicts.

"You can't blame him, mistress," said Pordu. "It is no small thing to work with addicts. Some of them are bound to die."

"They'll all die in the citadel if we do nothing," said Asti, coming up behind them while strapping on his sword and ax.

Rella smiled. "You look good in your new uniform, Asti." She had used up a lot of favors and one conjured sword to have those uniforms made, but it was worth it to see a semblance of a cohort around her once more.

"I'm proud to wear your colors, Rella of the wild fae," he answered, with a smile.

The mountain elves obeyed no one's laws and had at first refused Rella's offer of a uniform and weapons. Eventually, after seeing Patrice and her sisters strutting around in their new brown leather kilts and breastplates, and hefting their blue-and-green shields with the distinctive white flash in the center, they relented. However, the mountain elves only ever wore it in battle. The rest of the time, they wore their ordinary clothes. Rella couldn't help but admire their independence.

The elves went first, approaching the slave camp silently and unseen. Once in position, they signaled for Rella and the others to join them. Then, they attacked as one.

Rella knew that taking the guards was going to be the easy part, for they had the advantage of surprise. True to their reputation, the elves gave no quarter. Rella watched Beatty sneak up behind a dark fae guard almost twice his height. Without hesitating, he swiped his sword across the backs of the man's knees, crippling him and bringing him to the hard earth before the man could summon his battle magic. The crippled warrior's lightning wand clattered to the ground, alerting the other guards and prisoners.

Beatty never missed a beat. Within seconds, he stood on top of his enemy's prostrate body, his ax hacking him to pieces. The look of surprise on the man's face was still there in death.

While the wild fae made short work of defeating the other guards, he lifted the wand and shouted, "Father of Fedric?"

"Here!" The big warrior stood, raised his arm, and caught the wand as it circled in the air. "To me!" he shouted jubilantly. At once, the prisoners separated into two distinct groups. One a cluster of starving warriors, the other twitching addicts. Unfortunately, their addiction wasn't preventing the growls of warning issuing from their ranks. Rella doubted they had the focus to use their magic efficiently at this point, but they could cause a lot of chaos.

Patrice, her sisters, and Rella ran between the opposing groups, throwing captured lightning wands and swords to the exhausted warriors. Then they formed a shield wall, facing the addicts with the others behind them. At once, Fedric's father came up behind her. "Where is my son?"

"Later. What is your name?"

"Didn't Fedric tell you?"

"If he had, I wouldn't be asking," said Rella, keeping her eyes on the now-confused addicts milling in front of them.

"I am Viktar of Casta, Rella of the wild fae. Don't you know me?" His deep voice sent chills of recognition racing down her spine.

"Of course you are!" Rella's heart soared in recognition. Viktar had trained all her father's officers, including her. Now he served Calstir. Even in her father's time, the great man had found life at court difficult. She'd only seen him rarely after she left the officers training school. "And you know who I am. So, do we fight each other, or these dragon's-blood eaters?" she said, without turning to face him.

"I have no reason to fight you, Princess."

Rella wished she could believe him, but it was hard to trust anyone loyal to her brother. Despite Viktar's dislike of court, he wouldn't be here if he hadn't responded quickly to Calstir's call to arms. "Then let's see what we can do with this lot. Ideally, we need to pen them into a warded cage. Then confine them individually, so that they cannot hurt themselves or one another."

"You sound like you've done this before," said Viktar, his voice cold and hard despite the deprivation his body had suffered.

"You know very well that I have." Just then, a few addicts who'd picked up stones started throwing them at the wild fae shields. "They don't even have the sense to use their magic," she said. "We need to move them away from here before they realize there is no more dragon's blood for them."

"I hate to imagine what will happen then," said Viktar.

"Trust me, you don't want to know," said Rella. Just then, she saw Gimrir descending from the heights, a frown marring his brow. She marveled once more at how this ancient tree spirit fae could move about the forest so quickly. "Here comes some help."

Fedric and the mountain elves, led by Beatty, secured the perimeter and herded the addicts from behind. They started to place wards as they went, ensuring the addicts couldn't move toward the boats. Rella and Patrice's sisters banged their sword hilts on their shields, and with every bang sounding around the camp, they took a step forward. It had the effect she wanted. It confused the addicts even further, and they fell back.

Viktar had his group lined up, and they followed Rella's shield wall—a proud show of numbers only, for they were weak from hunger. Eventually, they confined the addicts to a small space expertly warded by Beatty's men. "That is good for now, but we must get away from here as quickly as possible," said Viktar, his eyes scanning the camp for his son.

"You need nourishment, and to talk to your son. I need to talk to Gimrir," said Rella, turning at last to face the famous warrior and letting him see her face. To her surprise, he didn't flinch at the sight of her changed features.

"You knew about this?" she said, waving a hand to indicate the mark spilling onto her face and her dark brown eyes.

"I am sad to see it, Rella. Your father would be too. However, I'm sadder still that your sacrifice went unrecognized in Casta. Lady Kemara should be banished, and Calstir needs a lesson on loyalty." The great warrior's bright blue eyes held hers, and she saw his feelings written there.

"No, Kemara was right. I should never have rescued Calstir. I brought this war to our people."

"Some wars are worth fighting, Rella."

"You would think that, Viktar. Still, if I had gone to the Dark Emperor as I promised, we could have had peace." She looked away from his penetrating blue gaze. "I refused to pay the price. This war is my fault."

His hand reached out and lifted her chin, forcing her to look directly up at him. "Even with this," he said, indicating the changes in her face, "you look so like your father, Rella of the wild fae. This war is not your fault. The Dark Emperor took advantage of you. Had you gone to him, he would have made war on Casta anyway. It is Casta he wants, has always wanted. Calstir is a fool not to recognize the truth of it. And, even worse, not to value his sister."

The light in the old warrior's eyes dimmed in sadness, and Rella gasped at his show of emotion. She wanted to be that young girl again—the one who'd climbed up on this warrior's knee and begged stories of ancient battles.

He laughed. "Now you know why I spent little time at your father's court. I never could hide my feelings, as I should. It's a useful trait in war—I could rage and rant, and everyone said how fierce I was. How great at inspiring our young troops."

"But as soon as the politics took over..."

"Ah, then I had to leave, and your father saw sense in that. He was my dearest friend and knew I preferred the simple life. He always kept me apprised of what was going on. He sought my counsel, but only through letters."

"You didn't mind that some of my father's ideas were, in fact, yours?" said Rella, guessing.

"No. Never. Besides, they weren't mine. Your father was a great king with many wonderful insights. He just enjoyed hashing out the details with me."

"I think you are too modest."

Viktar's head dropped to hide the small smile escaping his mouth, but Rella, being so much shorter, saw it. "I'm glad my father had you to help him."

"Now, Rella, where is my son?"

"First, you must eat. I have arranged for clean food. It's not fancy. I had to ask Clar to help me conjure it from our rations, but we're scouring the woods for whatever is available, and Pordu has shot a deer. Dinner will be plentiful," said Rella, hoping Fedric was now prepared to face his father.

"Can all wild fae conjure like you and Clar?"

"No. Our gifts are many and diverse. I will send Fedric to you," she said.

CHAPTER 6

That evening, Gimrir sat scowling in the corner of the hut once used to hold lighting wands, his long limbs folded awkwardly. He always stood so tall. Rella couldn't ever remember seeing him sit down in all the time she'd known him. It spoke to his exhaustion.

"I'm sorry to have involved you in this, my friend," she said, offering him some wild mushroom soup.

He lifted his long-fingered hand and ran it over his face. "I'm sorry too. It is too much for me. There is little I can do for them."

"You have them settled for the night. That is something," she said, placing fresh bread next to his soup.

"I only copied your recollections of the way your Captain Bernst contained addicts. The light fae helped me, but those demented souls fought like demons. Then I had to sedate them, even though I know it is not good for them. Until some Crystal Mountain healers arrive, it is the best I can manage. They are so many," he said, picking up his spoon.

"I wish I'd been able to wait for the healers, and not involved you, but I couldn't. I needed to help now. I'm sorry," said Rella.

"No, you did right. These addicts would have killed one another unless we contained them. Unfortunately, we have done all we can," said Gimrir.

"The light fae who are not addicted will be able to clean up after them and keep them safely warded until help arrives," said Rella, gazing through the doorway at the strange sight. Like giant chrysalises, the addicts were wrapped in canvas and strung between poles or trees. They'd used hammocks taken from the dark fae stores, then modified them. The sailcloth strapped their limbs tight against their bodies so they could not harm themselves or others with attempts to use their magic. Special wards covered them so that even if they escaped their physical bindings, they could not go far.

They appeared peaceful, but when Gimrir's potion wore off, the cries for help would begin. Asking, pleading, begging, bargaining, threatening—it was a familiar pattern. She'd seen her brother go through it all. Calstir had suffered for weeks before emerging more or less himself.

Gimrir leaned back against the wall. "That was good, thank you."

"You're welcome," said Rella, removing his empty bowl.

"What will happen next? I have no experience of dragon's-blood addicts."

"Puking, swearing, shivering. They will think they are dying and that this is some strange torture we are putting them through. Some will understand, but even they will have moments when they will try to kill us. All they want is dragon's blood. They will say or do anything to get it."

"Perhaps the short time they were addicted will help them recover more quickly than your brother," said Gimrir, one of the few people who dared to mention King Calstir's past addiction.

"Not from what I understand of this addiction," said Rella, heartily wishing it were so, but refusing to encourage false hope.

"I will return to camp as soon as the Crystal Mountain healers arrive. They do not like my kind, nor I, theirs. Besides, I have enough work in the camp to keep me busy," said Gimrir.

"Why do they not like your kind, Gimrir? I thought they'd dedicated their lives to healing. Why don't they want to know about your healing magic?" said Rella.

"They treat only light fae, never humans or dark fae, and they will very rarely heal halflings. Whereas I will happily ease the suffering of any creature, even a simple worm."

"But why are they so fussy about their healing? The Crystal Mountain libraries must contain many books of ancient knowledge. Their potential is vast," said Rella.

"They gather knowledge greedily and hoard it like a crow hoards anything that sparkles," said Gimrir. "They strive for perfection. In that way, they are very like the light fae they serve. Not like me—I don't like extremes. They think my healing is tainted, not pure enough."

"Probably because they are light fae. At least they were before becoming this reclusive sect of healers. I'm not sure what they are now," said Rella.

"Of course. They still recruit among the light fae, you know?" said Gimrir.

"I didn't know that. Ever since the Crystal Mountain healers came to Halfenhaw to help Dagstyrr's addicted brothers, they've wanted to get their hands on me. I know all light fae want to kill me on sight, so I wasn't surprised. From a young age, all light fae are conditioned to kill those who turn dark, but those we call the crystal fae want to capture me and subject me to their tests like an experiment. It makes no sense."

"They must think you have something to teach them. As I said, those healers hoard knowledge like misers hoard gold," he said. "I'm surprised they agreed to help your mate's brothers. They are halflings, are they not?"

"Yes. Dagstyrr's mother is Princess Astrid. A powerful light fae princess," said Rella. "Her first three sons have strong fae abilities, especially Erik."

"But not the fourth, your mate. Their father is Earl Magnus if I'm not mistaken—a human."

Rella smiled. "That's right, Dagstyrr is human."

"He must be exceptional to have won your love, Rella," said Gimrir, returning her smile.

"Anyway, I will be gone before the Crystal Mountain healers get here," said Rella. The last thing she needed was a confrontation with crystal fae.

"Very wise," said Gimrir.

"We would be lost without you, Gimrir. Your work grows daily. Have you thought of taking an apprentice?"

"I have one," he said, allowing a small smile to escape his serious face. "A little girl who is keen to learn all I can teach her. Unfortunately, she is human," he said.

"Why unfortunately?" said Rella, once more struck by the diverse prejudices that infected her world.

"Don't look at me like that, Rella. I mean that she has no understanding of energies the way fae do. It is necessary to teach her to recognize energy before she can learn to heal."

"Surely, that is impossible. Humans cannot read energy."

"All living things can, Rella, and she is coming along better than I thought possible. Either it is because she is young, and therefore more malleable and open to my teaching, or perhaps because she has a distant ancestor with a drop of fae blood. Who knows?"

"What is her name?"

"Sally. A silly name, I grant you, but she will not change it. When do you think the healers will be here?"

"Pordu and Asti left earlier today with three other of Beatty's mountain elves. They will listen out for word of Crystal Mountain healers this far south. With luck, they won't need to go all the way to the Crystal Mountain," said Rella.

"I heard there were some at Halfenhaw."

Rella's stomach clenched at the mention of Dagstyrr's home. How long ago was it that she'd sat on a windowsill overlooking the vast Halfenhaw forests while reading ballads? Her soul cried out for Dagstyrr. Where was he? Had he caught up with Captain Bernst, as Rella intended he should? Was he even now making his way to rescue the dragons? She closed her eyes. An image of his laughing face swam in front of her. Soft hair curling over his collar, eyes bright with amusement, then darkened by passion.

"I said, there were still some at Halfenhaw," said Gimrir. "You are tired too, Rella. You must rest. We have a long journey tomorrow. The wild fae camp will have moved on, and we must catch them up."

"Sorry, Gimrir, you are right. I am tired."

They awoke to the screams and curses of the crazed addicts. Rella had forgotten how badly it set her nerves on edge. On the *Mermaid*, there had been only four of them. Now, over one hundred fae addicts created a barrage of sound that threatened the sanity of those who heard it. Being fae, they used what little magic they could summon to compel the listeners to do their will.

The skiff bringing in today's supplies of dragon's blood had been intercepted by those light fae who had resisted the poison. Rella hadn't watched, but knew the warriors had taken pleasure in dealing with the boatmen themselves.

Viktar appeared where the women had slept looking ready to kill someone—now. Rella approached him cautiously, hoping it was the addicts and not Fedric's state that had him so riled up.

"Viktar, who do you want to kill first, them or me?" she said, nodding toward the addicts. With one hand on her sword hilt and green magical energy bubbling from the fingers of her other hand, she halted a few feet from him.

The old warrior gazed down at her, gripping the hilt of his sword. "I told you, you have nothing to fear from me, Rella."

"Even after seeing your son? You do know it was my magic that turned him?" As she spoke, Rella gauged the emotions on his face. He was no ordinary light fae, and she was not sure whether the feelings he showed were true.

"You saved his life."

"At a price. Though not one we intended," Gimrir's voice stole softly from behind Rella.

"He's an impetuous boy. Well-meaning, but he needs schooling," said Viktar, his eyes never leaving the unusual sight of the ancient spirit-fae.

"He gutted himself. Did he tell you? Made a good job of it too," said Gimrir.

"Aye. Can I assume you were not available to help my son, spirit-fae?" Viktar's voice was dark and dangerous.

"My name's Gimrir, and yes, I was available. However, your Fedric had done such a good job on himself that it took all the magical energy of both Rella and myself to push his slippery bits back into place. Never seen anything like it. I told her we should have let him die."

Viktar's face hardened into a mask, and then he bowed low in high fae style, honoring both Rella and Gimrir. "You have my sincere thanks. If ever I can repay your work, let me know."

"He cannot return to Casta, Viktar," said Rella. She, of all people, knew how devastating this would be to his family. All the plans they had for him were gone. He could never take his father's place, nor would he find a bride amongst the light fae families. If he was their only son, their line was now finished.

The old warrior sat down at the makeshift board and accepted a cup of mead from Patrice, his eyes never leaving the dark fae warrior maiden. No doubt he wasn't used to seeing such powerful dark fae warriors up close, and especially not serving him mead.

"I know he can never return," he said. Drinking down the sweet liquid, he wiped his hand across his mouth as Dagstyrr might do. Rella couldn't help thinking that it was very obvious he was not a courtier. He had few manners to recommend him. Unlike Fedric, whose ways declared him the light fae fop he was.

"You hoped he'd be your eyes and ears at court, I'm thinking," said Jul, refilling his beaker with mead.

"Aye, I did," said Viktar, not at all put out at Jul's ability to read the situation correctly.

"He looks the part," said Rella. "However, I'm not sure

his temperament is suited to court life. You said yourself: he is impetuous."

"What is there for him now?" The proud light fae warrior shook his golden head.

Rella sighed. "He could cut his hair and pass for human, but sooner or later, he's sure to use his magic. Humans don't like that. If he is honest about who and what he is, I might be able to find a place for him."

"You would do that, after all the trouble he brought you?" said Viktar.

"I was thinking of Captain Bernst. He is a good judge of men. I promise only to keep him with me until I confer with Bernst," said Rella, unsure how long her companions could stomach him.

"He did it to save me. I am very proud of him, Rella."

Rella couldn't help smiling. "I know. Have you told him how you feel?"

"Of course. However, life as he knew it is over," said Viktar, his sad eyes like sparkling blue jewels in the gloom of the tent.

"You and I understand that, but I'm not sure Fedric fully understands what it is like to live the life of a dark fae." said Rella. "I will not keep him against his will, Viktar. If he offends my people, he must go."

"I know my life has changed, Father," said Fedric, striding forward and helping himself to a cup of mead. "You've made it quite clear. I'm sorry to have spoiled your plans."

The young fae was sullen and resentful. Just the attitude Rella didn't need. "You don't need to stay with us," said Rella.

That changed his attitude. "I am honored to serve Rella

of the wild fae," he said, with a small bow, his voice soft and respectful all of a sudden.

Jul and Sophy took that moment to sit on either side of him. Rella knew the girls were suspicious of light fae, but none of them appreciated the degree of disrespect Fedric was showing his father. They sat closer than was necessary, then inched closer still. Fedric smiled, unsure of what was happening, but enjoying the proximity of the two beautiful warrior women.

"Does he smell?" said Sophy.

Jul sniffed the air. "Aye, of light fae courtesans, I'm thinking," she said, smoothing her hand up his lean thigh.

"Well," said Sophy, gently running her hand through his hair, her mouth inches from his. "We can deal with that."

Viktar glanced sideways at Rella, who kept her face stubbornly neutral. They both saw that Fedric had no idea what was in store for him. Rella didn't mind a bit of horseplay, but she wasn't sure this was the time or place for such games.

She opened her mouth to protest, but a small shake of Viktar's head halted her. *Very well,* thought Rella. After all, Fedric's superior attitude had been irritating everyone for days. *Let them have their fun.*

Rella and Viktar left the cave with Gimrir, knowing that Sophy and her sisters were about to give Fedric a sound drubbing. She trusted it would not go too far. However, they would not go gently on him.

The girls had done as she had suspected and stripped the young man of his weapons, his clothes, and then his dignity. They'd given him a few bruises, but no real harm had come to him. Viktar had managed to make the lad see it as an initiation, rather than a humiliating drubbing.

A week later, a messenger came to inform Rella that a large contingent of Crystal Mountain Healers was closing on their position. Leaving those who were free from addiction to supervise the addicts, Rella and her companions left for the wild fae camp taking Viktar and Fedric with them.

CHAPTER 7

Back at the wild fae encampment, Rella sat her horse in the high woodlands. Her mare was the one Dagstyrr had called Morning Star, and the name suited her, for she was always ready for a run in the morning. Whenever she rode Morning Star, her thoughts turned to Dagstyrr, and she blamed her yearning on the horse, though in truth, her longing for him grew with every passing moment.

It was not without good reason that her people always mated for life. Bonds between mates were tightly sealed.

She had returned to camp without ever reaching her goal of Thingstyrbol, but she did not feel defeated. Shaken by what they'd found, they all needed time to digest it. The Dark Emperor's evil rule was far more devastating and ambitious than she'd imagined. He wanted a dragon, and was prepared to sell prisoners to get one. What wasn't he capable of? She must be on her guard.

Glad to have been instrumental in rescuing her father's friend, Rella knew Viktar would prove useful in the days to come. He'd asked to stay and help ease Fedric into his new life. Rella was happy to oblige. Viktar had been her father's best strategist and close friend. She knew his size and light fae features stood out like a beacon in the camp. He drew mixed looks from the wild fae, who were all dark by nature. So she dare not give him any official status—the wild fae would never tolerate that—but perhaps she could show them his worth.

Below her, hundreds of people were strung out along a track two miles long. They were like a nomadic village. Everything you needed was there, or someone with the ability to make it was. Recently, she'd noticed more and more warriors joining their numbers—precisely what she needed. She was starting to rethink her idea of infiltrating the palace with a small group. But if she was going to attack Thingstyrbol head-on, she needed many more warriors—a proper army.

For now, warriors patrolled the line, helping where needed and bringing a sense of safety to the people who carted all their worldly goods to follow her—believing they were safe with the wild fae. These men and women were not cowards. They'd refused to serve the Dark Emperor, as was their right, and now they found themselves dispossessed. Rella wondered at the stupidity of the man. The Dark Emperor needed them far more than they needed him.

It was as if he was on a rampage of destruction just for the hell of it. His goals and motivation escaped her. Rella knew how important it was to understand your enemy in order to defeat him, and so she was left deliberating in ignorance.

Her own goals were simple enough, and she made no secret of them. First, she was going to defeat the Dark Emperor and place a new Dark Queen on the throne at Thingstyrbol.

If Dagstyrr hadn't freed his dragons by then, she'd find him and join his quest. Undoubtedly, he was speeding down the coast right now, perhaps on board the *Mermaid*, on his way to Hedabar. Drago and his kin were suffering. How much longer could the ancient dragon wait for release?

"My lady," said Fedric, gripping Morning Star's bridle.

"What is it, Fedric?" The young fae was still having trouble fitting in. He vacillated between confident arrogance and ingratiating helpfulness. The truth was, he was lost. He'd done what he thought was right to rescue his father, never dreaming the consequences to himself would be so dire. Rella, of all people, could understand that.

"Father sent me to invite you and your ladies to a feast."

"Tell Viktar we'd love to come. As long as he has plenty of Samish wine," added Rella with a smile. A social evening would be an excellent opportunity for Viktar and the dark fae to build a rapport before working together to attack Thingstyrbol.

He bowed and left. Rella wondered how Fedric felt about sharing a table with Patrice and her sisters after their last encounter. It must have hurt his pride.

The young man had promise, but Rella was not in the business of training young dark fae. She was thankful his father had remained with him for now, but she knew sooner or later Viktar must return to Casta. She only hoped tonight's dinner wasn't his way of saying farewell, because if anyone could plan a successful attack on Thingstyrbol, it was Viktar of Casta.

～

Dressed in a beautiful green silken gown studded with shimmering moonstones and embroidered with images of white ghost-toadstools, Rella made her way to the women's tent. Patrice and her sisters had also received luxurious gowns conjured by the seamstresses they sheltered and generously paid for by Viktar, as was the custom at light fae feasts. The host always provided the gowns. Rella had made it plain she wanted no extravagances among those who followed her, but she'd forgive Viktar this once. He had no idea just what a luxury this was.

When she entered, the sisters were admiring them-selves in a small hand mirror. Warriors didn't carry large mirrors around with them. "My, you look stunning," said Rella.

The sisters all blushed like schoolgirls caught trying on their mother's evening gowns. Rella laughed. "We deserve this, don't you think, ladies?"

"I do," said Jul, smoothing her hand down a deep pink silk gown.

"After having to listen to those poor addicted creatures, we certainly deserve this. I still can't get the sound of their screaming out of my head," said Clar as she twirled, holding out her violet skirts.

Patrice was stunningly regal in a red fine-woolen gown embroidered along the edge with blue forget-me-nots. Sophy was in bright blue, and Nan in pale rose pink. Their dark looks and lithe bodies suited the gowns well. Rella recognized an expert hand had crafted them.

Rella also knew this was just the thing to distract them from the horror of the slave pens. "Viktar's way of thanking us," she said.

"I'd have rescued him anyway," said Nan, teasing her raven hair into a wave at her temple.

"Aye," said Patrice, "he needn't thank us. You must make that clear, Rella."

"Don't worry, he already knows. With these gowns, he's thanking us for agreeing to attend his feast."

"Seriously?" said Patrice.

"It is customary among my...among the light fae."

The sisters laughed. "We don't need fancy gowns to be enticed to eat," said Sophy.

"Just the smell of decent food is enough to have us fighting over our place at the table," said Jul.

"One more thing. I ask that you all be respectful of Fedric tonight," said Rella.

A lighthearted moan went up from the sisters. "He's not so bad as long as his father's around," said Clar, kindly.

"Viktar knows his son can be difficult. I think that's what this is really about," said Rella. "Viktar can't stay here forever. One day, he must return to Casta, leaving Fedric with us."

"Perhaps we could persuade him to stay," said Sophy, a gleam in her dark eye.

"Last I heard, he was happily mated. There is no reason to think that's changed," said Rella, a warning in her raised brow.

"Do light fae *always* mate for life?" asked Clar.

"Yes," said Rella, putting a stop to their speculation.

"What, they don't even get to try them first?"

Rella smiled. "I didn't say they couldn't *try* them. There is a lot of fun to be had without actually mating."

Laughter erupted in the tent. Like Rella, these women were warriors in touch with their body's needs, and they were not shy to talk about it.

"Come on," said Rella. "We don't want to be late." Just as she lifted the tent flap, a young man stepped toward her with a tray of head garlands—each one designed to comple-ment a different dress. Rella smiled while Patrice and her sisters delighted in sorting them out. "Oh yes, true light fae style," she said.

"Really?" Patrice laughed. "Perhaps they're not so bad after all," she said, lifting a garland of red roses interspersed with the occasional blue forget-me-not—a perfect match for her dress.

"Forget it," said Sophy. "Imagine a whole room full of Fedrics."

"Ugh," chorused the others.

"Here, Rella, this must be yours," said Nan, handing her a wreath of green foliage studded with white roses and ghost-toadstools.

Rella paused. The wreath brought back memories of so many things. Perhaps that was what Viktar wanted. Toad-stools for the Dark Emperor who she was going to defeat, the wild forest foliage for the wild fae, and the scent of roses for Dagstyrr, needing only peppermint to make it a perfect representation of her life now. Of course, Viktar couldn't know her favorite scent was roses and peppermint. She'd used it sparingly since leaving Dagstyrr at the cabin so long ago. The memories that scent brought were powerful.

Jul, the youngest and smallest sister, came forward and expertly placed the garland on her hair, where her twisted braids already decorated her head. White ribbons fell down the back, and Jul weaved them into her long blonde braid. "You are very good at this, Jul," Rella teased. "If you ever want a recommendation as a lady's maid," she said, then watched the dark fae warrior's eyes turn black at the insult.

Jul turned and stared down her sisters. "Not one word, any of you, ever," she warned.

Her sisters raised their hands in surrender.

"We wouldn't dare," said Patrice, laughing. "You'll make us all bald with the next batch of shampoo."

"You are the best among us at dressing our hair; you shouldn't be ashamed of it," said Sophy. "I only wish I could do it."

"Well," said Jul, standing back to admire her handiwork. "I'll teach you."

"Thank you, Jul. It's wonderful," said Rella, amazed at the sisters' ability to turn instantly from fierce warriors to silly girls, then back again. They were strong and independent, unafraid to be themselves. It was that strength Rella would rely on to take her into the Dark Emperor's palace.

"Let's go," said Patrice, leading the party down the hill to the large tent Viktar had commandeered for the event.

The table, set with shining silver and crystal over white linen sparkled in the night. Glass globes hung from the roof of the tent, sending light dancing into all the corners then out again as the breeze caught them. Greenery from the forest festooned the table and walls. Viktar greeted each of them at the tent flap, and then passed them on to Fedric, who seated them with style and grace.

"Rella, my dear, thank you for allowing an old man this indulgence," Viktar said, indicating the tent with his hand. "I know you don't stand on ceremony here, but I was missing home."

Rella couldn't help but smile. "You honor us, my lord. It is a good reminder of happier times."

He held both her hands in his. "Even if they will never come again?"

"Especially so," said Rella, thinking she would never be that girl again.

"I'll let you in on a secret. None of us are who we once were. Life changes us. It is up to us to make sure those changes enhance who we are and do not diminish us," he said as if he'd read her thoughts.

"Oh, Viktar, sometimes you remind me so much of my father," said Rella. "That is just the sort of thing he would say."

"I hope I'm not making you morose. That was never my intention."

"Never. It is good to remember those we love. Especially when they are no longer with us," Rella said with a smile, allowing him to escort her to a seat at his right hand—a place of honor. The greenery scented the air. Rella breathed deep and relaxed into her cushioned chair.

There was not a large crowd, but enough to warrant a lute player and several servers. The young musician sat on a stool in the corner, strumming his instrument to a gentle tune.

Rella noted with interest that Viktar had invited most of her best warriors. Five male dark fae warriors were seated around the table, each looking as uncomfortable as the next. They gave the gowned women sidelong glances, never having seen their comrades dressed like this before. Viktar was very astute to have worked out that these were her leaders in the short time he'd been with the wild fae. Then again, he'd trained most of her father's officers. He had an exceptional eye for leadership.

There was no representative from the mountain elves. Rella wondered why, but would not insult Viktar by asking him. Perhaps Beatty and his kin didn't fancy a night of high light fae pomp.

Wine and mead flowed freely, and the conversation was all about what they would find at Thingstyrbol. Rella felt their excitement grow. Fedric, she was happy to see, served the most exquisite delicacies to Patrice and her sisters first. He paid attention to them, making sure their plates and cups were always full, and soon, they were laughing together. Hopefully, he'd forgiven them, and this wasn't just an act to please his father.

Viktar might have difficulty hiding his emotions, but Fedric was raised to spend his life at court and easily hid his feelings.

As the night progressed, Rella started to relax and enjoy the excellent food and company. The Samish wine flowed, and soon the dark fae were dancing traditional folk dances to the surprise of Viktar and Fedric. "I never expected my guests to be the entertainment," he said quietly to Rella.

"The wild fae love to dance. That they are doing so here is an honor. Very few outside their own culture see this kind of spectacle," said Rella. The women were leaping and dancing as wildly as the men. Born warriors, even their dances reflected fighting moves. The dance mesmerized all who witnessed it.

"The story tells of a warrior maiden who rescues her lover from a troll living high in the White Mountains," said Rella. "Unfortunately, he has fallen in love with the troll's daughter and has no intention of leaving. He calls his brothers to help him defeat the maiden and her sisters. The brothers all fall instantly in love with the sisters ignoring their brother, who is fighting for his life against the warrior maiden."

"I can see that now, thank you, Rella," said Viktar, watching the dance. "What is happening now? Has she killed him?"

"She has struck a death blow. He is dying. So close to death, the spell put upon him by the troll's daughter is destroyed. The warrior maiden is distraught. She has killed her love."

"So, what happens now?" said Viktar, watching the dancers whirl ever faster.

"She and her sisters turn into a storm that destroys the home of the troll and his daughter. The White Mountain is brought down to sea level, and the trolls all drown."

"Vengeful indeed," said Fedric, who'd been listening.

"Well, there is another version where the brothers all marry the sisters, and a prince comes along and falls in love with the sad warrior maiden. She falls in love with him, and they live happily ever after. However, humans dance that version."

"That is interesting," said Viktar. "Humans must have learned the story from the dark fae. They might not even have realized the tale weaver was dark fae."

"Yes, that is possible," said Rella, sipping her wine. "Likely even."

"Perhaps you might honor me later by dancing something from Casta with me?"

"It would be my pleasure."

Rella watched Fedric disappear and hoped he wasn't up to anything that might upset the company, but he returned quickly with a large dish of steaming sausages that he placed in front of her.

"What is this, Fedric?" said Viktar with a frown.

"It is a special dish of sausages, Father. I have it on good authority that Rella particularly enjoys a spicy sausage," said Fedric, with a smirk.

A hush fell on the crowd. Was Fedric trying to insult her? Spice prickled her nose. She couldn't help lifting a sausage as memories came flooding back of the night Dagstyrr introduced the crew of the *Mermaid* to his father's recipe. Keeping her eyes on Fedric, she bit into it.

"Dagstyrr," she whispered, her eyes closing.

"What are you saying, boy?" bellowed Viktar, on his feet and dangerous.

Rella reached out a shaking hand and gripped the old warrior's sleeve. "I think I have a visitor, Viktar."

Just then, a small figure ran into the tent, dodging any attempt to stop him. "Princess Rella!" he shouted. "I'm here. I told them you liked a big spicy sausage!" He stood grinning from ear to ear, one arm spread wide, emphasizing the empty sleeve on his other side. "I'm dark fae now, too. So here I am. Come to join you," he said, thumping his chest with his hand.

The whole company stood ready to slay the boy who'd just insulted their leader. Rella's hand waved them to sit.

"And I can fight now too! The captain's been training me," he said, brandishing a large dagger.

"Billy," she said breathlessly. Rella was almost brought to tears by his obvious delight at being with her again. Knowing he had no idea of his insult, she opened her arms to him. Billy knelt like a warrior and saluted her. She would not shame him with a hug, so she did all she could and saluted him back.

"Not the Billy you told us about?" said Patrice.

"The same," said Rella, smiling.

"You told them about me?" said Billy, rising.

"I did, Billy," she said. A single tear escaped her eye, and she swiped it away.

CHAPTER 8

Trying to hide the turmoil surging through her, Rella wondered why Billy had come to her first and not Dagstyrr...unless something terrible had happened to him? She didn't want to think about the alternative—that he hadn't forgiven her for deserting him.

Billy had told them that Captain Bernst was anchored beside the wild fae forest—and that was not good news. Why wasn't the *Mermaid* on its way to Hedabar? Rella and Viktar left Billy entertaining Patrice and the other warriors while they went in search of Captain Bernst. He was camped a couple of miles away, down by the wide estuary.

Viktar must have sensed her apprehension because he'd insisted on accompanying her, and she was too distressed to object. They were unusually silent as they made their way to the sailor's camp.

The smell of the spiced sausage was still on her hands and in her head. Rella felt as if she was losing her mind. All she could think about was Dagstyrr and how, despite herself, she hungered to see him. Still, her anger at him started to build with every step. He should be far from here rescuing Drago so they could be together forever.

She must defeat the Dark Emperor alone. He dare not risk injuring himself at Thingstyrbol, for he was their only way of communicating with Drago. Why did he make it so complicated?

Was he injured?

Rella allowed her feet to glide over the forest floor, barely touching down. She used her magic to speed her journey, and Viktar followed suit. Something terrible must have happened to Dagstyrr. Why else would Bernst be here?

"Wait," said Viktar, putting out a hand to restrain her as they drew near the sailor's camp. "This could be a trap."

"Billy would not lead me into a trap."

"Not knowingly. There is something wrong with the boy. Even I could see that, Rella. Don't tell me you didn't notice."

"He was just glad to see me," she said, remembering Billy's strange words: *I'm dark fae* he'd said. A chill ran up her spine.

She slowed her pace. "Yes, there is something not right," she said, knowing how badly Billy had been traumatized at the Casta court when he lost his arm below the elbow. Could something worse have happened to him since to cause his mind to desert him? She needed to find Dagstyrr.

"Let's take it a bit slower," said Viktar, "just in case." Together they slowed their pace, listening and watching like hunters in the night. They looked for anything that seemed out of place or sounded a warning to their acute hearing. The night sounds in the wild fae camp were many—small animals, burrowing insects, the rattle of dry leaves on the forest floor, and that was only the backdrop to snores, the tread of a sentry's feet, a child crying in the distance, and a dog barking—but nothing untoward reached them.

At last, she came to makeshift tents erected hastily along the shoreline. She recognized the *Mermaid* sitting offshore in deep water and one or two of the crew, who doffed their caps as Rella and Viktar passed. There was also a pair of magnificent longships dressed for war and pulled up on the shale. They must be the *Viper* and the *Knucker* that Captain Bernst had demanded as payment from Earl Magnus for rescuing his sons from Hedabar. The water sparkled silver in the moonlight, bringing a sense of wonder to the scene.

None of the tents looked any different from the others. Rella stood looking around the dark forest for Dagstyrr but saw no sign of him. Nor could she sense his aura of protection, which always heralded his presence. And where was Captain Bernst?

Rella calmed her growing panic and searched using all her fae senses. Then she saw Bernst sitting with his back against a tree. It was a favorite pose of his. She suspected he sat like that to replenish his fae energy whenever he came ashore.

Rella led Viktar toward the one-eyed man lounging on the ground beneath a horse chestnut tree. "Good evening to you, Captain," she said.

"Good evening to you, Rella of the wild fae. Strange company you keep," he said, nodding in Viktar's direction. He didn't move from his place as they approached but went on whittling whatever he had in his hand.

"This is a friend," she said, refusing to sound defensive.

"Oh, aye. Last time you had light fae friends, they stripped the clothes off you and tried to kill you. How's he different?" he said, indicating Viktar with his knife, but not deigning to look up at him.

"Princess Rella is quite safe with me," said Viktar, his deep voice sounding a warning.

"Viktar is a friend of my father's. I have known him all my life," said Rella.

"What's he doing here?" said Bernst, obviously not convinced.

"His son was having some trouble, and..."

"And you dashed in and saved him," said Bernst, raising his eyebrow. "A nasty habit you have there, Princess."

"It wasn't that simple," said Viktar, immediately jumping to Rella's defense.

"It never is," said Bernst, getting to his feet and putting out a hand to Viktar, "Captain Bernst, off the *Mermaid*."

It was Viktar's turn to raise a perfectly arched eyebrow. "I've heard of the *Mermaid*, sir."

"She's a good ship," said Bernst as the two gripped hands.

With a snort, Viktar said, "She's a bit more than that."

"Ah, you do know of her."

"By reputation only. We've never been formally introduced."

"Well, perhaps that could be arranged," said Bernst, obviously having summed up the mighty light fae warrior in front of him and decided he liked him. "I'm not promising anything, mind."

"The honor would be mine, Captain."

All this time, Rella's senses were searching for any sign of Dagstyrr. When she still couldn't find him, she turned to Bernst. "Where is he?"

The captain turned his one eye to her. "He's here. He's not very happy with you, though."

"Then what are you doing here?" she said, furious. "I have little patience for games."

"He wants two hundred of your dark fae warriors. He says I can pick them," said Captain Bernst.

"Is that all?" Rella fumed amid the sound of Viktar laughing. "Where is he?"

"Don't know exactly. Took 'imself off as soon as we landed. Wanted me to meet with you. That's why I sent Billy."

Rella knew the captain of old, and this was just his style. He never approached anything head-on. He preferred to sidle up to it and launch a sneak attack. "Why do you want two hundred more warriors? You only have three ships."

"I don't. I like to travel light, as you know. Dagstyrr wants them. If he can load each ship with a hundred warriors, each taking a turn at the benches, he'll be able to launch a direct attack on Hedabar."

"You don't think it's a good idea?" said Viktar, always ready to discuss battle tactics.

"No, I don't."

Viktar paced back and forth, his long hair flowing around him. His blue gaze turned inward as he considered the captain's words. "From what I've heard, the citadel is a stronghold. I think it's a good plan. It would be even better with more men, though I couldn't give any precise advice without seeing it, or a model of it."

"We only have three ships," said Bernst, his smile pasted on his weathered face.

"If he makes an assault on the citadel and is unsuccessful, this vizier will only strengthen his fortifications. He'll be pre-warned," said Viktar.

Bernst rolled his eyes. "That's what Dagstyrr says. I say, let's sneak in with a small crew, free the dragons, and get out as fast as we can."

"You are trying to save one hundred and sixty-eight drag-ons, not counting hatchlings or eggs—not steal a diamond necklace. No. You need more men," said Viktar thoughtfully. "Many more."

"They are dragons! They can fly. Once we've opened the doors for them, they can carry their hatchlings and eggs. All we need to do is get in, break their chains, and get out," said Bernst. "Simple." His frustration told Rella that he'd already had this conversation, or similar conversations, with Dagstyrr many times over.

"Viktar is the best strategist my father ever had. He knows what he's talking about," said Rella. The last thing she needed right now was these two at odds with each other.

"So, you have two hundred dark fae warriors sitting about twiddling their thumbs, do you?"

"Of course not," said Rella. "I need all the warriors I can muster to launch an attack on Thingstyrbol."

Viktar turned to Rella. "You aim to attack the palace en masse now?"

"You don't think it's a good idea?" she said.

"I have no idea. I've never seen Thingstyrbol...or the citadel," said Viktar.

"I have," said Rella, remembering her one trip to the palace of Thingstyrbol and shivering at the memory. "Originally, I had planned an attack of just twenty or so elite warriors. However, more and more warriors are flocking to the wild fae camp. They deserve to be a part of taking back the Dark Queen's throne."

Yes, she wanted every warrior she could find beside her on that attack. They could keep everyone else busy while she sought out the Dark Emperor. She was determined he'd fall to her blade. Her brows drew together in a deep frown.

Viktar put his hand on Rella's shoulder to comfort her,

then turned to Bernst. "I've never seen Princess Rella react like that to anything, and I've known her all her life."

"Aye, the Dark Emperor is truly something worth a grimace." Bernst gave an exaggerated shudder. "I met him once. 'Twas enough. But Rella will get the better of him, I'm sure. After all, she's the same girl who led the rescue of four light fae from the citadel. It had never been done before or since. Rella did it though," said Bernst, pride of ownership in his voice.

"If anyone could pull that off, Rella of Casta could," said Viktar, clearly claiming her victory as one for Casta.

"Will you two stop it?" said Rella. "It does not make me weak to admit that I'm not looking forward to another meeting with that revolting creature, but I *will* meet with him, and I *will* kill him. That's a promise."

"I never doubted it for a moment," said Bernst, with a gentle smile.

Viktar looked at the grey light shadowing the summer sky to the east. "The night is almost over. Let's meet tomorrow after we've had time to rest and digest what we've spoken about here tonight."

"Aye, I think this calls for a war council, right enough," said Bernst.

"Noon, my tent," said Viktar.

Bernst spat on the ground, barely missing Viktar's highly polished boots.

Viktar's eyes flashed a warning.

Rella supposed Viktar must appear very arrogant. He was a man used to giving orders and having them obeyed without question—just like Bernst. Tomorrow could be interesting.

She took a deep breath, searching one last time for any sign of Dagstyrr. There was none. "Tomorrow sounds good, gentlemen—noon at Viktar's tent. Billy can show you the way, Captain," she said, lightly touching his arm. She turned and led Viktar back into the wild fae camp with a heavy heart.

Dagstyrr must not have forgiven her after all. Well, she wasn't going to go chasing around after him. Did he expect her to hand over her best warriors? Hurt at his refusal to meet her had turned to anger. He obviously didn't crave her presence as she did his.

"Your Captain Bernst is an interesting fellow," said Viktar, about to leave Rella outside her tent.

"Yes, he is. He's a good man to have on your side in a tight spot," said Rella, unable to keep the exhaustion and disappointment from her voice.

The knowledge that Dagstyrr could be with her now yet refused to contact her left her feeling isolated like never before. He was her mate. She must have hurt him very badly. Didn't he understand it was for his protection?

"You'll need your strength and your wits about you tomorrow. Get some rest," said Viktar.

"I will."

"I'm looking forward to planning these assaults," he said, with a gleam in his eyes.

Rella laughed. "I can see that." She reached up on her toes and kissed his cheek as she had done when she was a child. His scent of steel and leather laced with cologne and silk, reminded her of her father. "Goodnight, Viktar, and thank you for a wonderful evening. Even if it didn't end the way you had planned."

"Goodnight, Princess," said Viktar, bowing and taking his leave.

She lifted the flap of her tent only to be pulled roughly inside.

"Dagstyrr." His name fell from her lips. His energy was everywhere, no longer a gentle protectiveness but a suffocating wall of passion that left her breathless. He held her wrist and dragged her around to face him—she didn't resist.

"Who is Viktar, and how exactly had he planned to end the evening?

CHAPTER 9

"Don't tell me you're jealous," said Rella, seeing the conflicting emotions of a protector and a wounded lover warring on his face.

His eyes were the darkest blue of midnight, searching her face for answers in the dim light of her tent. Rella had never seen him so angry. She couldn't help the thrill of excitement coursing through her—he cared as much as she did. After thinking she wouldn't see him, this show of male ownership was strangely reassuring.

Dagstyrr pulled her to him. His eyes locked on hers, his arms wrapping around her, declaring his desire, as his mouth claimed hers. One hand cupped her jaw. She felt the rough callus of his thumb graze her cheek, reminding her he was human. How could one man be so harsh and so tender at the same time?

Rella met his insistent mouth with demands of her own. Her vow to not fall into his arms the minute she saw him—shattered. How could she be angry with a man whose touch turned her into a bubbling volcano of need? She pushed her hands through his hair, gripping it; she needed to hold on to something before she spiraled out of control. The beard he'd grown since they parted tickled her skin, reminding her of his long absence.

She pulled away, breathless, torn between wanting him and duty. Her eyes searched his face. "Why are you here?"

A small frown marred his forehead. "Not now, Rella," he snarled, sweeping her up and carrying her to the simple bed of straw and furs.

Passion rose in her like the hottest fire, clouding her brain. The heady mix of safety and love that always came with his presence wrapped around her, and she was free to give herself completely.

He lifted her to her feet, then turned her away from him and started to unlace her gown. Suddenly she felt like a girl on her wedding day, shy and unsure. The soft garment fell to the floor, and she stepped out of it.

Dagstyrr pulled the wreath from her head. "Since when did you wear flowers in your hair?" he said with a laugh before loosening her braid.

She turned to him and unlaced his shirt, sweeping her hands up his body, removing the linen so she could press against the warmth of his chest.

Afraid to speak lest their anger at each other destroy this precious moment, Rella continued to undress him, raining light kisses over his scarred body while he gazed at her with unashamed love. Then, with a gasp, he lifted her onto the furs. His body was always so warm. She wasn't sure whether that was his natural state or the influence of Drago, but she luxuriated in his embrace.

They were in a world of their own where nothing and no one dared intrude. Both intoxicated by the passions deep inside that demanded to be quenched before anything else. Rella's magical energy of blue sparks and green puffs that manifested whenever they made love danced around them like a celebration, as his hands danced a magic of their own across her body.

His eyes blazed with passion as he possessed her like she was a finely tuned instrument he'd long ago learned to master. He was hers. The thrill of possession drove her desire until she wanted to take control, and he let her, but only until his desire pushed him to take her completely. Hard and driven, he pulled her down and possessed her until their bodies moved as one, and they cried out together in release.

Joy flourished in Rella's heart. This man was everything to her, and the wonder of it left her in awe. A tear slipped down the side of her face. She turned to him, but his eyes were closed, his breathing returning to normal.

He must have sensed her watching him, for he opened his eyes and raised a hand to wipe the tear from her cheek. "Whatever is the matter, Princess?"

"Absolutely nothing," she said.

He pulled her closer to his side and wrapped a fur around them. "A tear is not nothing."

"You make me happy."

"Do I now?" he said, his hand running down the length of her back to cup her bottom and pull her even closer.

She snuggled against his side, the familiar protective shield that covered him bringing her peace and comfort. In truth, the only time she felt truly safe was here, within his arms.

Dagstyrr woke to find the sun filtering through small holes in the tent. It was bright enough to let him know it must be near midday. He lay watching dust motes dance in the beams, not wanting to disturb Rella's sleep. She no longer smelled of roses and peppermint. That made him sad. It spoke to how long they'd been apart. He would remedy that.

She was his woman. They should be together always, but she'd taken it upon herself to leave him and go after the Dark Emperor on her own. Dagstyrr had sworn he wouldn't forgive her for that, but how could he be angry with her after the night of passion they'd spent together? It wasn't as though she'd seduced him. If he remembered correctly, he hadn't exactly been a reluctant participant. A smile crossed his lips. If memory served him right, he'd instigated it, not her.

Despite the urgency of rescuing Drago, he searched his conscience for excuses to stay with her a little longer. Surely a few weeks would make no difference? Then he remembered the overwhelming pain and despair that came with Drago every time Dagstyrr communed with him. Of course it made a difference. When you were living in hell, every moment was as a lifetime. Still, he must not allow his compassion for Drago to push him into acting rashly. To attack the citadel unprepared would spell disaster, and he was promise bound unto ten generations. He couldn't afford to get it wrong.

His family in Halfenhaw didn't even know about his promise to Drago on their behalf.

Dagstyrr knew he was walking a fine line of conflicting duties and desires. As soon as he had the men he needed, no matter what was happening here, he must set off for the citadel.

He bent and kissed her forehead. She mumbled something about sausages, which reminded him of how hungry he was. Slipping out of bed, he pulled on some clothes, then padded barefoot to the tent flap.

He surprised the two guards on duty outside her tent. They both wore the brown leathers popular amongst the wild fae. He'd hardly call it a uniform, but their shields wore Rella's device, and their spears were real enough.

Billy sat on a patch of grass some feet away, watching the tent. He sprang up and came to Dagstyrr, carrying a basket of fresh bread rolls and mead in his one hand. "Take this to Princess Rella," he said imperiously. Then, turning to the guards: "I told you there was a human in there."

The two men looked at each other, looked at Dagstyrr, and then one whispered, "Pay no attention. We think he's head-struck."

"No, but he is injured," said Dagstyrr. "Don't let him get into any trouble."

"Don't worry, we all know about him after last night."

"What happened...Never mind," said Dagstyrr, taking the fresh bread inside and setting the basket on the bed. No doubt he'd hear tales of Billy's latest escapade from the crew.

"Wakey, wakey, sleepyhead." He shook Rella's foot. "I've some fresh bread and cold mead here," he said, pulling the bottle from the basket.

Rella stretched like a kitten awakening in the sun, twisting her spine this way and that, then stretching out her limbs. Eventually, she opened her eyes and smiled up at him. "You really are here?"

"I am." He leaned forward and kissed her. She was an erotic picture of loveliness lying there in the dappled light. Her long limbs exaggerated her lithe body and made an art piece of the dark mark twisting up her body to land on her face. Strands of golden hair sparkled in a sunbeam, but her dark eyes were wanton. He gazed into their depths and forgot about breakfast.

She moaned her pleasure as he stretched out naked next to her and trailed his mouth along the length of her thigh. Cupping a perfect breast, he brought his mouth down to claim hers as she wrapped her legs and arms around him.

"My Lady, are you dressed?" A man's voice sounded, loud and irritated, from outside the tent.

Dagstyrr and Rella froze. She looked up at him. "What time is it?"

"I don't know," he said. "Tell whoever that is to go away before I kill him," he growled, tracing kisses down Rella's neck.

She laughed. "I can't."

"Then tell him you'll come when good and ready, and that it might be a week or two."

He felt her stomach push against his with every bubble of laughter. "I can't." Then he watched her face calm, and her eyes left his. "Seriously, what time is it?"

"Seriously, I don't know. About noon, I'd guess," said Dagstyrr, knowing now that their lovemaking was doomed.

"Noon!"

Dagstyrr rolled aside to let her up, unable to help the moan escaping his lips. "What's so important it can't be postponed?"

"You," said Rella, pulling on an assortment of leather clothes that looked like they'd seen better days.

"Me? What have I to do with anything?"

"Beatty," she called "Tell them I'll be right there."

The man huffing and puffing his frustration outside their tent left.

"What have you to do with anything? You want my men."

"Of course I do, but why should that involve anyone other than you and me?"

"Because," she said, sitting and pulling on a high boot, "there are other people involved besides us. I organized a war council for noon today at Viktar's tent."

"Why didn't you tell me?" said Dagstyrr, jumping up and pulling his shirt over his head for the second time that morning.

"Who said you were invited?" said Rella, pulling on a second boot.

"I'm the one who wants the men, remember?"

She turned on him just as he was pulling on his boots. "Why weren't you there?"

"Where?" he asked, genuinely perplexed.

"Last night. Why weren't you there? You let Bernst do your talking for you. That's not like you, Dagstyrr. What are you playing at?"

She stood, looking every inch a fierce dark fae warrior. One hand on her sword hilt, the other hand raised to hold him back—with magic if necessary. Dagstyrr admired her crazy mix of exotic siren and fierce warrior. "I was afraid of what would happen when we saw each other."

"I wouldn't have hurt you."

"That wasn't what I was afraid of," he said, grinning and closing the distance between them. He enjoyed Rella's momentary confusion. "Think of what *did* happen when we saw each other."

"You're not that special, Dagstyrr of Halfenhaw. I wouldn't have ravished you in front of the crew. Oh, you are infuriating." She turned to leave.

He reached out and grabbed her arm. "I love you, Rella." He felt her still.

She turned and looked up at him. "I can't think why."

"I fought the urge to come racing after you for weeks. I think about you day and night. You are constantly in my head and my heart. Don't try and deny that what we have is beyond ordinary bonding," he said.

"I deny nothing, but until I've put to rights the wrongs I've brought upon my people and you have rescued your dragons, we can't afford the luxuries ordinary people have."

Her words cut him deeply. She spoke the truth he didn't want to face. "What luxuries do ordinary people have that we may not?" he whispered, barely able to trust his voice.

Gazing into the depths of her dark eyes, he was mesmerized by the complicated feelings stirring inside him. He'd give his soul for her, but even that wouldn't be enough to save her or his family. He was promise bound to a dragon.

"Ordinary people can have a home, a family. Until we fulfill our tasks, we dare not have either."

"Is that what you want?"

"I want what you want, Dag." Her hand came up and cupped his chin. "Don't make me say it here and now. It will soften me, and I must go and be Rella of the wild fae in a war council."

He pulled her into his embrace and kissed her as if his life depended on it. She melted against him, but he pushed her away. "We'll finish this tonight," he said with a grin.

Rella rolled her eyes. "Very well." She turned and exited the tent.

"Wait." He caught her up. "You still haven't told me. Who is Viktar?"

CHAPTER 10

A hush fell over the company as Rella entered the tent with Dagstyrr by her side. His warrior bulk presented an unknown challenge to those already assembled, but they'd know he had no magic in an instant. She suppressed a smile, proud that these mighty fae warriors found it necessary to evaluate a mere human as a threat. It spoke volumes about his presence.

Viktar stood in full battle gear, looking every inch the powerful commander that he was, his steel-blue fae eyes quickly assessing the newcomer. She saw Dagstyrr's gaze meet his without flinching—a feat for anyone.

Rella ignored Viktar and Dagstyrr's overt appraisal of each other. She knew both men well enough to trust that it would not come to blows.

"So, you are Dagstyrr of Halfenhaw," said Viktar, at last offering his right arm. Dagstyrr gripped his arm with his right hand in the way of warriors everywhere, and the whole company appeared to exhale a sigh of relief.

Stiff and formal though they were being, Rella hoped they'd soon be allies, or better yet, friends.

"Viktar of Casta? Of course. My mother speaks highly of you," said Dagstyrr, visibly relaxing as understanding dawned. Here was the legendary commander of all Casta's armies.

"I trust the fair Astrid is well?" said Viktar.

"She was the last time I was home."

Rella couldn't help noticing the lie but understood it. The last time Dagstyrr saw his mother, she was standing on the shore while Dagstyrr sailed away on the *Mermaid*. Her three eldest light fae sons were dragon's-blood addicts, and her youngest human son was sailing with the dark fae. Princess Astrid had stood bravely next to her husband, Earl Magnus, waving off her son as her world crumbled around her.

Captain Bernst lolled in a corner, his weather-beaten features and drab clothing in stark contrast to his glittering host. Deep in the shadows, Billy sat intent on some cobweb or other in the fingers of his one hand. The boy was so focused on whatever he imagined was there, he barely acknowledged Rella. Yet he managed to throw a scowl at Dagstyrr before returning to his task.

"Dagstyrr, this is Beatty, leader of the mountain elves." Beatty gave a curt nod. The elves never touched others unless it was necessary. Then she went to Patrice and Jul. "Ladies, may I introduce Dagstyrr of Halfenhaw."

Patrice stood with her arms folded, raking him up and down with danger in her dark eyes. Eventually, with a small smile, she held out her arm to him. "Interesting choice, Rella," she said, laughter in her voice. That she found him attractive was obvious. Unlike light fae, dark fae often mated with humans. The question was, would she give Dagstyrr the honor he was due as a warrior?

Dagstyrr's smile at Patrice's overt assessment bordered

on flirting—lucky Rella wasn't the jealous type. Though, she admitted, it did irk.

"This is my youngest sister, Jul," said Patrice. "The one with the brains."

"It is a pleasure to meet you, lady," said Dagstyrr, bowing low over the hand Jul held out to him. "How many more sisters are there to swell our ranks?"

"Three," said Jul. "Patrice leads our house in battle."

Until this moment, she hadn't realized how important it was to her that these warriors respect her choice of mate. He was as much part and parcel of her world as they were, and they must accept him. No matter that he was human—he was her chosen mate.

"Dagstyrr, this is Fedric, Viktar's son." Fedric stood in the shadows, a younger, slimmer version of his father, but without his commanding presence. Rella guessed he was still coming to terms with his brown eyes and future prospects.

"Honored to meet you," said Dagstyrr, going up to him and taking his arm. The shadows lifted as the young man stepped forward, bringing his eyes into the light. Dagstyrr turned immediately to Rella, questions in his raised brow.

Fedric scowled.

"I healed his wounds," she said. "Too much dark magic entered his body. A lot has happened recently. It will take some time to bring you up to date."

He knew nothing of the aborted attack on Thingstyrbol, or the light fae slaves. She smiled to herself when she realized why she had been so tardy—they'd been too engrossed in each other last night to allow the world to intrude on their happiness.

It was a situation she'd have to rectify.

After the introductions, Viktar acknowledged the gathering was now complete, and Fedric closed the tent flap. Rella pulled a silencing ward over the tent. Some of what they had to discuss here was not for everyone's ears.

Rella opened the conversation. It was important that the newcomers didn't misread the structure making up the wild fae. "I want you all to understand that although I command the warriors known as the wild fae, once Thingstyrbol is taken, that will change."

"Even Patrice and her sisters?" said Viktar.

Rella felt Patrice stiffen beside her. "Patrice, Sophy, Jul, Clar, and Nan are highborn ladies of the House of Threme. They outrank you, Viktar, and are full-blood dark fae warriors. We fight together because we choose to, and because we have a common enemy. So, yes, once that enemy is defeated, many will return to their homes and duties, including the Threme sisters."

"I had no idea your position was so precarious, Rella," said Viktar.

"It is the way of the dark fae," said Captain Bernst. "We sign on for a campaign like a sailor does on a ship. After that, we can leave anytime it suits us."

"A strange concept, I must say," said Viktar.

"It keeps us honest," said Bernst. "Nothing worse than having men under you who don't want to be there. It encourages discontent." With a smile, he raised his cup of mead in a salute to Patrice and drank it down. She lifted hers to him and also drank.

"The trick is to make them want to be there," said Viktar.

Rella knew Bernst was enjoying the consternation etching its way across Viktar and Fedric's faces. They were just now beginning to realize that working with the dark fae was going to be a new and very different experience for them. Here, there were no glittering regiments and cohorts to command.

Viktar wanted to guide his son through the transition to the dark fae before returning to the rest of his family in Casta. The sooner the boy learned how things worked in his new world, the better.

"So, you are promise bound to a dragon?" said Fedric, sounding as though he didn't believe one word of it. Why should he? Dragons hadn't been seen in Casta or the surrounding countryside in many generations.

"That's about the size of it," said Bernst, looking him in the face for the first time.

Viktar stared ahead. "I saw our people trapped and fed dragon's blood. It takes hold immediately. The dragons are there all right," he said, his face a picture of light fae immobility, giving nothing away.

Rella glanced at Dagstyrr's questioning look. From the moment they'd first met, she'd kept things from him—no more. "The Dark Emperor enslaved light fae to sell to the vizier of Hedabar," she said softly.

"Surely he's not short of gold?"

"The price was not gold," said Viktar. "He wants a dragon."

Rella watched Dagstyrr stiffen. "I will warn Drago," he said.

Beatty stepped forward and faced Viktar. "Those freed slaves are the lucky ones. The Crystal Mountain healers will see to them. Ask Rella here what it's like in the citadel. Captured fae of all kinds are drained of their magic energies. Even mountain elves, dryads, and others who have no battle magic."

"But their magic energies are strong," said Bernst.

"Milked like goats," said Rella, remembering the awful truth of what resided in the citadel.

"How can you know so much?" said Fedric. "I thought you were in and out of the citadel in a short time."

Astute, thought Rella.

"The fae imprisoned there cannot replenish their energies," said Dagstyrr. A gasp from several people interrupted him. "Eventually, they lose their magic."

Viktar's head turned toward Rella. "They are mad then?"

Rella looked away at the mention of madness. "Aye," said Dagstyrr, whose frown reflected his memories of the place.

"They don't live long," said Rella, recovering her composure. "The dragons, on the other hand, live long lives imprisoned in the citadel's depths."

Viktar stood and paced the tent. Eventually, he sat back down, his fists crashing on the table. "Dragons are our kin by magic. Why do we not know of this?"

At that, Billy jumped up and stood fearlessly in front of the great Casta warrior. "I'll tell you why, you piggin' light fae piece of shit!"

Rella stood quickly. "Billy! If you..."

Viktar extended his arm to halt her. "No, Princess Rella, let him speak," he urged.

The boy's eyes gleamed with hatred. "This is what happens when someone tells the truth in Casta." He pulled his empty sleeve up and showed the scarred stump of his arm. "Tried to kill me, you did, but Rella of the wild fae saved me. Her and the captain saved me. Now I only sign on dark fae ships, 'cause Rella and me are dark fae now."

"All right, Billy, you come here now," said Bernst.

"I'm telling the truth. The truth is Casta is a bunch of murderin' liars." Billy stood his ground, sneering at the great warrior. "Care more about their fancy clothes than their people. Don't trust them!"

"Billy, go see what's keeping lunch. Tell cook we want spiced meats, just like Dagstyrr here showed us," said Bernst. "You've had your say, and now it's someone else's turn."

The boy bounced on his toes for a moment while he considered the captain's orders. Eventually, he turned. "Aye, aye, Captain." Then he turned back to Viktar. "Don't think I'm afraid of you. I'm not."

"I never thought for a moment you were, Billy. I commend you for telling the truth," said Viktar.

The whole company sighed with relief as Billy exited. He'd brought up a sensitive matter, and now Rella must explain it. "The court at Casta thought to bury news of Hedabar and leave their prince rotting in a cell," said Rella. "I couldn't see the big picture then. Even if I had, I doubt I could have left him to rot."

"What is the big picture?" Dagstyrr challenged her as always.

She smiled up at him, in part to wipe the sneer off Fedric's face. "That my brother will never be the king he could have been before his time in the citadel. That the Dark Emperor wants war with Casta at any price, and that my broken promise is only the excuse he used."

"Oh, there is something you're forgetting," said Bernst.

"What's that?" asked Rella.

"He still wants you for his queen."

"Nonsense." Rella shivered, denying what she knew to be true. "He could have anyone he wants."

"Except you," said Bernst.

"Well, we have two problems taxing us today," said Rella, ignoring the pitying look from Patrice. "Firstly, how am I to attack and defeat the Dark Emperor at the fortified palace called Thingstyrbol? There must be one assault on the palace, not a long, drawn-out siege. I want him dead the day we attack. Secondly, how can Dagstyrr launch a successful rescue of the dragons without taking men away from my attack on Thingstyrbol?"

"They are, remarkably, the same problem," said Dagstyrr, whose voice had remained silent for a while.

"How?" said Fedric, who hadn't taken his eyes off Dagstyrr since his appearance in the tent.

"They are both assaults on fortified edifices by forces that are smaller than we need to ensure success," said Dagstyrr.

"You are correct," said Viktar, approvingly.

"Dividing my forces is out of the question," said Rella, understanding that they were finally getting down to the reason for this meeting. "I need every warrior I have to attack Thingstyrbol. Most of them have only joined our ranks in the last ten days."

"If—and I mean *if*—you use your whole force against Thingstyrbol and win, your army will then be free to help rescue the dragons," said Viktar.

Rella stared at him. "I will win, Viktar. I have to. It is the only way to put a stop to this senseless war. Once the dark fae restore a traditional queen of their choosing on the throne at Thingstyrbol, the Casta armies will go home. Peace will once again hold dominion."

"A pretty picture," said Dagstyrr. "Are you sure it's what Calstir wants?"

"Of course it is," said Rella, not wanting to imagine her brother wanted to continue this war. She had started it, and she would put an end to it.

Patrice stood. "The human is correct. Calstir is enjoying

his victories more than ever. He's claiming all the lower shires as light fae territory. Why do you think our wild fae numbers here are so great?"

"The Dark Emperor claims all the territory he wins too," said Viktar. "I see no difference."

"I do," said Dagstyrr. "The difference is, once Rella defeats the Dark Emperor, whoever sits the throne of Thingstyrbol will have her work cut out for her. It will only be the beginning of long, drawn-out peace negotiations to reclaim all her territory, and that's time I don't have.

"If you lend me the warriors I ask for, I will return with dragons," he said, unable to keep a smile from his mouth.

Captain Bernst leaped to his feet. "Don't say another word. Damn it, haven't you learned anything? Don't make promises you can't keep, especially where dragons are concerned. You don't know when they are listening."

Dagstyrr towered over him. "Every day, those creatures suffer pain we cannot imagine. Whether I am promise bound or not, I have to save them."

The enormity of his task brought silence to the room.

"How many ships do you have?" asked Viktar quietly.

"Three, but only ninety men," said Dagstyrr, just as quiet.

"I know where there is another one," said Viktar. "The guards were drilling us on sitting the benches so we could row ourselves down to Hedabar. The healers only took one ship, the *Drake*, up to the Crystal Mountain. The *Spider* lies abandoned."

Dagstyrr frowned at Rella.

"A ship belonging to the Dark Emperor," she whispered, which did little to erase his tense brow. He hated to be kept in the dark. However, she trusted he'd go along with her until she could fill him in on the details. A ship was a ship, and that was what interested him.

"I've no doubt the Dark Emperor will have retrieved it by now," said Captain Bernst.

Patrice stood and smiled. "My sisters and I had it brought up to the large Elfin Cove. It is well warded. No one will find it."

Surprised, Rella smiled her approval. "Well done!"

"Doesn't mean I intend to hand it over to your human, Rella," said Patrice.

"Of course not, and his name is Dagstyrr, meaning bringer of the battle storm. Once you get to know him, I think you'll find it appropriate," said Rella with a smile. She could see Patrice's interest quicken.

Viktar coughed to regain their attention. The tension in the room was growing and could very quickly erupt into chaos. That was the last thing Rella wanted. She needed all the help she could get, and there was no better strategist than Viktar of Casta.

"Viktar, putting aside our different agendas for a moment, how would you suggest we launch our attack on Thingstyrbol...and on Hedabar?" she added at the last minute.

"I thought you'd never ask."

"Then you have a plan. Will you be with us?" asked Patrice.

"I'm afraid not. I must return to Casta before too long, but my son will be with you."

"Fedric is no Viktar," said Patrice, her dark brow raised in amusement. She'd voiced what everyone was thinking. "How can we trust your plan, if you won't be there to see it through?"

The young fae warrior had his father's height, but not

his composure. He visibly bristled at Patrice's criticism but did not comment. Either he was learning or was under strict instructions from Viktar.

"Aye," said Beatty. "What's to stop you planning an attack sure to fail—then leave us to our fate? You'll get rid of hundreds of dark fae and an inconvenient dark fae son all in one day."

The mountain elves were always a suspicious lot, but Rella realized Beatty was only saying what others would think. A hush fell over the assembly. Silence stretched until no one dared to break it.

Eventually, Viktar's voice rumbled through the tent. "Beatty is correct. There is no reason for you to trust me. However, I give you my word that I will help plan attacks on both Thingstyrbol and Hedabar by assessing your forces' strengths and weaknesses and the strengths and weaknesses of your targets. Besides, you need me."

The tension in the war tent grew. Viktar couldn't always hide his arrogance.

"More dark fae refugees join the wild fae every day. It's a huge task to weed out those who are real warriors and those who simply want to fight. I can do that faster than anyone here, and I can teach them to fight as one by placing the experienced warriors in the right positions. That way, we make sure the less experienced have strong sergeants peppered among them."

Silence met his speech.

"Come on," said Viktar, struggling to stay patient. "You are all leaders in your own right. I want to help. You don't trust me? Fair enough. Judge for yourselves."

Rella didn't want to be seen as championing the light fae. At the same time, she knew Viktar of old. He would never betray her. "I do not doubt Viktar's ability as the best strategist of our time. However, I have learned the hard way always to protect myself."

Turning to Viktar, she said, "What we are also wondering is, once you have helped us decide our plan of attack, what will stop you returning to Casta and informing Calstir of our plans? He is your liege lord and could use it against us."

"Aye," said Beatty. "With all the wild fae warriors at Thingstyrbol, the rest of our people would be easy prey for the likes of Calstir. To say nothing of a bargaining token to toss at the feet of the Dark Emperor."

Mutterings of assent filled the tent. Rella saw the big fae's head drop and knew he was thinking on his feet. She was also aware of Fedric's growing resentment as he glared at her from the shadows. She understood it. To question his father's motives was an insult; no one in Casta would dream of doing such a thing. Hopefully, Fedric was about to learn something.

"Rella of the wild fae speaks the truth," said Viktar, lifting his head. "No man, not even an old man such as myself, can serve two masters. Therefore, I ask to remain among you until after we attack the citadel at Hedabar. I will 'sign on,' as you say, for these two campaigns only. That way, I can serve Rella as I served her father before her without betraying my new king. Once I return to Casta, I will finally swear my oath to King Calstir."

Dagstyrr stood up. "My mother often spoke of the integrity of Viktar of Casta. What he is proposing is hard for such a man. However, in helping us defeat the Dark Emperor on our terms, he is still serving King Calstir, is he not? Using his experience to help us lay out a plan to save the dragons—well, isn't that helping Casta too?"

"Aye, the war will be over either way," said Bernst,

rubbing his chin. "I can see that. As long as he stays here and we have his sworn oath as a fae lord, he won't try and contact Casta."

Patrice looked at the mountain elves' leader, and they exchanged a nod. "Beatty and I agree, but we want the sworn word of his son as well."

It was Viktar and Fedric's turn to exchange nods. "We agree."

"The first assault must be Thingstyrbol," said Viktar. "After that, we sail for the island of Hedabar with as many as we can muster."

"Agreed," chorused Patrice and her sisters.

"Aye," said Beatty.

The last to agree were Dagstyrr and Bernst. "I only hope the taking of Thingstyrbol goes quickly," said Bernst, throwing a truculent look at Dagstyrr.

Rella knew she needed to lighten the mood of the gathering. Overall, she was pleased with their progress. Bringing such diverse peoples together was challenging. Now, they must get down to detailed planning.

Just then, Billy entered the tent with a basket of fresh bread rolls on his arm accompanied by three dark fae servants bringing spiced stew and an array of condiments, with sweet cooled mead to wash it down.

"Perfect timing, Billy. We could do with a break," she said, unable to keep the triumph from her voice. She had what she'd come for: their agreement to attack Thingstyrbol first and no warriors going off to Hedabar until afterward.

"Tell me, Rella," said Viktar. "How do you pay your army? I can see everything is in short supply among the wild fae, yet you appear to find the resources you need."

"Most are here because they choose to be. I certainly have no gold to pay or outfit an army," said Rella.

"A Dark Queen on the throne of Thingstyrbol will be payment enough," said Patrice, passing out steaming bowls of fragrant stew. "We dark fae have many talents and know well how to barter for what we cannot conjure ourselves. Besides, there are hundreds here who are not warriors, but sell the fruits of their labors in return for our protection."

"Why do you think we are so poorly dressed, and live in tents that leak water on our makeshift beds?" said Rella.

"So, who will pay the army once the threat of the Dark Emperor is gone, and we are on our way to Hedabar?" said Viktar.

Rella's heart soared when he said 'we'. It spoke to his full commitment.

Captain Bernst leaned forward. "I will. Thanks to young Dagstyrr."

"What do you mean?" said Viktar with a frown.

Rella rolled her eyes. "He means the gold Earl Magnus paid him for healing and transporting his three sons to Halfenhaw."

"I see."

Rella knew Viktar didn't like her precarious position. In Casta, an army that wasn't paid might desert on a whim. The wild fae were different, but reliable in their way. It had taken her some time to come to terms with that, and now she had to make Viktar see it too. "Viktar, warriors fighting for the freedom of their families and ancestral land are very motivated."

She watched as Viktar thought for a moment before nodding sagely in her direction. "You are right, Rella."

Rella left the tent with Dagstyrr. She'd promised herself she'd no longer keep things from her mate, so now she must fill him in on the details of the slave pens. It might help him trust Viktar and Fedric. Dagstyrr had barely taken his eyes off Fedric during the meeting, and Rella knew he didn't trust the young fae.

"Fedric gutted himself?"

"He did. It was a very foolish thing to do."

She watched Dagstyrr come to understand the sad story she'd just relayed to him.

"That creature is a monster. Selling slaves to Hedabar—disgusting." His fists shook with a need to break something.

"That is why Viktar and Fedric are here. There is no light fae intrusion into the wild fae, rest assured," she said, uncurling his hand and taking it in hers. Immediately, she felt him relax.

"So, Fedric didn't think he'd end up dark fae?"

"I'm not sure what he thought would happen. He's impetuous."

"And brave. Give Fedric his due."

"Aye."

"So, if you hadn't found the slave pens, I'd have been too late. Your sneak attack on Thingstyrbol would be over."

"Yes."

Dagstyrr's warm hand slid down the back of her leather tunic to land at her waist. It was hard for them to keep their hands off each other when they were this close. "You might have been captured."

"No, I would never have allowed that to happen."

He turned her toward him. "Rella, you will not die. I won't let you." Strong emotions enhanced his protective energy and threatened to overwhelm her. Bright with passion, his eyes conveyed so much more than words ever could.

Rella reached up and cupped his face. "Everything happens for a reason."

"We still have a lot to discuss."

"Aye."

"No more running away."

"No," she said, hoping she could keep her word.

"I mean it, Rella. Don't ever do that to me again."

CHAPTER 11

Dagstyrr watched his beloved march down to the receiving tents, where a commotion heralded a batch of newly arriving warriors. His spirits lifted, with the knowledge that soon Rella might have the troops she needed to face the Dark Emperor with an army. When the time came, he'd be with her, ready to extend his protection against magic to her. They'd fight alongside each other like ancient warrior lovers.

However, guilt at delaying his rescue of the dragons gnawed at him.

Dagstyrr took his meal and wandered through the camp until he found a quiet spot where he could talk to Drago unobserved.

Checking that he was alone in the small clearing, Dagstyrr put down his bowl and turned his back on the camp. He reached out to Drago. The oppressive weight of the dragon's presence almost made him fall to his knees. Something was wrong. Drago usually managed to control the influence he exerted on Dagstyrr's body.

What has happened? said Dagstyrr, dreading the answer.

Today, the vizier took my daughter's eyes.

Left speechless by the horror of it, all Dagstyrr could ask was, *Why?* The surge of pain from Drago was almost too much to bear.

She could not find his longship.

A chill ran up Dagstyrr's spine. *What's the name of the longship?*

The Spider.

Damn.

Do you know where it is?

I do.

Don't tell me of its whereabouts. Don't even think about it. If I don't know, the vizier can't make me tell.

Is the Drake *all right?*

Burnt to a crisp. Went down with all hands, but it wasn't enough. The vizier had ordered both ships destroyed after they fell into the wrong hands.

Dagstyrr thought of what Rella had told him. About all the light fae as well as the Crystal Mountain healers aboard the *Drake*. All those innocents dead, and what a terrible death it would have been. The lucky ones would have drowned. *I'm sorry he hurt your daughter.*

Even if she killed so many?

Yes. How was he going to tell the others who even now congratulated themselves for having saved so many? "No one deserves such cruel punishment for failing to fulfill a command. What is your daughter's name?"

Syra. She is my youngest, not yet a mother.

Tell her not to despair. I am coming.

Is that why you contacted me?

The hope in Drago's voice was unmistakable. Dagstyrr

sighed. *No, I need more time. I don't want to land without suffi-cient forces. We have only one chance to do this, Drago.* Dagstyrr felt the dragon's heat and fury flow through his body.

Make it soon, Dagstyrr of Halfenhaw.

Drago left as suddenly as he'd arrived. The surrounding woodland came slowly into focus as Dagstyrr's eyes returned to normal. Whenever he spoke to Drago, his eyes became the dragon's eyes. Drago had no eyes, just two burning pits of flame where they once were before the vizier had blinded him.

Billy threw a bucket of water, splashing the tree stump where Dagstyrr was sitting. The charred wood smoldered. "That dragon needs to mind his temper. We don't need him setting our woods on fire," he said with authority.

Dagstyrr didn't have time to react to Billy chastising Drago. He was surrounded by wild fae, all of them watching him while down on one knee, as if in homage.

Feeling uncomfortable with all the attention he was garnering, Dagstyrr stood. He hadn't meant to make a scene. He'd thought he was alone. Viktar and Fedric stood against the forest line, Fedric leaning against a tree eating an apple as if watching a fairground spectacle.

Viktar approached him, his long legs striding across the clearing. "I've heard of dragon-talkers, but never thought I'd be privileged enough to meet one. Never mind witness him conversing with his dragon. It is truly an awesome sight."

"Drago's..." Dagstyrr's voice sounded deep and rough. He coughed to clear the effects of Drago. "His eyes were taken by the vizier."

A buzz went up among those present. These people were not happy to hear of Drago's plight. Dagstyrr suddenly realized he could ensure their loyalty now. Once

Thingstyrbol was taken, they'd sail with him instead of dispersing to their homes. "Today, the vizier took his daughter's eyes."

"You're dragon-promised to rescue him?" said Viktar.

At that, a chorus of shouts went up. "Take me with you!"

"I'll sail with you."

"I'm your man."

Dagstyrr stepped forward. "Yes, I need warriors. Anyone willing to sign up must speak to Captain Bernst. I think most of you know him."

"Is Bernst sailing with you?"

"Yes, he has the final say on all recruits," said Dagstyrr, knowing Bernst could assess dark fae warriors faster and more accurately than a human could. Shouts came from all directions, and Dagstyrr knew he had as many men as he was willing to take. If he could persuade Patrice to lend him the *Spider*, he could sail with almost four hundred warriors. For the first time, he dared to hope his quest might stand a chance.

"I've sailed with Bernst before; he's a good man," said a large dark fae warrior sporting an array of knives and axes.

"Then that is our next quest, after Thingstyrbol," said Dagstyrr, shaking the man's hand. He was surrounded by dark fae, and not all of them were warriors. Ordinary housewives approached, offering to do his laundry and mend his clothes. Artisans of all kinds offered their wares. Anything he needed to help rescue Drago was his for the asking. He and Viktar were almost overwhelmed by the enthusiastic crush.

Dagstyrr looked up and smiled at Rella, standing in a high clearing, but one look at her face wiped the joyful grin from his face. She stood with spear in hand and a look of thunder on her face. Fedric stood next to her, whispering behind his hand.

Whatever poisons the young lordling was dripping in her ear were working. Dagstyrr watched her eyes darken and her body tremble before she marched away.

CHAPTER 12

Furious at Dagstyrr undermining her with the new dark fae warriors, Rella stormed into her tent with the Threme sisters hard on her heels. She needed to calm down so she could think straight and plan her next move, but Patrice and her sisters raged with her, adding their strong emotions to hers.

Reeling from the audacity of it, she fought to control her rising battle magic. Had he done that on purpose? Why had he shown Drago's eyes? She could still hear Fedric whispering in her ear—*to steal her warriors*. Her heart said no, he would never betray her, but Rella of Casta understood what it was to be betrayed by the very person who was supposed to protect her. *It can't be happening again! Not Dagstyrr. Not him.*

She tried to slow her breathing as she paced back and forth; dark green energy continued to escape her fingertips at odd intervals, a testament to her distress.

"Who does he think he is?" said Sophy.

"He's human!" answered Patrice. "Oh, I know, the

dragon-fire eyes are impressive, and he's pleasing to the eye, but he's just a human."

"His story's a good one. I'd be for him myself, if it wasn't for the fact that he's just undermined our whole mission to attack Thingstyrbol," said Clar. "Everyone wants to run off to Hedabar now and rescue dragons. Are they so short-sighted?"

"It's not just a story," said Rella, angry with herself for defending him.

"Oh, don't you start taking his side," scoffed Nan.

"I'm not! I'm only saying it's not a story. It's real," said Rella, remembering Dagstyrr's compassion for the wounded creature and the promise the dragon pulled from him in a moment of sympathy without any understanding of the consequences. If it hadn't been for Rella foolishly carrying the dragon's-blood pellets for her brother, Dagstyrr would never have met the dragon, never been promise bound. Was she doomed to create chaos whenever she endeavored to do good? If so, what did that mean for her attack on Thingstyrbol?

Was this attack yet another disaster she was about to create?

Doubt rose in her gut like a coiled serpent. Rella loved Dagstyrr with every inch of her being. She'd happily give him all the warriors he asked for—after Thingstyrbol.

"How dare he try to steal our troops?" said Patrice, her voice low and dangerous.

"I hope he didn't mean to do it," Rella said, remembering how Dagstyrr had warned her against trusting her brother, King Calstir. She hadn't listened, going against his advice and her own instincts, and then Calstir had betrayed her most spectacularly.

Dagstyrr knew how devastated she'd been by that

betrayal. He understood why she blamed herself for this war and her reasons for attacking Thingstyrbol. He would never betray her. Yet, she had seen it with her own eyes. Even that fool Fedric could see what was happening.

If Dagstyrr betrayed her, Rella wasn't sure she'd survive with her sanity intact. Was this the moment she started slipping into madness, as the prophecy proclaimed?

No, she reassured herself. It was in the wrong order. *First, you will kill. Then you will enjoy it. Then comes madness,* she quoted in her head. Rella had never enjoyed killing, and she'd been careful to never use magic to kill since becoming dark. However, the prophecy was old, ancient. Might it be misinterpreted? If she were destined to go mad, it must be *after* she put an end to this war!

Rella continued to pace up and down as she attempted to rein in her anger and hurt.

She'd leave Dagstyrr as soon as she felt the madness take hold. She loved him too much to subject him to the slow, dangerous deterioration of her fae mind. "Why? Why did he do that?" Her fists pounded on the table.

"If he's stupid enough to make a promise to a dragon, then he's stupid enough to cross a light fae mate," said Fedric, entering the tent and interrupting her.

"Did no one think to put up a silencing ward?" said Patrice, raising her hand and warding the tent against listeners. Then she rounded on Fedric. "Don't you dare call him stupid. You gutted yourself—on purpose. Remember?"

Fedric raised his hands in surrender before perching on the edge of a table. "I've told my father to forget planning for today. Dagstyrr impressed him too, though I can't think why. It's not as if he gains anything by being a dragon-talker with scary eyes."

"Fedric, you are only showing your ignorance," said Sophy.

"If Drago spoke to you, you'd fry in seconds," said Rella, unable to keep the contempt from her voice.

"If he can converse with his dragon, they can help each other when the time comes to rescue the dragons," said Jul, obviously thinking ahead.

"How many dragons is he supposed to rescue?" laughed Fedric.

Rella stared hard at the arrogant young lordling. "One hundred and sixty-eight dragons, not counting hatchlings or eggs," she said.

The expression on Fedric's face froze. She knew he was trying to ingratiate himself with the wild fae, but disbelief was written on his arrogant face for all to read. Eventually, he lowered his head. "I still don't see why that is so spectacular," he mumbled.

"Dragons are our kin," said Rella. "No fae, light or dark, can converse with them. Yet Dagstyrr, a human male, does."

"That means," interrupted Jul, "he's descended from the first human boy to ever converse with a dragon without having his brain boil in his head."

"I'm supposed to believe that old legend?" said Fedric.

"No, you're supposed to believe your own eyes," said Rella. "You saw the smoke and felt the heat come from him as his eyes turned to fire. Could your body withstand that?"

"I don't know. Anyway, I thought the dragon-talker's eyes were supposed to become the dragon's eyes, not fire," said Fedric.

A hush fell on the women as they looked to Rella to answer for them. She cast her mind back to the day Drago appeared beside the *Mermaid*. Saw once again Dagstyrr's arm arching across the sky as he tried to dispose of the drag-

on's-blood pellets. She remembered the fear gripping the
crew as the colossal beast dived into the water. Then his
broad angry head emerging beside the boat, close enough to
reach out and touch his snout, with the sea boiling around
the *Mermaid*. "Drago is blind. He hunts by sense of smell.
Where his eyes once were, there is fire. You *are* seeing his
eyes in Dagstyrr."

"I see."

"No, you don't, Fedric. When was the last time you saw a
dragon?" said Patrice.

"Never."

"When did you last hear of anyone seeing one?"

"Never."

"They are our kin," said Sophy. "Yet it is generations
since we've even seen one, never mind communicated with
them. Here we have a nest of one hundred and sixty-eight
captive dragons we knew nothing about, and the only
person who can communicate with them is Dagstyrr of
Halfenhaw—a human."

"That makes him more precious than anyone else here.
Fae, light or dark, are easier to replace than Dagstyrr of
Halfenhaw," said Jul.

"So, what you are saying is, if it came to a choice, you'd
save that human over anyone else here?" challenged Fedric.

"In a heartbeat," said Rella, very much aware it would
not be his ability as a dragon-talker that would compel her
to save him. He was her mate, and that's why he was so
dangerous to her. She'd forget everything if he were in
danger and rush to his side.

"Me too," said Patrice. "Sorry, girls."

"No problem, I'd do the same," said Sophy, the other
warrior sisters nodded their agreement.

"I don't understand you. If there is one dragon-talker out

there, there must be others," said Fedric. "Has he no brothers?"

"All his brothers are light fae. Addicts rescued from the citadel at the same time as my brother, Calstir. Drago won't hear of them assisting in any way," said Rella. "Dagstyrr and the crew of the *Mermaid* are sworn unto ten generations to set them free."

"Ten generations? That's harsh. Even for a fabled dragon," said Fedric, unable to keep the sarcasm from his voice. "However, no matter how special this human is, you cannot allow him to dance in here and sweep up your best warriors for an expedition bound to fail."

A hush fell over the gathering. Rella stared at him, unable to move. There, he'd said it. He'd said what most people were thinking, but no one would dare to speak aloud. No one believed Dagstyrr could free the dragons. Was she naïve to believe he could? Or was she just love-struck? Most irritating of all was that the little lordling was doubly right: Rella could not allow Dagstyrr to take her warriors.

Over the commotion, she'd heard him say, '*First Thingstyrbol*' but the talk all through the camp was now of Hedabar and dragons. His quest had captured everyone's imagination. How was she going to convince people that Thingstyrbol must come first? These were dark fae warriors. A dragon rescue was very appealing to their sense of romantic adventure. Whether he'd meant to or not, Dagstyrr had undermined the authority she'd worked so hard to earn.

Dagstyrr needed to be alone after talking to Drago. It wasn't just the exhaustion that came with the heat of his presence; it was the emotion. Sometimes the weight of Drago's suffering threatened to overwhelm him, never more so than today.

He should be happy with the reception he'd received from the wild fae warriors, but the look of pain on Rella's face when she'd seen them flock to his side spoiled any thrill he'd experienced. How was he going to convince her that he would die before being betraying her?

Walking alone through the forest, he pulled a flower, rubbing the soft petals between his fingers, releasing their scent. He touched the bark of trees, the familiar smell of pine and cedar reminding him of home. Shadowed by a green canopy he walked on, until he came to a small water-fall spilling into a pool.

Sitting down on a mossy rock, Dagstyrr allowed the spray of the mountain water to cool him. He smiled when he saw it casting a rainbow down one side of the waterfall—simple magic. The real, everyday kind of magic humans could trust.

He didn't hear Viktar come through the forest until he was near. Either it was the noise of the waterfall, or Viktar chose to let his feet touch silently on the forest floor. Not simple magic. Not the kind you could trust.

"I'm sorry to disturb you." The high light fae warrior stood a respectful distance away.

Dagstyrr stood up. "You don't disturb me. I'm going for a swim," he said, hoping the man would take the hint and leave. High light fae lords cleansed themselves with magic or indoor pools, not forest waterfalls. Also, all light fae were notoriously bad swimmers. Something to do with carrying the weight of their magic in their bones.

Viktar surprised him. Laying down his staff, he removed his sword belt with a smile. "I think I'll join you."

Sure it was a bluff, Dagstyrr undressed and dived into the icy depths. The silky water flowed over his skin like a balm as he plunged deeper into the clear amber water, wiping away Drago's hot, dry presence. When his lungs would take no more, he surfaced, just in time to see Viktar diving naked into the pool.

Dagstyrr swam toward the waterfall until he was directly underneath, and water cascaded over his head, threatening to drown him. There was nothing in the world like a forest pool for refreshing body and soul. He wasn't fae. He didn't understand the energies the light and dark pulled from the sky and the earth, but he understood this. Like he said. Simple magic.

Viktar kept a respectful distance, diving and surfacing on the other side of the pool, almost as if he enjoyed it. Dagstyrr had never known any light fae who could swim without using magic, but he had to admit, Viktar looked as if he knew what he was doing. The pure physical strength it took was impressive. Viktar was a big male warrior with a lot of powerful magic, yet he chose not to use it despite the weight of his magic dragging him down.

When Dagstyrr noticed the ends of his fingers wrinkling up like a white sourberry, he took one last dive, then reluctantly made his way to the edge and pulled himself up. Viktar was already out. He'd used magic to dry himself, and his long blonde hair fell perfectly down his broad back. As Viktar pulled on his shirt, Dagstyrr couldn't help noticing a small scar on his arm, and a chill shot through him.

He quickly dressed, then turned to face the warrior lord. "What are you?"

Viktar looked puzzled. "What do you mean?"

"I've never seen a fae swim like that, and you have a scar on your arm," said Dagstyrr, indicating on his own arm exactly where the scar was.

Viktar threw back his head and laughed. "I can swim because my father insisted I learn the old-fashioned way. He lost a younger sister to the water when they were children, so he was made to learn, and insisted I did too. It is all recorded in our family history if you don't believe me."

They both knew such light fae records were in the bowels of Casta's Lineage Library, well beyond Dagstyrr's reach. "What about the scar?"

"Ah, now, that is not recorded," said Viktar, drawing his finger the length of the scar and smiling, before tucking in his shirt and finishing getting dressed.

Dagstyrr felt cold water drip from his hair down the back of his shirt as he fastened on his sword belt. "Light fae never allow scars to mar their bodies. So, what are you?"

A smile played on Viktar's lips. "Someday, Dagstyrr dragon-talker, I might tell you about that scar. For now, suffice to say, I keep it as a reminder."

"You forget. I've been to the court in Casta. I've seen the ancient and the young without a wrinkle, blemish, or scar. Their clothes without a crease fitted perfectly to their perfect bodies. Yet, you want me to believe the great Viktar of Casta, leader of all the armies, and confidant of the king, chooses to keep a scar on his arm?"

"I'm rarely at court. When I am, you'll find me in the tilt-yard or fencing gallery. Calstir's father was my friend. He put up with my eccentricities. If he could deal with it, so can you," said Viktar, his expression icy.

"Now you serve Calstir?"

"I've not met with him since he returned to Casta. Has he changed?"

"I've no idea. He was a dragon's-blood addict when I met him. I wouldn't trust him. You do know what he did to Rella?"

"Princess Rella is very like her father, but sometimes she trusts too easily," said Viktar, his bright blue eyes piercing.

"You mean me?" Dagstyrr threw back his head and laughed.

"What is so funny?"

"Of all the creatures in the world who would betray her, I am not one of them."

"What do you call conspiring to take her warriors?"

"I didn't. I sought privacy before I talked with Drago. Oh, come on! You know there are spies from both Casta and Thingstyrbol who would love to undermine Rella. Find out who first found me and brought the audience to watch. Then, let me know—for that's who's trying to undermine her authority, not me."

Viktar watched him closely, as if he could read the truth of his words in the air about him. "You are cut off from your surroundings when you talk to your dragon?"

"Yes. No, sometimes." Dagstyrr sighed. "It's not that simple. I'm still learning," he said, knowing he'd exposed his vulnerability to the great warrior, and furious at himself for it. He didn't trust Viktar.

Dagstyrr stood from pulling on his boots. "It is time to return, and fix this mess."

"Can I help?"

"No. This is between Rella and me."

"I am her strategist. She will come to me for guidance," said Viktar.

"She will come to you for your expertise, yes, but only after she and I work this out together."

"You are sure of that?"

"I am. I respect the great Viktar of Casta when it comes to strategy, but you are not infallible," said Dagstyrr, thinking of the boat laden with addicted light fae and Crystal Mountain Healers burning up under a dragon's fire and sinking to the ocean's depths. Viktar had advised Rella to send them north onboard the *Drake.*

"I don't pretend to be infallible. That is why I keep my scar—to remind me," said Viktar, a small frown forming between his eyebrows.

He knows I'm holding something back, thought Dagstyrr. *Well, let him. I must protect Rella from this information; otherwise, she'll blame herself for all those deaths.*

"I will discuss what happened today with Rella," said Dagstyrr, setting off for camp.

"She has a temper, you know," said Viktar, calling after him.

Dagstyrr didn't turn around, but acknowledged Viktar's comment with a wave of his hand. He *did* know she had a temper, and that was what concerned him. How was he going to calm her down before she killed him?

CHAPTER 13

Dagstyrr raised his wooden shield in front of him before opening the tent flap. Rella stood there like a goddess ready to dispense punishment. Fortunately, her bolt of blue battle magic glanced off Dagstyrr's shield boss and ricocheted upwards. A smoldering rent let the blinding sunlight burst through.

Patrice nodded to her sisters, who rose from the table to leave. When Fedric appeared reluctant, Clar and Sophy took an arm each and marched him outside with them. "No one will disturb you, mistress," said Patrice.

"Calm down, Rella," he said, dropping his shield and daring to step inside. It was probably the worst thing he could have said.

"Don't tell me what to do," she said, blue energy sparking from her hands to fizzle on the floor. "Haven't you humiliated me enough for one day? Using Drago to ensnare the loyalty of my people—that was a low blow, Dagstyrr." Another bolt of battle magic flashed across the gap between them, and a choking haze of green crept along the floor and stopped short of his feet before sliding harmlessly up the

sides of the tent then dissipating. A bolt of blue quickly
followed. Dagstyrr ducked instinctively, and it landed on a
chair that exploded into fragments.

"Stop it, Rella, unless you intend to kill me. I didn't..."

"Don't tell me what to do!"

He'd never seen her so uncontrollably angry and knew it
was born of hurt. Why could she not direct this kind of
anger against Calstir or the Dark Emperor or the vizier of
Hedabar? Why him?

He guessed that she'd been living among the dark fae so
long that her ability to contain her emotions was gone. "I'm
not telling you what to do. I only want to make you understand what happened."

"Draw your sword."

"No, Rella. Please." If they drew swords, it would mean a
real fight between them. Rella's magic couldn't harm him
thanks to his mother's protective energy field, which
shielded him from magic—but a sword could kill. His
weapon could just as easily injure her, even if he only
intended to block her.

It was no use. Rella was in a blind rage that demanded
action. He drew his weapon as she bore down on him. Her
piercing eyes had never been darker, revealing her very soul
—raw and vulnerable. She advanced on him with a fierce
passion born from the pain of betrayal.

What had he done to her?

Later, as her limbs started to slow with fatigue, Rella gazed
at the wreckage surrounding them. Large rents in the roof
showed where her strikes had bounced off Dagstyrr's

protective shielding and torn holes in it. Broken furniture littered the tent.

Even if she couldn't use magic against him, she was a highly skilled warrior who knew what she was doing. But Dagstyrr had proved an equally skilled opponent. She was yet to score a direct hit. Even against her fae speed, he met every blow. He refused to attack. Did that mean he felt guilty?

Once more, they faced each other, swords drawn, panting with exertion.

"Enough, Rella," said Dagstyrr, straightening and putting down his sword. "I am not going to fight anymore."

Her initial fury had dimmed but still smoldered under the surface. Their long struggle had left her tired and frustrated. "Pick it up. I will not attack an unarmed man, even one who has betrayed me."

"I'm glad to hear it."

"Pick up your sword," she said.

"No." He sat on the floor, breathing heavily and covered in sweat.

"Damn you!" She screamed, throwing her weapon to the ground. Their fight had been long and spectacular, but it was over. She needed every one of her warriors for her attack on Thingstyrbol. He had to understand that. She would not face that vile creature shorthanded.

Rella looked at the human male sitting on the floor of her tent, his dark blue eyes gazing up at her, wary and watchful. He had her heart and her body, but that was all. He did not rule her. And she would not let him steal her army.

She walked over and righted a chair. Underneath, a bottle of mead had escaped the carnage. She grabbed it before sitting and lifting the bottle to her lips. The sweet cold liquid quenched her thirst. "What am I to do with you?"

She watched him rise slowly to his feet.

"Wrong question," he said. Then he looked around for a serviceable chair, eventually finding a stool. He brought it to sit in front of Rella so that they faced each other. Watchful, he held out a beaker for some mead.

Rella's eyes never left his as she poured the sweet liquor into his cup. "So, what is the question I should be asking?" Her voice was cold enough to send shivers down the rank and file of her followers, but he showed no fear. It was either stupidity, or he felt safe with her—and Dagstyrr wasn't stupid. He knew she wouldn't hurt him, because to hurt him meant hurting herself. However, he must know she could make his life very difficult.

They held each other's gaze until his eyes crinkled at the sides, and she knew he wasn't as sure of himself as she'd thought. "What are we going to do now? That is the question."

"There is no 'we' where my warriors are concerned. I am in command. I make the decisions."

"You and I both know that isn't true. These people are fickle and will decide for themselves."

"Oh, my love, you may have impressed a few dark fae halflings with your display, but the lead warriors have already promised to follow me," she said, bluffing. Rella watched his face for a clue that he wasn't as sure of himself as he sounded. She found none.

"You misunderstand me," he said, his eyes roving over her face.

Rella raised her hand to the mark on her face. It was automatic, and it annoyed her whenever she did it. "We both have tasks to perform. Mine is paramount. I must put a stop to this war between the Dark Emperor and Casta. Every day, people die because my actions started this war. It must stop."

"Yes. Yes, you are right. It must stop, and it will," said Dagstyrr. "We have had this argument before. I still maintain this war was inevitable. The Dark Emperor is far too ambitious. If you had...if you had gone to him as agreed, this war would still have happened. Why can't you accept that?"

Rella was glad to hear him stumble on his words when he spoke of her going to the Dark Emperor. Despite their differences, she was his woman. "Perhaps, but you cannot know that for certain."

"Yes. I can. If you don't believe me, speak to Viktar. I'm sure he would agree with me."

"You've talked to him about this?" Was there no end to his interference?

"No. We have not spoken about Calstir or the Dark Emperor, so you can be sure he speaks his true mind to you."

"There you go again, telling me what to do." Rella knew it was petty, but he had to stop it, or she'd go insane. "Calstir is Viktar's liege lord, not me," she said.

"I understand they have not met since the death of your father, so he can't have sworn allegiance yet. Also, I get the feeling he favors you, rather than your brother," said Dagstyrr.

Rella had that impression too, but could she trust it? She'd made so many mistakes, and she carried them with her like a litany of failures. The first was defying the Casta council and rescuing Calstir. The second was going to the Dark Emperor for help. The third, carrying those stupid dragon's-blood pellets with her to ease Calstir's withdrawal.

If it weren't for that mistake, Dagstyrr and the *Mermaid*'s crew would not be dragon promised.

The fourth—believing Calstir could persuade the council to let her stay in Casta—was her worst mistake so far. Trusting the brother she'd just rescued from a living hell. At least the rest could be put down to ignorance. Calstir's betrayal was the result of sheer stupidity on her part. Everyone saw it coming but her.

"How soon can you march on Thingstyrbol?" said Dagstyrr quietly.

Rella looked away. This man could read her like a book, and he would see her insecurity written all over her marked face. But if she couldn't trust him, then she was indeed doomed.

"We are aiming for two weeks hence. It is the time when we think the Dark Emperor will be most vulnerable. Most of his troops will be housed in villages some distance away, preparing to attack Casta once more," she said.

"You have spies in his palace?"

"Of course."

"He will have spies here."

"I know, but what can I do about it?"

"Keep your plans to yourself. Tell no one."

Rella laughed. "How can I do that? My warriors are not like Casta troops. They are the wild fae, displaced by war and owing homage to no one. As you so rightly pointed out, they come and go as they please. If they thought I was keeping secrets, I'd wake in the morning to an empty camp," she said with disgust.

"Ah, I see a glimpse of Princess Rella, leader of her cohort of Casta warriors," said Dagstyrr, gently taking her hand in his own. "You and I must work together, my love. It is the only way."

She felt the rough skin of his fingers brush her palm then close around her sword hand, making it appear small and soft in contrast. "You are right. Part of me still yearns for the discipline I commanded in Casta. I sometimes wonder if I'll ever truly understand the wild fae, even if I am one of them."

"Together, we will work it out. Besides, once you are queen in Thingstyrbol, you can command discipline again. You can teach your troops all you know."

She laughed. "Dagstyrr, I have no ambition to be queen of the dark fae."

"Good," he said sounding relieved. He smiled at her, a twinkle in his eye.

"Oh, you think I would give up a throne to be with you?" She laughed. Dagstyrr always brought out the best in her. If she didn't kill him first, they might have an exciting future together.

"To rule has never been your ambition," he said. "If it were, you'd be queen of Casta right now, and Calstir would be rotting in Hedabar. Tell me, what is it you do want, Rella? I don't believe I've ever asked you."

She let herself gaze deep into his hypnotic eyes. She wanted so much: to kill the Dark Emperor, to see an end to the war, to save the dragons, and then to go away with him to some mountain retreat where no one knew them and start life anew. Perhaps they could build a home similar to Halfenhaw. Instead, she sighed and said, "One thing at a time. For now, I want to stop this war by killing the Dark Emperor."

"Do you have a replacement in mind? You know you cannot leave the throne empty, or anarchy will rule. A civil war could be far worse for these people."

"Yes, I have a replacement in mind," said Rella, imagining Patrice wearing a glittering crown with her warrior sisters surrounding her.

"You're not going to tell me, are you?" he said, smiling.

"No."

"Very well. Let's go and talk to Viktar about how we're going to win Thingstyrbol for the dark fae."

"Thingstyrbol is not your fight, Dagstyrr."

"Yes, it is. You are my woman. Your problems are my problems. We must show the wild fae a united front you and I."

"You mean that?"

"I do. Besides, Thingstyrbol should be fairly straightforward as long as we have enough warriors. It will be a good training ground for them before we tackle Hedabar."

"Whatever happens, it will not be as easy or as simple as you think. The most important thing is that you remain safe. Without you, we have no hope of rescuing Drago," she said, not saying that if anything happened to Dagstyrr, it would destroy her. He was her everything.

"We could do with some time to train the troops and assess their skills. How long before you want to attack?"

"I told you, two weeks," said Rella. She liked that he found it so easy to accept her as commander. As long as they presented a united front, people should get the message.

"Then we have no time to lose," he said. "Viktar is enquiring into who brought the crowds to watch me talking to Drago after I took steps to make sure I was alone. We might find the Dark Emperor's spy."

"I'm sure he has more than one. The only people we can trust are the Threme sisters, Beatty and his men, Viktar, and Bernst," said Rella, thinking. *There are so few.*

"I'm not sure I trust that many," said Dagstyrr.

"What do you mean?"

"What about Fedric? I saw him trying to influence you in the forest."

"Aye, I think he fancies himself as someone with influence. Don't worry, everyone sees through him," said Rella a little guiltily, knowing his poisonous whispers had helped inflame her temper. "You are right, though. Fedric is one to be watched."

"What about Viktar?"

"I trust him implicitly."

"Do you know he wears a scar on his forearm?"

Rella saw Dagstyrr's eyes darken whenever he spoke of her mentor and knew it would take time for the two men to see eye to eye. "Yes, I do."

"Isn't that a bit strange?"

"No, it is a souvenir." She laughed.

"Mmm. Viktar told me it was to help him remember."

"Well, it is, I suppose. I gave it to him when I was two years old."

"You!"

"We were having dinner in my father's private dining room. As it was only friends and family, Calstir and I were allowed to sit at table. Our teachers strictly controlled our magic so that we'd not harm anyone."

"I remember my mother doing that with my brothers," Dagstyrr mused.

"So, the talk was of strategy and awareness of others, as was usual when my father and Viktar got together. Viktar boasted that he was always alert for danger. That no one could ever surprise him."

"Don't tell me. You speared him with a butter knife," said Dagstyrr, laughing.

"A meat knife. If I hadn't been sitting on his lap at the time, he would have seen it coming. Years later, to my shame, he related the tale to our year at the cadet academy —leaving out names, of course. It was his favorite story, and he repeated it often."

Dagstyrr laughed. "I think I might grow to like your Viktar after all. Let's go and find him."

"But first, hold me," she said, knowing it would lead to more. Viktar could wait.

CHAPTER 14

Viktar sat by a campfire with Fedric, entranced by the songs of the wild fae minstrels. Their size and long light fae hair bright in the firelight drew wary looks from rest of the audience. The dark fae ballads, which told tales from long ago, captivated Viktar's love of tradition. Fae history remembered in poetry for future generations to recite and learn who they were.

Rella and Dagstyrr slipped quietly onto the bench next to father and son, careful not to disturb the musicians. Food was passed around the gathering from one to the other. But nothing disrupted the flow of the tale.

Both Viktar and Fedric were still as statues, captivated by the young woman, drum in hand, beating out the rhythm of her tale against the music of the harp behind her. As Viktar reached for a morsel of wildfowl from the tray, he suddenly noticed Rella and Dagstyrr. "So, you didn't kill him then," he whispered to her, before passing the food on and turning once more to the music.

Rella glanced at Dagstyrr. They both had silly smiles on their faces, like children caught misbehaving. She reached down and insinuated her hand in his. The warmth and feeling of protection his touch brought soothed her spirit amid her crazy life.

The tale being told onstage was an old one, full of stirring episodes and passionate love affairs. Rella could see Fedric was spellbound, or perhaps the young woman who so expertly weaved the tale with her hypnotic voice had something to do with his expression.

Viktar stood carefully and eased his way to the end of the benches, indicating that Rella and Dagstyrr should follow him. They followed the old warrior out of the circle and through the forest.

Once inside the confines of his tent, Viktar placed wards so that no one but themselves would hear their conversation. He poured Samish wine in delicate crystal cups and signaled they should make themselves comfortable on the pile of silk cushions surrounding the low table in the center of the tent.

Rella smiled at Dagstyrr, who still managed to look awkward on reclining cushions.

Then the three of them sat in silence, sipping their wine. Rella knew a lot depended on what was said here tonight. The stakes were too high to blunder in without first thinking it through.

Viktar broke the silence. "So, as you are both still alive, I take it you two have come to some agreement. Are you going to tell me?"

Rella and Dagstyrr glanced at each other. Viktar's ability to read her was very disconcerting. Then again, it was what Viktar did best—read people.

"Yes. Nothing has changed. We attack Thingstyrbol in two weeks with as many warriors as we can muster, then on to Hedabar." Dagstyrr's voice rumbled across the small space bringing reassurance.

Rella knew he was making it all seem too easy. "Once a queen is back on the throne at Thingstyrbol, we must expect some warriors to stay with her. However, many more will flock to Thingstyrbol to guard her. It may mean the end of the wild fae. If nothing else, our numbers will be greatly reduced."

"Why?" said Viktar.

"If the Dark Emperor had not usurped the last queen, there would be no wild fae, no dispossessed fae at all. The wild fae will welcome her and look to her for protection as they return to their homes in dark fae territory once again," said Rella.

Viktar nodded. "I have no doubt many will want to stay and help establish the new queen, but I saw the looks on their faces when Dagstyrr talked with Drago. Warriors will follow him. What you must do is prepare these warriors to fight as one."

Dagstyrr was learning to respect Viktar's abilities. "Yes, their lack of discipline is unprecedented. What worries me is, whether these warriors are capable of fighting like a cohort or a crew."

"Beatty is even now preparing to take the mountain elves up to the villages surrounding Thingstyrbol to gauge the Dark Emperor's strengths and weaknesses. They travel fast and blend in easily with those living along the route we must take to reach there," said Rella. "While they are gone, we must work these warriors hard."

"That's all very well, but until we find out who is spying for him, the elves will be in grave danger," said Dagstyrr.

"Spies are everywhere. That doesn't change. There is always someone with a grudge or greed enough to sell information for gold. The trick is to let them think they know what is going on. Which is why we must keep details of our plans to a select few," said Viktar.

"You are right. I'm surprised Englesten hasn't put in an appearance," said Dagstyrr.

"The Ghost King?" said Viktar.

"Who?"

"That's what the mountain elves call him, the Ghost King."

"He introduced himself as Englesten when he came to visit Dagstyrr and me on the day of the first battle," said Rella, remembering the pain she'd felt watching the beginnings of the war she had started. The Dark Emperor had proved himself a scourge on the land and all the diverse dark fae inhabiting it. It was up to her to put an end to him.

"Englesten is interested in one thing," said Dagstyrr. "Freeing his family from the vizier's citadel. He could care less about Thingstyrbol. I keep expecting him to turn up and chastise me for delaying my attack on Hedabar."

"Well, if we want to mount a full-scale attack on Thingstyrbol in two weeks, we must get to work," said Viktar standing and approaching the war table set up where his bed should be.

Several hours later, as dawn was piercing the eastern skies, the large table in Viktar's tent held two scale models, one of Thingstyrbol, the other of Hedabar.

The model of Thingstyrbol fascinated Dagstyrr. It looked like something out of a nightmare told to children to keep them close, like a fairy castle made of living trees with turrets and bridges. However, this castle was black and covered in what looked like a suppurating mold, except for a glassy section of the wall linking two square towers. There was a lacy fragility about the roofs and the bridges that lent it an ethereal quality.

Rella had fashioned it from memory using a small piece of a mossy stick before turning her attention to making a model of Hedabar. That one he recognized. The wharf where boats unloaded into the warehouses, the narrow streets, even the inn where he'd stayed, and the citadel that dominated the small town, all perfect in every detail.

He looked across at her frowning down on the models she'd made and wondered about the accuracy of the Thingstyrbol model. It seemed too bizarre to be real.

"How accurate is this one?" he said, pointing to the dark mass on the edge of the table.

"I know what you're thinking. I spent weeks in Hedabar, so that model is accurate. Thingstyrbol is too. I guarantee it," she said.

Dagstyrr's eyebrow rose as he considered it.

"Do you doubt me?"

"No," he assured her. "Not at all."

"Then what is it?"

"I think I know what is bothering Dagstyrr," said Viktar. "The place looks as though it could fall about your ears at any minute."

"Which adds to the danger," she said. "It's worse when you're there. Creatures living inside have their nests in every corner. It is damp and warm, with water dripping down and rotting away all the beauty that was once there. I fear the very foundations might be compromised."

"Then it didn't always look like this?"

"No, though I can only go by hearsay," said Rella. "When

the queens ruled the dark fae, Thingstyrbol was said to be a palace of joy and wonder. I imagine it was clean as well."

Viktar sat and poured some wine. "That is the genius of the Dark Emperor. When he decided to challenge the Dark Queen's rule, he did so with slurs about her forgetting her roots. He pointed at the sparkling beauty of Thingstyrbol as an anathema. He broadcast that she was aping Casta and that soon there would be no difference between the light and the dark if she were allowed to carry on."

"That is ridiculous," said Rella.

"I agree," said Dagstyrr. "Light and dark are both true paths of magic determined centuries ago. Even I know that. It has nothing to do with how the palace is decorated."

Rella laughed softly. "So, you are an expert now?" she teased.

Rella sensed something was wrong with Viktar. He'd fallen very quiet. It wasn't like him.

She studied him as the old warrior composed his countenance to one of neutrality. Then it dawned on her. "Viktar, you saw me use both light and dark magic, blue *and* green."

Rella was so used to her dual magic that in the safe confines of Viktar's tent, she'd been lulled into a sense of complacency and used both to make the models, forgetting her old friend had never seen such a thing. She remembered her first reaction to it and imagined the conflict warring inside him. He'd hidden it well.

Was he just too much of a gentleman to comment?

For a long time, Viktar said nothing, his face a study of stony detachment. Then he stood and came to take her hands in his. "When Fedric told me of it earlier, I dismissed it. I should not have."

"Of course. He saw the start of our fight, Rella," said Dagstyrr.

"When you started to construct the model of Thingstyrbol, I thought I'd imagined it. I have never met a light fae turned dark before. I assume it is normal?"

Dagstyrr and Rella exchanged glances. "I don't know," said Rella.

"Is this the fate that awaits my son?" said Viktar, obviously shaken.

"Tell no one, Viktar," said Dagstyrr. "We don't understand it ourselves."

"We must watch Fedric, and see what happens," said Rella. She didn't want to be any more different than she was already. If this was normal, so be it. If not, the fewer people who knew about it, the safer she'd be. Unfortunately, Fedric knew, and he couldn't keep his mouth shut.

Viktar let go of her hands and poured another cup of wine, which he downed. "In years past, from time to time, someone would appear claiming to have both dark and light magic at their fingertips. Most were fakes, marketplace con men earning a living by amusing the throngs. One or two demonstrated minimal powers to manifest both dark and light. They usually became court favorites, feted and brought out to impress visitors, but they were all—a little mad."

Rella gasped.

"Rella's magic is strong," said Dagstyrr, sitting down opposite Viktar and leaning forward. "She is not a spectacle to entertain the court. You are privileged to have seen this; keep it to yourself."

"Don't challenge me, human," growled Viktar.

Rella couldn't ignore what Viktar had said about being a little mad. A shiver of fear rose from where it dwelt in the furthest corners of her mind, where she tried to keep it locked it away. "Viktar will not betray me. Will you?" she said, coming to stand beside Dagstyrr, her hand on his shoulder, wanting to make it very clear to Viktar where her loyalty lay.

"Of course not," he said. "I will spell my son, so he will not remember. If the same happens to him, it will bring back his memory."

"Tell me how I'm different from the others you spoke of," said Rella.

Viktar nodded. "Your intentions are different. You have nothing to gain from this phenomenon, no audience to con out of their pretty silver."

"I might," said Rella. "If people are so quick to follow a human dragon-talker, think how they will flock to follow a fae princess with one hand dispensing light magic, the other dark."

"Is that how it works?" said Viktar.

"There is already a price on your head, Rella," said Dagstyrr. "Don't make it worse."

"Dagstyrr is right," said Viktar. "Don't forget the stain of madness also follows those who turn dark—not that I believe it," he added quickly. "You are perfectly sane. I have no doubt of that."

It was good to hear him say it, but for how long would it remain true? Dagstyrr's hand covered hers where it lay on his shoulder. His warmth was a familiar comfort amongst all this talk of marketplace freaks and madness.

Rella trusted these two men above all others. She would listen to their counsel, but the decision of where and when to attack Thingstyrbol was hers alone. Knowing she could show her dual magic and rally the wild fae to her side was reassuring, but it would be a last resort. "For now, no one must know," she said.

"You must keep an eye on Fedric," said Dagstyrr.

"I will," said Viktar, looking tired. "One day, Rella, everyone will know."

"Perhaps," she said, knowing the future was impossible to predict. "Until then, it is our secret."

"By the way, it was Billy," said Viktar, turning to Dagstyrr.

"What do you mean?"

"Billy brought the others to watch you talking to Drago."

"So, not a spy then."

"No, nor someone trying to undermine Rella. Just an addle-headed boy trying to win favor with the dark fae," said Viktar. "You must keep a watch on him. He is more dangerous than you think."

CHAPTER 15

It was almost noon when Rella and Dagstyrr arrived
back at her tent, exhausted and ready to grab a couple
of hours of rest. Rella wasn't looking forward to
sleeping amongst the devastation she'd created the night
before. To her delight, Patrice and her sisters had been there
first. She might have known.

The women had used their magic to recreate her tent
more or less as it had been before her fight with Dagstyrr.
She stood just inside the tent flap, admiring their work.

"I think you owe someone a present," said Dagstyrr,
starting to strip off his clothes.

"Is that the way it works in your father's house?"

"No. In my father's house, we get to lie in our mess until
we've cleaned it up ourselves. That is why I suggest you owe
someone a very nice gift for all this," he said with a
disarming smile, and indicating their spotlessly clean and
tidy surroundings.

"Patrice and her sisters," said Rella, easing her tired
body out of her leather uniform. "I can feel their presence in
this magic."

"Then I shall get them something I think they'll like," said Dagstyrr.

"You don't have to. I can look after my warriors myself. Or are you hoping to win over Patrice so that she'll lend you the *Spider*?" said Rella, warming the clean water in her bath with a twist of her fingers before stepping into the scented water.

"I'm sure a little token won't hurt my cause, but no, that is not why I would like to make a gift to her and her sisters. I feel responsible for the mess. If I'd been more careful who saw me..." A bar of soap hit his shoulder.

"You're starting to sound like me. It wasn't your fault. It was Billy. Let's leave it at that. Still, you can get the women an appropriate gift if you like. There is a goodwife new to the camp with some exquisite and expensive embroidery. I'm sure they'd appreciate something from her stall."

"Mm, expensive, you say." He picked up the rose-and-mint-scented missile and advanced on the bathtub. "And exquisite. Just so I get this right, which piece of embroidery had you earmarked for yourself?" he said with a grin, joining her in the tub despite her protests.

CHAPTER 16

The newest recruits, Drago's plight, and Viktar's insistence on training brought a renewed sense of purpose to the camp. They also lifted Rella's spirits—or was that Dagstyrr's influence? A broad grassy plain near the beached longboats rang with the noise of armed men and women exercising with their various weapons. The sounds of war echoed across the tents, galvanizing people to work harder at their tasks. Rella watched from the hill as Viktar and Patrice walked among the fighters, clearly assessing their abilities.

After talking with Dagstyrr, Viktar and Patrice had agreed that no magic was allowed during practice. Without magic, faults in technique were soon exposed. Deprived of the magic they'd otherwise use to strengthen and speed up their limbs, the trainees were not doing well. Their heavy practice weapons frustrated the dark fae warriors and Rella could see them stamping the ground, unused to being so confined. In a battle using magic, fae feet barely touched the earth.

She felt Dagstyrr approach. "They're a sorry lot," said Rella.

"Mm, they are. But if these warriors practice without magic, think how much faster and more accurate they will be in battle once they start using it again." he said.

"You don't have to convince me. I only hope the younger warriors don't become too discouraged," said Rella, pointing out a young dark fae who had withdrawn and was sitting upon a stump with his sword resting across his lap.

"Maybe I can help," he said, his bright smile mischievous.

"Dagstyrr!" she called after him, as his long stride ate up the ground between her and Viktar. A lot of the women stopped what they were doing and watched with her. Rella felt a spike of pride, knowing he was her mate. She followed slowly in his wake as the two men conferred, but when they waved to Patrice to join them, she quickened her pace. "What are you up to?" Rella asked when she reached them.

"I think it's a good idea," said Patrice.

"What is?"

"To help us raise morale, Dagstyrr wants to challenge all comers," said Patrice. "Since he's human, they'll think him an easy mark. Then he'll show them the advantage a well-trained warrior can have without resorting to magic."

"We could make a contest of it," said Viktar. "Use of magic would mean automatic disqualification."

"I'd let them determine the penalty for using magic," said Patrice. "They will make their own rules anyway. You might as well let them do it from the start."

"Where is Beatty?" said Viktar.

"Beatty and his men are in their tent hatching a new plan to gather up-to-date information before we advance on

Thingstyrbol," said Rella. "It's taking longer than I'd expected."

"I was surprised to find elves among the wild fae," said Viktar.

"They may not be fae, but they've always worked with the dark fae, so I made them welcome. Besides, mountain elves are excellent spell casters. The best you will find anywhere," said Rella.

"And they can fight. I was impressed when I saw Beatty's men take down the guards at the slave pens," said Viktar.

"I hope they have their plans in place by tonight," said Dagstyrr, reminding everyone that time was of the essence. Every day Dagstyrr delayed, Drago and his family suffered.

It took about half an hour for the warriors to decide who would challenge the human knight, and in what order. Once they'd placed their bets, the dark fae formed a warrior's circle. Rella knew the odds for the bets would change with each round. Having sparred with him herself, she also knew just how good he was.

Dagstyrr had grown up practicing with his three light fae brothers and had developed some interesting techniques to compensate for his lack of magic. He was expert at anticipating moves.

Patrice joined her, "So, should I bet on the human?"

"Do what you think is right," said Rella. "Just don't get in the ring with him. You might get a few surprises."

The tall warrior threw back her head and laughed. "That's what I thought. Viktar and I will call the rounds and come to his defense if someone forgets and uses magic," she said with a wave as she joined the crowd.

"They might get a shock if they do," said Rella quietly to herself as she watched Patrice and Viktar position themselves on opposite sides of the circle created by the dark fae warriors.

She watched the contest from the vantage point of the hillside. Dagstyrr was quick to defeat the first two warriors, and now the dark fae were regrouping. They changed the order of the contest and re-wrote the bets.

This behavior was intolerable to light fae or even humans, but to the wild fae, it was perfectly normal. Rella found herself thinking more and more about Beatty and his men. The mountain elves were a great asset to any army. They rarely came down to the lower lands. Their stature made it hard for them to blend in. Which was ironic when she thought about it, because they were known for their stealth and ability to infiltrate enemy camps.

Scouting for the wild fae was taking a significant risk. The Dark Emperor was nasty when crossed. Even his followers feared his temper. Despite the sunshine on her shoulders, she shivered.

"Well, you'd better stop that before you attack Thingstyrbol, Princess."

She turned swiftly. "Englesten. Where did you come from?"

"I came to see Beatty. That's some task you asked of him." The ancient mountain elf's beard and hair were snowy white. His elongated fingers were twisted and wrinkled like oak twigs. Rella couldn't help glancing at his feet. She often wondered whether a mountain elf's soft leather boots hid elongated toes or very long feet.

"Is it too much for them? Should I tell him not to go?"

"Not at all," said Englesten. "Beatty will go."

"Is something wrong? Why do you have to speak with him?"

"No more than usual. I also wanted to check on young Dagstyrr. I'd expected to hear he was on his way to free those dragons before now."

"He needs more ships."

"Ah."

"I suppose he's going to help you defeat the Dark Emperor first?"

"Don't worry. He's an accomplished warrior. He knows what he's doing," said Rella, irritated. Englesten showed up at the strangest times, and always seemed to know far too much about her business.

"He mustn't be hurt," said Englesten. "We need him strong and confident to rescue those dragons."

"Tell me, Englesten, is it just dragons you want him to rescue?" She knew he must have another reason for monitoring Dagstyrr's progress.

"Just dragons," he said. He pointed down at Dagstyrr, who was now facing his sixth opponent—the toughest one so far. "Is he supposed to continue till he falls dead?"

"Of course not. He knows what he's doing, elf."

"Would they know when to stop it? He's human. They're not."

"You have a point," said Rella.

"Well, are you going to put a stop to it, or must I?"

"You will leave it alone, Englesten," said Rella, turning his way, her eyes flashing a warning he understood.

"You're a cold mistress," said Englesten, pointing at her with his elongated fingers.

"Yes, I am mistress here, and as cold and as hard as I need to be. Don't ever forget it."

"Do you want Beatty's men or not?"

"Is it up to you?"

"It might be."

"It either is, or it isn't."

"Argh!" With that, he disappeared back into the forest within seconds. He was very fast. Rella hoped he wasn't returning to Beatty, but she thought not. All that interested Englesten was Dagstyrr and the dragons. The last time he'd turned up, he'd ignored her completely.

She'd made enquiries about Englesten since his last visit, back at the cottage. And she'd discovered that he treated all women with contempt, no matter their rank. The mountain elves never allowed their women to come down from their mountain homes. Beatty said it was to protect them because humans and fae could be cruel to their race. Rella understood the truth of that, but it didn't explain Englesten's attitude toward her.

Dagstyrr now faced his tenth and last opponent. Sweat dripped from his hair into his eyes, and Rella wanted so much to wipe it away with a wave of her fingers, but she dared not help him in any way. Someone might detect her assistance and cry foul. Too much silver and gold changed hands as each man challenged him.

Dagstyrr's new opponent was the young dark fae she'd observed earlier. He was as tall as Dagstyrr but thinner and, of course, he was fresh. She watched the young warrior hefting his sword to familiarize himself with its weight. He stood on his toes, his calf muscles giving his stance a spring, a readiness to jump in any direction.

Dagstyrr walked casually back and forth, swinging the great sword she had made for him as if to gauge its weight. He was loosening muscles stiff from wielding his weapon. She saw his hand go up and rub his neck as he rotated his shoulder.

Was he *truly* that tired, or was this one of his famous feints? The young fae was looking more confident with every move Dagstyrr made. Rella saw he was drawing the young man in. Showing him what he wanted to see so that he'd start the fight overconfident. It wasn't fair.

Then Rella thought of why Dagstyrr had learned to fight like this, of all the scars on his body. Scars he couldn't wave away with a burst of energy from his fingers. It was indeed fair. He'd earned the right to teach the wild fae.

The round started quickly. With astonishing speed, Dagstyrr had the boy on his knees. But the boy jumped up at once, a frown marring his youthful features. As the fight continued, Rella realized that he was the best opponent Dagstyrr had faced so far—definitely trainable. He was already incorporating lessons learned from watching the others. He saw some of Dagstyrr's feints in time to clash swords where others had ended up with his blade at their throat.

Rella was a highly trained light fae warrior, good enough to rise through the ranks and become the leader of her cohort. Yet, the first time she'd sparred with Dagstyrr, he'd managed to teach her a thing or two. This boy stood no chance, but she hoped Dagstyrr wouldn't trounce him. He needed some pride if he was to be one of her leaders. She could see his raw ability even as he hit the dirt again.

She needn't have worried. Dagstyrr allowed the round to end in a draw—much to the dismay of those betting on their favorite. No one had bet on a draw.

Rella made her way down to the field and marched right up to the young fae. "What is your name?"

"Reckless," he said.

She laughed. "Well, Reckless, how would you like to train with my guard regularly?"

She saw him try to hide the grin sliding across his face. "I'd like that very much, mistress, but there is something you should know. I'm a halfling."

"That doesn't matter," said Rella. "Patrice, here's one for you. His name is Reckless. Any nonsense, and you know how to deal with it."

Then she turned her attention to Dagstyrr, who was sitting on a stump smiling at her, sweat dripping off his face. "I thought you'd notice that one."

She wrinkled her nose as she approached. "You need a bath."

Dagstyrr stood. "I have a better idea," he said, sheathing his sword and taking Rella's hand.

"The waterfall?"

"Yes, the waterfall," he said with a grin.

CHAPTER 17

"We daren't risk too many," said Beatty. "We don't like drawing attention to ourselves. If people see more than one or two of us at a time, they will become suspicious. Our kind rarely travels in large groups."

"So, what do you propose?" said Dagstyrr, handing around drinks to Beatty and his men, who managed to lift the proffered cups with their strange, long, knobby fingers far more delicately than he'd have thought possible

"Six of us will set off. We'll keep to the deep forest where no one will see us. After a while, we'll leave one behind and continue," said Beatty. "Some while later, we do the same again. Now we are four. We continue like that until we are only one."

"You mean only one will enter the villages surrounding Thingstyrbol?" said Viktar, a frown marring his forehead.

Dagstyrr wondered again whether this man really was light fae. He looked light fae, but he certainly couldn't hide his emotions well enough to be a courtier.

"That's right," said Beatty.

"What if something happens to him?" said Dagstyrr.

"Less chance of that if I'm alone. I will take the last leg of the journey," said Beatty.

"What's the advantage of leaving men behind?" said Rella.

"We know there are spies in Thingstyrbol and here in camp. Those left along the way will notice anyone moving in both directions."

"What if they're innocents going about their daily business?" asked Viktar.

"Oh, we won't challenge them. We'll note who they are and when and where they move," said Pordu with a grin.

"Good thinking," said Viktar, grinning back at him.

"Of course, the other advantage is, we can relay a message faster. Each man has only a short section to run, and you know how quick we are," said Asti, with a wink.

"Do you know of one named Englesten?" said Rella.

Beatty and the other mountain elves froze.

"So, you do know of him," she said. "Tell me, what is his story?"

An awkward silence permeated the gathering, as Beatty and his men shuffled their feet and looked one to the other until they reached some silent agreement. "We do not speak of him. Why do you ask about Englesten?"

Now it was Rella and Dagstyrr's turn to exchange glances. "He visited us some time ago," said Dagstyrr, not giving anything away.

A gasp went up from the mountain elves seated on Viktar's cushions. Then they fell into an animated discussion in some strange language Dagstyrr had never heard before. Given the looks on their faces, neither had Rella or Viktar.

Viktar poured more Samish wine, then sat back

patiently while the mountain elves argued among themselves. The only discernable word was "Englesten."

Eventually, they stopped talking and drank down their wine, frowns crinkling up their already wrinkly faces. They were not happy. Dagstyrr, Rella, and Viktar sat quietly, drinking their wine and saying nothing.

Beatty broke the silence. "We have agreed to speak of him. We will not ask you to keep silent, for we don't believe you can."

Viktar's chest heaved at the insult—the accusation that they were incapable of keeping a secret rankled—but Dagstyrr shook his head at him, and their light fae host sat back.

"No insult is meant. It is our way. We either speak of something, or we don't. We never ask people to keep secrets," said Beatty. "Englesten should be our king. Many still think of him as the true king."

"I believe he is called the Ghost King," said Viktar.

"Aye, that's right," said Pordu, eyeing Viktar with suspicion.

"Why call him the Ghost King, if he is not your king?" said Rella.

Beatty glared at Rella. For a moment Dagstyrr thought Beatty would change his mind and refuse to tell them about Englesten. Then the elf took a swig of wine, and started his story.

"Just as he was about to ascend the throne, word reached the court that the vizier of Hedabar had captured his sister. His father was dying. Englesten and his half brother stayed at court but sent every other family member on a quest to free his sister. You can guess what happened to them." Beatty drank down his wine and lifted his cup for a refill.

Dagstyrr saw it was hard for Beatty to talk about this to

strangers. The other mountain elves tensed in sympathy. He filled all their cups before sitting down.

"They were all taken," said Rella, in a whisper.

"Aye. We are not fae, but evidently the vizier has a need for our kind. News reached us of their capture the same day as his father's funeral. Englesten was due to be crowned the next day. In an agony of grief and guilt, he foreswore his throne. He abdicated in favor of his half brother, whose name we never say. It is our custom never to mention the given name of our king. He is simply the Elf King."

"Is he a good king?" asked Viktar, getting quickly to the point.

"He is," said Pordu.

"So, what happened to Englesten?" said Dagstyrr, keeping a close eye on Rella, aware of the similarities in her own tale, a dying king, a captive family member. Except Rella had not stayed home.

"He disappeared into the woods for many years. We didn't know whether he was alive or dead. The Elf King looked for him and decreed that whoever came across him must give him food, shelter, clothes, whatever his want should be. That he should never be accosted, hurt, or restrained."

"So, his half brother sought to look after him," said Viktar.

"Of course," said Pordu. "Englesten's suffering is our suffering."

"Eventually, we started to hear of him turning up whenever anyone talked of breaching the citadel," said Asti.

"We are not surprised he turned up to see Dagstyrr, only that it has taken him so long. He will be keeping his eye on us now," said Beatty. "But we are not here to speak of our

Ghost King. Viktar needs more information to strengthen his plan of attack. That is our job."

"You've proved invaluable in the past," said Rella.

"Aye. We are mountain elves and can infiltrate the villages surrounding the castle and along the route. We are welcome in the gatherings of the dark fae and can obtain the latest gossip. However, we are not trained tacticians."

"What are you saying?" said Rella.

"We think it best if someone trained to attack castles is with us," said Beatty.

"I agree. I'll go," said Viktar. "I'd like to see Thingstyrbol for myself and gauge its strengths and weaknesses. Rella's model is expertly devised, but I can learn more from the real thing."

"With respect, Viktar of Casta, you are big and obviously light fae. You'd stand out like an orchid in a cow field," said Beatty.

"I'll go," said Rella. "I'm dark fae, and I'm small. I can do this."

"No," said Dagstyrr, jumping up. "The wild fae need you here. I'll go. I'm human. No matter my size, no one sees me as a threat. I can disguise myself as a sea trader wanting to sell something small. Pretty stones or jewels, perhaps?"

Pordu stood up and raised his hands. "The decision is ours, and we've already decided Dagstyrr is the best for the job. One big human is, as you say, no threat to the fae."

"Dagstyrr can't go!" said Rella. "If anything happens to him, who will free Drago and his family?"

"I've already volunteered. Besides, as Beatty says, I am the best for the job."

"What about Drago?"

"Believe me, Drago is my priority. Once Thingstyrbol is returned to the dark fae, more warriors will sign up with me to attack Hedabar. As Viktar so plainly put it, I need far more warriors than either of us can muster at this point."

"We might lose the warriors we have trying to take the palace," said Rella.

"That is a risk I have to take. Hopefully, if the war with Casta is at an end, more of the dark fae will flock to the new Dark Queen's banner. With luck, enough of them will want to sail to Hedabar," said Dagstyrr.

"Releasing tortured dragons will appeal to their sense of justice," said Rella.

"Every day it becomes more urgent," said Dagstyrr. "When do we leave, Beatty?"

CHAPTER 18

Dagstyrr and Rella walked the Night Market set up by the traders and artisans under striped awnings. Their booths, set up under the trees, were lit up by pretty lights and fireflies darting here and there creating an enchanting place to stroll. The scent of night flowers and candy treats permeated the air as couples wandered hand in hand before bed.

They found the embroiderer, and Rella helped Dagstyrr to select some pretty hand-stitched ribbons for Patrice and her sisters as a thank-you for tidying Rella's tent after their fight. Then he smiled as if he had not a care in the world before selecting a stunning piece he somehow knew she wanted for herself. Had she gazed upon it too long? It was a velvety white cushion of the softest fabric. In the center, there was silk embroidery of fantastic swirling bright blue and intense sparkling green—her colors.

He then whispered to the woman in some negotiation they kept secret. They giggled and laughed together like conspirators. If the woman hadn't been old enough to be his grandmother, Rella would have been jealous. She hugged her cushion as she admired the way Dagstyrr treated everyone with so much respect. The old woman agreed to have the pieces sent to the individuals he'd bought them for, and Dagstyrr smiled while slipping something into his pocket. Perhaps he had another surprise for her?

They continued their walk, where he purchased some pretty blue, pink, green, and yellow stones, and a small selection of northern silver jewelry. Just the sorts of things a sea trader might have to sell.

Eventually, they returned to Rella's tent. Dagstyrr had just enough time to change his clothes and kiss her farewell before the mountain elves came for him.

Then, he was gone.

At least our parting would not be for long this time, Rella consoled herself over breakfast. Realizing Captain Bernst stood by her side eating his bread, and that she'd ignored him, she said, "I'm sorry, Captain. I find myself falling to daydreams at the oddest times these days."

"I can see you're busy planning something in your head, mistress," said Bernst. "I'll not disturb you any further." He turned to leave.

"I'm just unusually tired."

"Nothing to do with being up all night at the market, then watching Dagstyrr and the elves leave?"

Laughing, she turned to him. "Nothing gets past you, does it?"

"Well, I wouldn't go that far, but I've seen you sleep-deprived too often in Hedabar not to recognize the signs," he said.

"You are right. A good night's sleep is what I need, but first I want to talk to Patrice."

Rella finished her breakfast, then made her way to her favorite spot overlooking the training ground.

The warrior sisters were making fast progress training the newer recruits. Viktar and Sophy walked among the paired warriors, who were fighting hand to hand without using magic. Every so often, the two would stop and offer advice, or in Viktar's case, a whack with a wooden sword. *He'll never change,* Rella thought fondly.

She remembered her training days in Casta like they were yesterday. Viktar's idea was always to show, then teach, and if they still didn't learn, whack. He said people remembered lessons better when they brought pain, particularly arrogant young fae. After her first whack, Rella had determined never to earn another.

Viktar famously predicted a warrior's future after just one practice. He was never wrong. Watching him now, she saw a hint of how he did it.

Future leaders learned by watching others—show. Sergeants learned by explanation—teach. Warriors learned by avoiding pain—whack. She smiled to herself. The great man appeared to have so many secrets, but all you had to do was observe him, and his methods revealed themselves. No wonder her father kept him away from court.

"What are you smiling at?" asked Bernst, coming up beside her.

"Memories. Are you following me?"

"Not at all. We haven't had much to smile about lately. I've just been teaching Billy to stick a man with a knife. Reminds me of the time I trained my firstborn."

Rella smiled. "In, twist, out, repeat?"

"Aye, you've got it. Some things never change. I told Billy to go for the gut, and not to try anything fancy."

"It might make him feel safer if he has a way to defend himself."

"That was my thinking."

"I miss him."

"Who, Billy?"

"No," said Rella. "Dagstyrr."

"He's only been gone a couple of hours. Don't worry, lass. I told Beatty and Pordu I'd have their hides if anything happened to him. He and I have some dragons to rescue."

"You're worried about him too."

"Of course I am. We're dragon promised to ten generations, and he's the only one who can talk to Drago. He is our best chance of success," said Bernst. "I fear our only chance, unless young Dagstyrr has an offspring hidden away that has inherited his special gift."

That was something Rella had never considered. Their time together was so precious they'd never discussed the possibility of Dagstyrr having a child. "I doubt it. I'm sure he'd have mentioned it if he had." The more she thought about it, the more she was convinced she was correct.

"Well, I can't ask his brothers to take his place," said Bernst. "They're addicts, and Drago warned us against using them. That would mean waiting until his brothers have grown children. Then I'll get the privilege of walking up to Halfenhaw's gate and telling the family the good news. Meanwhile..."

"Meanwhile, Drago and his kin continue to suffer."

"Aye," said Bernst. "And we lose thousands of warriors trying unsuccessfully to breach the citadel."

"I do understand, you know."

"I know you do, lass. But every time he talks to Drago,

the dragon's situation appears to have worsened. It was Dagstyrr's soft heart that made him promise in the first place, and now all these delays are eating away at him."

Rella didn't need Bernst spelling out the obvious. As an experienced commander, she was sure they were doing the right thing. After Thingstyrbol, she'd do everything in her power to raise as many ships and warriors as she could to attack Hedabar. Attempting to get away from the doubt gnawing at her, Rella said. "Last time, it was Drago's daughter. The vizier took her eyes. Why would anyone do that?"

"Control through fear. I've known enough sea captains who use it."

"He already has control. Drago keeps his family in line so that the vizier won't hurt them. So it makes no sense to blind Drago's daughter."

"Punishment?"

"For what?"

"I don't know, but I have a feeling."

"What? Tell me, Captain. I can take the truth better than leaving it up to my imagination. Do you think the vizier knows Drago talks to Dagstyrr?" said Rella, her heart skipping a beat. That would put them all in mortal danger long before he set off to rescue Drago. Just as Drago protected his family, so the dragons would protect their patriarch. If the vizier sent a dozen dragons to wipe out Dagstyrr and the wild fae—they would.

"No, I'm sure the vizier knows nothing. After all, it's been a long time since a dragon-talker lived among us. I just have a feeling our special human is not telling us everything."

"Mmm," said Rella. The captain was voicing what she'd been thinking ever since his spectacular talk with Drago was witnessed by the dark fae.

Dagstyrr and the mountain elves moved through the moonlit forest like ghosts. The human's long legs ate up the miles. Even so, he had trouble keeping up with the swift elves. He suspected they were slowing to accommodate him, for they looked as fresh now as when they'd started. He, however, was sweating profusely from the pace they set, to say nothing of having had no sleep.

As morning broke hot and thirsty in the forest, Beatty called a halt by a stream. After drinking their fill and topping up their water bottles, they climbed the hill to one side of the road below them, where they could rest unobserved.

"You see well in the dark," Dagstyrr said to Asti.

"Aye, but it was easy last night with a gibbous moon to light the way."

"Was there? I can't say I noticed. The forest makes every night dark to my eyes," said Dagstyrr, realizing he knew very little about these mountain men. That was another strange thing about them, always men and never women. He doubted he'd ever heard of a female mountain elf, never mind seen one. Perhaps, once he got to know them better, he'd get the opportunity to ask about it.

"Get some sleep," said Beatty. "We'll be off again as soon as the sun dips behind this hill. The going will be rougher, though. We can't follow the road any longer without drawing attention to ourselves."

Dagstyrr found a likely tree to lean his back against, then withdrew the ribbon from his pocket. He hoped its maker was as good a spell worker as she'd claimed. He watched the others select suitable places to sleep among the bracken before lifting the ribbon to his face and breathing in Rella's unique scent of roses and mint.

It was silly, but one of the things he missed most about her was that intoxicating perfume. If the spell worker was as good as her word, he need never be without it again. Perhaps he could have her make more. Rella could wear some in her braid? But maybe that was no longer fashionable; what did he know? The sun warmed the earth around him, and together with the scented ribbon, lulled him into a sense of perfect peace.

He awoke with a start. Someone had kicked him awake, and instinct warned him to keep quiet. The sound of carts on the road below reached their hiding place. Dagstyrr crept forward to lie under the bushes and watch the activity.

People of all kinds were marching toward the wild fae camp. Dagstyrr quirked an eyebrow at Beatty, and he replied with a nod. These people must be deserting the Dark Emperor. They were vulnerable to attack, and if that happened while Dagstyrr and Beatty's men were hiding in the forest above, it would spell disaster. Instinctively, those people would climb into the woods to escape, pursued by their attackers. Some might hide under their carts, leaving the warriors with them to fight off the enemy.

Dagstyrr tried to get a sense of how many warriors there were. He estimated one warrior per family cart, which was a better ratio than the wild fae had. His heart surged with hope as he realized this caravan was going to swell the number of warriors at Rella's command.

Beatty was kicking him again. The others were moving away. He wanted to stay and watch, but understanding the danger, he reluctantly crouched down and followed the elves out of sight of the dark fae cortege.

Once they were out of hearing range of the dark fae, they stopped to make some plans.

"That was a short rest," said Beatty. "But if we carry on we should be within range of my cousin's inn by nightfall. We can rest there for part of the night. Then he'll see us safely on the road in the early hours, before anyone is around."

Awakening to danger had produced an adrenaline rush that energized Dagstyrr, despite the lack of sleep. Now that the immediate threat was gone, exhaustion was catching up to him. He guessed they'd had about three hours of sleep. "It will be good to get a decent rest," he said. "I didn't expect you to have cousins in this area. Are there any more surprises I have to look forward to?" said Dagstyrr, not used to being kept in the dark.

"Oh, plenty, I should think," said Pordu. "Like we told you before, we don't talk of anything unless we're happy to have it common knowledge. We don't burden others with our secrets."

"I see," said Dagstyrr, knowing he was only touching the tip of a society that was still a mystery to him.

An hour after sunset, Beatty called a halt right in the middle of the swampiest forest they'd encountered so far. Every green patch of ground promising a firm foothold, turned out to be a mossy sponge releasing its water under their weight. Dagstyrr's boots were soon waterlogged.

"We must wait here 'til the inn's other customers are

gone home for the night. I don't want anyone to see us," ordered Beatty.

"Won't he have overnight guests?" whispered Dagstyrr.

"No, I've arranged for the inn to be empty, but he must accommodate his usual tap room customers or they'll get suspicious. So we must wait until they leave," said Beatty.

The sound of carts moving along the road far below them had been their constant companion throughout the day. Dagstyrr wondered that the Dark Emperor hadn't sent his troops to stop them. Then he remembered that the dark fae chose whom to follow, and when. It would go against their deepest culture for the Dark Emperor to interfere with them leaving—but would that stop him?

Dagstyrr sat sweaty and grimy, his clothes mud spattered and damp. Even his knees itched from the wet mud penetrating his clothes. He wished Beatty had chosen a drier place to stop. Then he found his leather water bottle almost empty. Looking around, he saw they were all in a similar position. Asti upended his flask. It was empty. So was Pordu's. Dagstyrr took a swig then tossed his bottle to Asti, who received it with a nod of thanks before drinking and passing it on to Pordu.

The other mountain elves, whose names he now knew were Mita, Clam, and Storr, were seated on a fallen log with Beatty, hidden beneath a large bush. They spoke in whispers and hand gestures in that strange language of theirs.

Dagstyrr wished he could understand it, but tried to respect their privacy, which was so important to them. Most people were happy to teach a few words of their language to others—not these mountain men. He sat as still as he could, while his clothes soaked up the moisture from the ground, and the creaking wheels of a dark fae caravan passed far below.

They waited until they heard the drunken babble of customers leaving the inn. Beatty waited a little longer before heading down to the inn alone. When he returned, it was with smiles and food. Dagstyrr ate gratefully. His stomach had felt empty for hours.

"There are only a few left. Once he signals that his patrons have all left, we'll go down. He has everything ready for us. Even a bed big enough for this lad," said Beatty, giving Dagstyrr a friendly pat on the knee.

"It will be appreciated, I assure you. Any chance of a bath?"

"Of course. Themdi is an excellent host. He often caters to humans."

Dagstyrr smiled. "I look forward to meeting him."

That was a lie. As the day had progressed, Dagstyrr had grown more and more aware of the differences between the mountain elves and humans. It wasn't just their appearance or their strange language; it was a fundamental difference that he couldn't put his finger on. If not for Rella's faith in them and their reputation among the wild fae, he'd find it hard to trust these little men.

CHAPTER 19

Two roads converged at the inn's gates. One was a spur of the road they'd been shadowing all day. The other, thick with greenery, hadn't been used for a long time.

Constructed of wattle and daub and reinforced with stout oak beams, the inn welcomed travelers with a dense thatched roof and roses around the doorway. Dagstyrr appreciated the well-crafted building from the dim light of a solitary lamp hanging in the cobbled courtyard. He and the elves hugged the shadows, skirting the stables until they arrived at the back door. Themdi may have seen all his patrons off, but drunks were unpredictable, and it was imperative they were not seen together if they were to stand a chance of infiltrating gatherings along their route.

Beatty led them silently through a low door into a storeroom filled with barrels, sacks, and split wood. It was all familiar and welcoming—his father's undercroft in miniature.

Dagstyrr made his way up a stepladder and into a kitchen where the stove still gave out some heat. A man stood at the door. He was short of stature but tall for a mountain elf. *He may be a halfling*, thought Dagstyrr as the man gestured for them to follow him through the deserted taproom and up rickety stairs to the attic bedrooms.

True to Beatty's word, Themdi had furnished a large bed and a warm bath for Dagstyrr. The mountain elves occupied a large room next to his. "We prefer to stick together," whispered Beatty, leaving Dagstyrr alone.

Dagstyrr put down his pack and weapons before stripping off his soiled clothes and stepping into the warm bathwater, where he washed off the mud and grime. Dressed in a clean shirt, he fell gratefully onto the bed. Who knew when he'd sleep in a bed next? Then he reached for the ribbon from his leather jerkin. He closed his eyes, and imagined Rella lying beside him. The perfumed ribbon usually evoked her presence, but tonight it only emphasized her absence.

With a sigh, he tied it around his wrist, rolled over, and fell into an exhausted sleep, ignoring his damp hair on the pillow.

It was the stench that awoke him, sending warnings flashing up his spine. Dagstyrr coughed amid the suffocating smell of earth and rotting vegetation. A primal scent, rich with all the decay of the forest, surrounded him. It was still dark, but someone, or something, was in his room. He lay still, opening his eyes just enough to see a tall shadow cross the floor at the foot of his bed.

The Dark Emperor!

On second glance, he saw that Rella's description of the creature was incredibly accurate. Insects and dead vegetation fell from the tall being's clothes as he moved, and Dagstyrr tried not to shiver in disgust. Who knew what was hiding in that cloak of his?

Fighting his instinct to rise and reach for his sword, he lay without moving a muscle. What was the Dark Emperor doing here? Did he think he could use Dagstyrr to reach Rella? Forcing his breathing to remain unchanged while he observed the creature, he tried to plan an attack, or at least a shouted warning to the mountain elves. Unfortunately, the dangerous fae stood between Dagstyrr and his weapons, which he'd carelessly left on a trunk on the other side of the room.

Were Beatty and the mountain elves still sleeping? He hoped this creature had no interest in them.

The Dark Emperor killed humans on sight. There was only one reason Dagstyrr still lived—Rella.

"Come now. I know you're awake. Don't take me for a fool, human." The man's voice sounded educated but cold. His eyes flashed like fire-rubies in the night, his whole being emitting a dread sense of power and corruption.

Dagstyrr opened his eyes fully only to find the Emperor's long face smiling down at him. He decided to play dumb. "Who are you? What are you doing in my room?" said Dagstyrr, attempting to pull himself up. But he couldn't move. Panic fluttered in his chest, and he ignored it. Now was not the time to appear vulnerable.

The Emperor threw back his head and laughed in scorn. "Why are humans always so transparent?"

Dagstyrr's mind was racing now. It wasn't magic holding him down; his mother's protective shield would have warned him of that and put a stop to it, even if he was sleeping. He looked down. His restraints were ordinary vines. Whenever he tried to move, they tightened around him—

pulled by Beatty and his men. Now that his eyes were fully open, he could just make out their wizened faces in the dark.

Intent on the Dark Emperor, Dagstyrr hadn't noticed anyone else in the shadows, but there they were, crouched on either side of his bed and pulling on the vines. "So, you are the spies?" said Dagstyrr, putting as much contempt into his voice as he could muster. His stomach lurched. Rella trusted these men. They knew her plans, and now they were betraying her.

Beatty harrumphed. "No. Don't call us spies. We're heroes."

"I will kill you all," growled Dagstyrr, his voice darker than the night. Asti flinched. How was Dagstyrr going to get word to Rella? Her precious mountain elves had betrayed her. "I hope you negotiated a good price. I hear I'm rather valuable in some quarters. For a human, that is."

The Emperor continued to smile down at Dagstyrr as he paced the room on extraordinarily long legs, one hand to his chin as if deep in thought.

"One thousand dark fae in exchange for one human," said Pordu. "Not bad, I'd say."

"You mean those people traveling the forest road?"

"Aye, that's right," said Beatty. "Dark fae. They are free now, thanks to us."

That explained why the Dark Emperor's forces were allowing them to leave. It had nothing to do with their culture. "So, you intended that I should accompany you right from the start?" Dagstyrr knew he'd been taken for a fool, and it irked him. He'd been led into a false sense of security by the wild fae, but he should have known to never trust the self-serving mountain elves. So should Rella.

"Of course."

"Mind you, it had to be your idea," said Pordu with a short snigger.

"Being the big hero, we knew you couldn't resist," laughed Asti, more confident.

"Enough!" said the Dark Emperor, raising his hand in command. "Get him out of here."

"If you unbind me, I will walk," said Dagstyrr as Beatty and his mountain elves hefted him onto their shoulders to carry him downstairs.

"I don't think so," said the Dark Emperor.

"Worth a try," replied Dagstyrr. He tested his restraints as they maneuvered his large frame down two flights of stairs made for those so much smaller. His bonds were tight. *Surely*, he thought, *breaking out of natural restraints should be easier than this?*

But the vines were green and newly cut.

They bundled him out the door and toward an elegant black carriage drawn by eight black horses with large plumes on their heads and winged feet. He'd heard of such horses, but always thought they were a myth. He was immediately impressed by the horseflesh, but as he looked them over, he noticed their eyes. They were sad beyond imagining, their spirits broken. These were not proud working beasts, he realized. These horses had been horribly abused.

The coach was an illusion too. This was not a coach made for comfortable transport. It was a portable jail cell made of iron—no wonder the horses were stressed, pulling all that weight.

The Dark Emperor's minions threw him into the coach so that he landed on the floor with his head against the opposite door and his legs sticking out. Without care for his comfort, they pushed his feet up and around to fit into the carriage, then locked the door behind him.

His feet were where his head should be. He managed to right himself and stick his head out the window. Unfortunately, the windows were too small to allow someone as large as him to escape. The metal-built coach had him caged as securely as any jail.

Beatty and his men were nervously preparing their bundles to leave. "You don't think this evil-smelling piece of refuse is going to let you live, do you?" said Dagstyrr.

He saw the elves hesitate. So, they knew how dangerous this was. They'd made a deal with a madman, and now they were nervous.

The tall Emperor let his head fall back as he muttered some kind of spell. Beatty and his men took a step back, eyes flashing warnings silently between them. They were not happy, not happy at all.

Pordu stepped toward the coach. "What do you know of it? We have paid the price to free the dark fae. An agreement between dark fae is *never* broken. Something your woman needs to learn."

Dagstyrr laughed. He'd quite happily strangle every one of the mountain elves himself, given half a chance. They'd betrayed Rella and all the wild fae. She'd trusted them, and this was her reward. Did they honestly think swelling her ranks by one thousand dark fae would make up for it? Somehow, he had to get a message to her. "Tell me again, what exactly was the bargain you made with this long stinky piece of garbage?"

"You, in exchange for one thousand dark fae. Simple," said Pordu. "The mountain elves become heroes."

"Ah, would that be exactly one thousand?"

"Of course," said Asti, letting his contempt show on his face.

"Not one thousand villagers and six elves then?" said

Dagstyrr, forcing a broad smile. He knew how dangerous this was, but reckoned it was his only chance to get a message to Rella.

Even in the shadowy night, he saw the elves' faces blanch. Immediately, they tensed and started to back away toward the forest. A scuttling sound behind them made them turn.

A host of crabs sidled out of the wet forest floor toward them. Claws raised, they nipped the air as if blindly searching for their next meal.

"There you are, my little ones. I told you there would be a feast tonight," said the Emperor.

CHAPTER 20

Ghastlier than any nightmare Dagstyrr could dream up, the crabs came crawling over the ground, making straight for the mountain elves who now knew what fate awaited them. The horror of their situation showed on their faces—a mixture of fear and disbelief. They backed away cautiously, looking for an escape. Pordu dashed sideways toward the forest, but as soon as he changed trajectory, more crabs came from that direction until he and his companions were surrounded.

Dagstyrr closed his eyes for a moment. He was angry at Beatty and his men, and would quite happily run them through with his sword, but no one deserved to die like this. To be eaten alive by crabs. One little bite at a time. How much of their flesh would be gone before death finally claimed them?

The Dark Emperor stood unharmed amid the carnage. The crabs gave him a wide berth as he conducted their feast. He used his long arms to wave them forward, yelling with delight when they reached their target. The elves were cursing and screaming, trying to jump clear of the morass of crabs that had turned the forest floor into a living carpet. One by one, the red and black crustaceans found hold and climbed men's clothing until they reached flesh.

Dagstyrr saw Asti pull off his coat to dislodge the dozen or more crabs crawling over his back—big mistake. They nipped through his fine lawn shirt, and bright splashes of blood blossomed over his torso.

The screaming increased as the crabs reached more tender parts. First, the neck and face—and it was only going to get worse. Dagstyrr slumped against the metal bench, not wanting to watch the carnage he couldn't prevent.

What kind of devil was this Dark Emperor?

Schooling his disgust, Dagstyrr called out to him: "I knew you were powerful. Evil even. I never thought you were stupid."

He was rewarded with a cackling laugh, which sounded disturbingly like that of an hysterical lunatic. "Don't think to save them, human."

"Oh, I can assure you, I won't. Those traitorous, lying little bastards deserve all they get," said Dagstyrr, with feeling.

A dark shadow passed in front of the coach's window, and a lean hand gripped the edge. "So, do tell. Why do you think I'm stupid?" said a sneering face that Dagstyrr knew to be the root of all Rella's nightmares.

The man's breath smelled foul, and his teeth were pointed and black with rot.

Dagstyrr tried to relax and look as though he had not a care in the world, which was difficult while trussed up like a pig ready for the spit. The screaming of the elves increased and spurred him on. He needed to get word to Rella's camp somehow. "My father... You have heard of Earl Magnus, I take it?"

"Certainly. Who has not? He tricked a light fae princess into marriage."

Stunned by that answer, Dagstyrr struggled not to be distracted by it. "Well, my father would say that you should allow at least one of them to escape."

"Why would I do that?"

"To enhance your reputation, of course."

"What do you mean?"

"This forest glade will be cleaned by morning. No sign of what happened here. No one to tell the tale..." Dagstyrr fell silent, allowing the idea to grow in the Emperor's head.

"You're sure this isn't some trick to save your favorite?"

"Give me one chance, and I'll run them through for you," growled Dagstyrr, trying to convince the Emperor. It galled him to think of the trust Rella had put in these traitors, but now one of them might be his only hope to get a message to her.

He watched the Emperor pace the ground, his head tilted as if in deep thought. "Come on," whispered Dagstyrr. For this to work, the Emperor would have to make a decision soon. Time was running out for the elves.

The Emperor stopped pacing as the screams from his victims increased. He waved a hand, and dark green energy flowed in a torrent from his fingers over the ground. Dagstyrr didn't dare appear too interested. He sat back, his expression neutral. The Emperor could change his mind at any moment, and this was Dagstyrr's only chance to let the wild fae know what had happened.

"Which one should I save?"

"I don't care."

"Three are dead now anyway," said the Emperor laughing his strange high-pitched cackle.

"Well, which one best serves your purpose? After all, there isn't much point if he just crawls off and dies."

"That one I think," he said, directing his magic energy in Pordu's direction.

Dagstyrr eased closer to the window and looked out. Crabs were pouring over the three mountain elves who had fallen to the ground, none showing any sign of life. Beatty and Storr were still fighting them off, their screams growing weak as they lost the battle to survive.

Pordu was suddenly free of crabs. His whole body was one bloody mass, but he was upright and walking. He loped cautiously for the tree line. He turned at the last minute to see the Dark Emperor wave him on. "Go. Spread the tale of what has happened here this night."

The terrified mountain elf turned his face to Dagstyrr. His big eyes, full of pity and regret, pierced the bloody night. Then, with a nod, he was gone.

Dagstyrr knew he'd make it back, but Rella trusted these men. Would she see through the lies he was bound to make up to cover up his treachery? Viktar of Casta would know a coward's deception when he heard it. Bernst would hear a lie too.

It didn't take magic to uncover a lie; it took experience.

The Dark Emperor climbed up on the coach and took the reins. The winged horses galloped along the road like ordinary beasts, spurred on by the frenzied cracking of the Dark Emperor's whip. Glad to be gone from the clacking crabs and bloody screams of the inn's courtyard, Dagstyrr concentrated on not being pulverized by the iron carriage's bouncing and rocking.

With hands and legs bound tight, he careened into the metal sides with every twist in the road. He tried to calculate how far they were from Thingstyrbol. Hours, he reckoned, even with flying horses—why were they galloping like any normal horse? Dagstyrr braced his legs against the right wall and his back against the left, preparing to ride it out.

His only hope was Pordu—a cowardly liar. Dagstyrr's only hope was that good men would see through the mountain elf's lies, and trusted they could convince Rella not to attempt a rescue. At all costs, she must stay away, or this monster would have her. Dagstyrr was under no illusion—he was only alive because he was bait.

Unfortunately, Rella was the rescuing kind.

Despite long days on the practice field drilling the wild fae, Rella found it hard to sleep. Just like she had last night and the night before, she crawled out of her bed and wrapped a blanket over her shoulders. It was Dagstyrr's blanket, but it wasn't enough to soothe the turmoil in Rella, knowing Dagstyrr was in danger.

The closer the time came for her to face the Dark Emperor, the more Rella knew she wasn't nearly as brave as everyone thought. It made her crave the incredible sense of protection and wellbeing that came with Dagstyrr's presence. He was her weakness.

Stepping outside her tent, she nodded to the guard and made her way to a rock, where she could sit under the stars and replenish her energies, both light and dark. The scent of pine and cedar filled the air under a sky sparkling with midnight stars.

Her guards watched from a discreet distance. They were used to this nightly ritual, but they had no idea why she did it. As dark fae, she could replenish her energy from the ground beneath her while sleeping, but Rella needed more.

The stars and moon were necessary to bolster her light fae energy, while the earth fed her dark fae energy. Both were vital parts of who she was, but the fewer people who knew about that, the better. She didn't need another target on her back.

Sitting beneath the carpet of twinkling light, she wondered whether Dagstyrr was lying in some forest glade, watching the same stars rotate slowly in the heavens. Once he returned, they'd take Thingstyrbol and kill the Dark Emperor. Only then would she be free.

"Good evening, Rella."

She hadn't heard Fedric's approach. "What are you doing sneaking around at night?" she said, irritated at being disturbed.

"I couldn't sleep," he said, ignoring her brusque words.

Rella sighed. When he was reasonable, it was difficult to be harsh with Fedric. He hadn't understood that healing such a terrible wound with dark magic would result in him turning dark. He had come about it with the best of intentions. "Why not?"

"I miss sleeping under the stars. I know it makes no sense. I understand that I need contact with the earth now, but I miss the stars' beauty," he said, sitting a little way from her.

"They are beautiful," said Rella, beginning to wonder whether Fedric was going to have both magic energies, like her. In some ways, it would make her feel better knowing it was normal for fae like them. However, she couldn't imagine Fedric keeping it to himself. He'd use it to gain every advantage he could as he carved out a place for himself in his new world.

They sat in companionable silence, soaking up the energy of the night. Eventually, Rella said, "What you need are some friends. You should make an effort to get to know more people."

The handsome fae warrior smiled. "It isn't easy with my father constantly reminding people that I'm light fae turned dark. However, I do like the company of Reckless. He's neither one thing nor another too."

"So, he doesn't judge you. It makes sense. You two are of an age, both skilled warriors, both with a lot to learn, and both needing to make a place for yourselves in the new world once this war is over," said Rella.

"Both needing a mate," said Fedric, his eyes seeking hers.

"I don't think either of you will have any problems on that score," she said, ignoring the way his eyes raked her body.

"True. However, it will be hard to find the right mate. One worthy of bonding with."

Rella laughed softly. "You really must lose that arrogant light fae streak running through you, or there is no chance of a dark fae woman taking you as a mate."

"Ah, that is my point exactly. I am a light fae lord turned dark. Who here is my equal?" he said casually.

Rella didn't want to believe what she was hearing. "How dare you?"

"You and I are the only two of our kind," he said.

Rella stood, her temper rising. "Be very careful, Fedric. Do not dare compare us. I chose to turn dark, while you simply made an error, never expecting to face this outcome. You have a lot to learn. I wouldn't be so quick to look for a mate if I were you. Remember, when we mate, we bond for life."

"Yet, you chose a human."

Rella knew he was foolish, young, arrogant, but she

didn't trust any of that would stop her from killing him if he dared to disparage Dagstyrr. "Leave now! Change your thinking, Fedric, or it will see you in an early grave."

"Perhaps you should change your thinking. You and I would make a powerful couple," he said.

The tall, elegant youth stood looking down at her, trying to ingratiate himself in all the wrong ways. A knowing smile tainted a twist of Fedric's lips. "Don't worry, Princess Rella, I understand. I must wait until your human dies, which he inevitably will soon enough."

In an instant, Rella stood over him. Her green battle magic was slowly choking the life from him as it swirled around his prostrate body. She trembled from head to toe, trying to control the rage knifing through her. Her every instinct was driving her to blast him from the earth for threatening her mate. All her fears for Dagstyrr coalesced into a blinding hatred of Fedric. She wanted him to taste the dark battle magic choking through every minute space in his arrogant body, to know he was dying and who was killing him.

Whatever you do, lad, don't move! Bernst's voice sounded in her head.

"Rella! Let him go!" Viktar's order rolled across the field, full of a compulsion only ever used in battle. Reserved for the direst circumstances.

Captain Bernst and Viktar came either side of her. They daren't risk touching her or she might accidently kill Fedric. Then Rella saw the confused pain on Viktar's face, and something inside her broke. Still shaking with rage, she pulled back from the youth at her feet and turned away.

Viktar went immediately to his son. Bernst ran his hands down her arms, keeping them tight to her body where she could do no harm. She sensed Bernst was using healing magic to help calm her, but the rage inside her would not die. He'd threatened her mate. All the primal urges of the fae were burgeoning in her now.

Eventually, she contained it to a small part of herself, and Bernst's efforts allowed her breathing to return to a semblance of normalcy. Her guards were carrying Fedric across the field toward his father's tent. It would be some time before he recovered.

"What on earth did he do to deserve that?" Viktar towered over her, his anger a palpable energy flowing from him in waves like courtly silk. "You almost killed him."

"I may yet."

Captain Bernst bravely stepped between them. "I think we need to hear her out."

Momentarily distracted by Bernst, Viktar took a deep breath. "Very well. What do you mean, you may yet? What could he possibly have said to warrant death?"

"He threatened my mate," said Rella simply, walking away.

Minutes later, Rella sensed someone following her. Who had witnessed her lose control? Still uncertain of her position as leader of the wild fae, she couldn't risk her reputation with rumors of madness. Though, in truth, the dark fae often showed their tempers and might understand better than most.

Whoever it was, they didn't exactly try to hide their presence. Fae could move silently when they wanted to—Billy!

"Billy, run ahead and light the lamps in my tent."

"How'd you know it was me?"

"We fae have our ways. Now, off with you."

"Aye, we do, don't we?" said the boy, happily running ahead.

Later, Rella poured mead into two cups and offered one to the boy. "Why are you not following Captain Bernst?"

Billy took the mead and downed it in one gulp before sitting on a three-legged stool. His head hung low, long strings of hair falling over his eyes. He flicked his hair back and said, "I hate to be the one to tell you, Princess, but I think he's the spy."

Rella carefully suppressed the laugh threatening to surface. Bernst a spy? No. Not ever. "What makes you think that, Billy?" she said, forcing a small frown to let the boy know she took him seriously.

"He and Viktar, that light fae, they've been sneaking off together and talking to newcomers."

"We need as much information as we can gather before attacking Thingstyrbol. These people might have important information. I'm sure there's nothing to worry about, Billy."

"I'm sure there is. You need me. I know you can't be everywhere at once. I understand," said Billy. "But I can keep track of them and report back to you."

"Captain Bernst is your friend, Billy. He even taught you how to defend yourself with a knife."

"He's sneaky. I bet he hasn't told you about the injured man what came in this morning. They've got him hidden in a tent. Everyone's abuzz with it. He's got things to tell, but they didn't tell *you* about him. Did they?" he said, nodding sagely.

Rella saw how it might appear to the boy. "They will tell me. I wasn't in the mood to listen tonight, that's all. Besides, if he's injured, they'll want to make him better first."

CHAPTER 21

The next morning, Rella wrapped her woolen cloak tight against the dewy mist rising from the river. A blue heron skimmed the water, looking for food. At her request, Patrice had brought the *Spider* up from the Elfin Cove, and together with the *Viper* and the *Knucker*, the fleet looked magnificent. Billy's misgivings had niggled at her all night, but she was determined to wait until her most trusted friends told her what was going on.

"We're ready when you are, Princess," said Captain Bernst, coming up beside her.

She looked down, embarrassed at her lack of control the night before. "How's Fedric?"

Bernst laughed. "Don't worry. He'll have the worst headache of his life for a day or two. No permanent harm done."

"Is that how Viktar feels?"

"I've no idea."

"I must apologize to him," she said, absently kicking a pebble.

"Don't bother," said Viktar, appearing at her side, his

stern face like granite in the morning sun. "I hope both you and Fedric have learned your lessons."

Rella struggled not to argue. If Fedric hadn't threatened Dagstyrr, she'd have kept control over her emotions.

Viktar must have sensed the feelings warring inside her. "If you let Fedric control you like that—he will."

"What do you mean?" she rounded on him, despite her promises to herself not to challenge him.

"I mean all good commanders must control their emotions—at all times. Not just on the battlefield. Rella, why do you think the courtiers in Casta are encouraged to show no emotion? They are not unfeeling. They are the commanders of our armies, and must never act on personal emotions," said Viktar.

She looked at Bernst at that revelation. The sea captain met her gaze and shrugged.

Rella started to understand how she'd allowed Fedric to control her by getting under her skin, and was struck by how easily he'd done it. "I must be more careful in the future."

"If it's any consolation, he didn't intend to threaten Dagstyrr directly. He's still finding out what he is now, and desperately looking for a friend."

"Well, he went the wrong way about it," said Rella, unable to keep quiet, "but he has to accept there are no others like him. He must choose dark fae, halflings, or humans for his companions."

"First, he has to forget the ideas of hierarchy drummed into him from birth," said Viktar.

"So, Captain, you were saying that you're ready to sail?" said Rella, wanting to change the subject. "Have you enough oarsmen?"

"Aye, it doesn't take long to train men to the oar when

they're motivated. Mind you, after a full day pulling an oar, some will regret being so hasty to volunteer."

"Eventually, they'll be stronger for it," said Rella.

"If they don't break their backs first," said Viktar with a knowing grin. "I discovered muscles I didn't know I had while practicing on the *Drake* before you rescued us from the slave pens."

"The *Mermaid* is keeping her usual shape?" said Rella, uneasy, knowing if the *Mermaid* was to navigate the river that ran past Thingstyrbol, she couldn't do it shaped as a seagoing barque. Her keel was too low in the water, whereas longships were ideal for speeding up rivers.

"Aye, she won't be going upriver."

Rella's head turned sharply. "Why not?"

"She won't approach Thingstyrbol. Says it's not good for her with *him* there," said Bernst with a frown.

"We need all the men we have to attack Thingstyrbol," said Rella, trying to keep the frustration from her voice.

"She knows what she's doing," said Bernst.

Both Captain Bernst and Dagstyrr had a relationship with the sentient being known as the *Mermaid*—Rella didn't. Unfortunately, everyone who knew the *Mermaid* bowed to her wisdom. Very irritating.

"Perhaps I could talk to her?" said Rella.

"You won't change her mind."

"No. You've always said that the *Mermaid* is very obstinate. We'll leave for Thingstyrbol as soon as Beatty and Dagstyrr return. They've been away three days. He could be back tomorrow or the next day."

"You're a bit obstinate yourself if you don't mind me saying," said Bernst with a grin.

"This is not the first time I've led warriors in battle," she said, instinctively putting her hand to her sword hilt.

"It's the first time you've gone up against the likes of him, though, isn't it?" said Viktar, able to hit the crux of the matter.

"I've known this was coming for a long time. I always knew I'd never be able to pay the price." Seeing the look on Bernst's face, she said, "Don't look so shocked."

"No dark fae would ever speak so plainly about refusing to pay the agreed price. I can only think you were light fae at the time and didn't understand how sacred a promised price is to us."

"True enough. I didn't fully understand at the time. But you should know I don't regret not paying it. This war would have happened with or without my help. I am convinced of it now. The Dark Emperor is an abomination, a scourge on the lives of all fae, dark and light. He must be stopped."

"And you're the one to do it," he said.

"Do you believe that?" said Rella, embarrassed at needing his validation.

"I do. Without Rella of the wild fae, no one would dare to attack Thingstyrbol. That place is the very root of us. Since the fae split into light and dark, many generations have held it in sacred awe—until him. Do you notice nearly all the wild fae warriors are young? None of them as old as Viktar or myself?"

Having been brought up in Casta where no one allowed age to mar a complexion, Rella hadn't given it much thought. "It had not occurred to me."

"No, it wouldn't. Those of us old enough to remember the dark queens find it hard to imagine attacking Thingstyrbol."

"But we must."

"Aye, that devil must be brought down once and for all. The tales told by the newcomers are becoming more horrific

every day," said Bernst, spitting on the ground to ward off
the taint of evil he imagined his words brought with them.

Rella wondered if Viktar and Bernst would tell her
about the newcomer in the tent now.

"Best not talk of it," said Viktar, quickly.

Apparently, they were keeping her in the dark about
something. Could Billy be right? What was going on behind
her back? "Patrice and the other warriors bring all their
important intelligence straight to me. Bad or not, I need to
know what's happening," she said, giving them one more
chance to tell her.

Silence greeted her statement. Both men looked as innocent as babes. That alone roused her suspicion, for Bernst
never looked innocent. She changed the subject. "As soon as
we march, this encampment will be struck and moved on."

"I don't suppose you're going to tell us where they'll be
going?" said Viktar.

"I don't know, and that's the way it has to stay. Gimrir
will lead them. He has an uncanny knack of knowing the
safest places, something to do with talking to the trees. The
last thing I want is the Dark Emperor launching a rear
guard attack on our loved ones," said Rella, unable to stop
thinking about Dagstyrr. Where was he?

"It's for the best, I reckon," said Bernst.

"Let's see your recruits, Viktar," said Rella, turning and
leading the way into the broad meadow that housed Viktar's
war tent. The scent of woodland flowers and the buzzing of
bees followed them all the way there. On a day like today, it
was hard to imagine the stink of blood and battle magic.
Rella took a last deep breath before entering his tent.

Six young commanders stood to attention as Viktar
entered, fully armored in bright blue-and-white Casta steel,
his braided hair falling down his back, ready for war. Rella

had to admit, he'd never looked more magnificent as he took his place at the table with the model of Thingstyrbol in the center. The commanders, dressed in varying shades of brown leathers, stood around the table, committing to memory every inch of the approaches to the palace.

Reckless saw her and smiled. A bright blush crept up his eager face. The others noticed and turned to her, but Fedric kept his head down. That headache must be hurting something rotten.

She was pleased to see Reckless among them. Clar and Nan, two of Patrice's sisters, were there, along with two other recruits; a man called Abar and his wife, Effa. Both of them looked like seasoned warriors in their battered armor and shining swords and axes.

Rella and Captain Bernst stood by the tent flap, listening as Viktar pointed out places where ambushes were likely. Those with knowledge of the villages and forest surrounding the palace had supplemented Rella's model, and now it took up the whole table. Pathways, hills, hidden dells, and cottages were now shown, making it easier for the leaders to plan their attack.

"I didn't mean to disturb you," she said, with a nod to the commanders.

"We're nearly finished, my lady," said Reckless.

"Yes," said Viktar. "Each of these six will lead a cohort in the attack. Each cohort has a single goal; once reached, those warriors hold their positions. I will pull a cohort of my own to one side. I can use those warriors to bolster any others that are struggling to reach their target."

"What about me?" said Rella, unable to locate her position on the three-dimensional map.

"You must take overall command," said Viktar. "I suggest here," he continued, pointing to a hillock far removed from the black battlements of Thingstyrbol. "You will get a good idea of how things are shaping up from this position. We can use the mountain elves as runners."

To her shame, Rella was relieved. To stay well back from that hateful place was a blessing. But this was her fight. Could she stand safe in the rear while others fought her battle?

"I'd rather be closer to the action," she said.

"I know. All new field commanders think that way, but if you're to direct the battle, you must position yourself here," said Viktar.

"Very well," she said, seeing sense in his thinking, but still feeling guilty.

"The warriors from the longships will land here and make for the black glass wall linking these two towers. It is the best defense the Dark Emperor has, and most likely where he'll retreat from the onslaught of the other cohorts."

"I don't want..."

"Rella, I've been over this a hundred times. Even you must bow to my experience sometimes," said Viktar, clearly irritated. "There will be over three hundred seasoned warriors and all the siege ladders we have. Dagstyrr's an experienced commander. Yes, there will be casualties, there always are."

Her eyes flashed to Fedric. His eyes were cast down toward the model, but a tiny twitch at the corner of his mouth spoke of triumph.

She stepped forward. "I will command from that hill, as you say, but only until the ships arrive. I will then join with those warriors and fight alongside my mate. The Dark Emperor will fall to my blade."

Her statement wasn't up for debate. Fedric looked up

now, surprise giving his light brown eyes a stupefied look. The boy had no idea who he was dealing with.

Viktar sighed. "Very well. However, those ships won't hit the shores until I give the signal. I want these other positions secure first. That wall will be the last target."

"I agree. Those positions should be secured first, but I will give the signal," she said, glancing at Bernst, who answered her with a tiny nod.

Whatever happened to her or the wild fae, Dagstyrr must never fall into the hands of the Dark Emperor. He had a promise of his own to fulfill to Drago. One he could not escape. When would he return?

CHAPTER 22

Captain Bernst left Viktar's war tent as evening shadows lengthened in the glade but then quickly returned just as the warriors were taking their leave. Rella had never seen him look so flustered. "What is it, Captain?" she said.

"Oh, I just wanted Viktar for a moment," said Bernst, trying to assume his usual casual attitude, and not managing it.

Viktar's head lifted quickly, but his smile was just a second too slow to reach his lips. "Captain Bernst and I are working on something, a surprise," he said, coming over to Rella and patting her shoulder. "You get some sleep, my girl. You must be ready to lead your troops at a moment's notice."

What were they scheming? Whatever it was, they must think her a fool not to notice. If there was something that Viktar and Bernst didn't want her involved in, chances were she needed to know about it. She forced a yawn. "Aye, you're right. I just wish Dagstyrr would return," she said, leaving.

Instead of going to her tent, she doubled back in the forest in time to see Bernst and Viktar exiting the war tent together. Long dark cloaks with large cowls masked their identities, but Rella would know them anywhere. She crouched in the undergrowth until they passed by her, then followed at a safe distance.

They kept their heads together, whispering so low, even her acute hearing couldn't make out more than the odd word. Suddenly, aware of being followed, she slid behind a sourberry bush and waited. Whoever it was, they were not fae. Not with such loud footsteps. "Billy!" she whispered. The boy appeared and snuggled next to her, bringing the smell of unwashed clothes and adolescence.

"You stink," she whispered.

"Aye, maybe, but so do they," he said, his eyes never leaving the cloaked backs of her most trusted advisors.

"Do you know where they're going?"

"Aye, the man in the tent is dying. I bet that man knows who the traitors are, and those two are going to shut him up," said Billy.

"Billy, Captain Bernst and Viktar are not the traitors," she said.

"Oh, no? Why are they skulking about at night then? Not wanting you or anyone else with them in case they're overheard. I bet they kill the man so he can't tell who the traitors are," said Billy. "Come on. We don't want to lose them."

Rella scrambled after Billy. The boy was deranged, but he was also very good at following Captain Bernst. She couldn't help wondering what they were doing and why they didn't want her to know about it. If it was something dire enough to upset Bernst, then that worried her. She'd thought him unflappable.

Rella and Billy followed the two men into the valley where newcomers were kept for a while until they understood the wild fae rules. Once inside the hustle and bustle of the newcomer's camp, they were able to follow a short distance behind Viktar and Bernst. As soon as they were within reach of the newest wagons and tents, the cloaked men hurried directly toward one tent set apart from the others.

Rella and Billy followed.

The tent appeared to be guarded by mountain elves, but not any she recognized. She stood back as Viktar bowed low to enter, followed by Bernst, who turned and looked around, no doubt looking for Billy—he was not quiet to fae ears. That's how Bernst always knew where he was. Which tonight, worked well for her. Any noise she'd made, he'd assumed was Billy.

Rella made her way to the tent, hoping to overhear them before being challenged by the guards. *What am I doing?* Spying on her closest allies did not sit well with her.

Viktar and Bernst were probably making final arrangements with the mountain elves to act as runners between the different cohorts when they attacked Thingstyrbol.

So why sneak about in the night?

Realizing how ridiculous she appeared skulking through her own camp, she stood tall and walked toward the tent. Billy raced after her, pulling at her leather jerkin. "Come away, my lady. They're bad men. Don't trust them."

"It's all right, Billy. They won't hurt us," she said, trying to reassure the boy. When they were fifteen feet from tent, the flap opened, and Captain Bernst and Viktar emerged. Billy raced for the cover of a wagon, sliding under it in a trice.

The grim faces of her advisors stopped her in her tracks. Bernst was wiping blood from the blade of his seaman's knife on his sleeve before sheathing it. He looked up guiltily before sighing and coming to a stop.

Rella advanced, not wanting to believe the horrible ideas Billy had planted in her head. As she drew abreast of the men, Viktar's hand flashed out and caught her arm. She turned to meet his eyes. He looked guilty as well. Shaking her arm out of his grasp, she carried on into the tent. He didn't try to stop her.

Inside, a man lay dead. Pordu! Her heart fluttered as she took in the many horrible injuries inflicted upon him. They looked like bites, but what kind? He must have been in agony, poor man. A wide gash across his throat told the tale of Bernst's bloody knife—the coup de grace.

She would have done the same.

She approached the bed slowly, closed his eyes, and rested his long-fingered hands across his chest. What had happened to him, and why did he suffer to return when he was so severely injured? A man like Pordu could have sought help in a dark fae village along the way, so there was only one answer. He brought a message involving the whereabouts of Dagstyrr and the others.

With a swiftness born of fury, Rella marched out of the tent and between Captain Bernst and Viktar. Taking them both by the arm, she said, "Gentlemen, we need to talk."

The Dark Emperor arrived at Thingstyrbol, still whipping his horses into a frenzied gallop. A flurry of activity met their arrival. Bruised and battered, Dagstyrr spilled from the coach onto the palace courtyard. An old mountain elf with a grin as wide as his face held the carriage door open. Dagstyrr gazed up at the dark towers surrounding the cobbled yard. The turrets reached high into a brooding night sky—he would not die here!

Rella needed him.

Drago needed him.

The Dark Emperor leaped down from his driving seat, fresh and enlivened as if the last few hours of his mad dash through the forest were no more than a summer outing. Looking around, Dagstyrr could see the exhausted horses were near the point of death. Their eyes rolled in their heads, and foam covered their hides as they blew long and hard on trembling legs. He'd be surprised if they didn't drop dead after that run.

Why on earth did the madman not let them use their wings? Then he noticed a wing fall to the cobbles as the beasts stamped the ground. It was a deception. These were ordinary horses with dyed eagle wings glued to their hocks.

"Madman" was right. If the Dark Emperor was using such petty illusions to impress his people, he was not nearly as powerful as everyone thought. Struggling to sit with his back against a wheel, Dagstyrr laughed aloud.

The Emperor stopped stretching his long limbs and advanced on him. "What's so funny, human?"

"I just wondered why someone as powerful as the Dark Emperor bothered gluing eagle wings to his horses. Why not find some real flying horses? Those are ridiculous!"

The Emperor leaned against the carriage with one arm, causing his living cloak to drape over Dagstyrr. "I suppose you know where I might find such beasts?" he said, his voice as low and as dangerous as Dagstyrr had yet heard.

"Of course not. They are a legend."

"And if you did hear of such a beast, you would tell me, right?"

"No."

"Ah, you think to trick me by being honest. I know you humans can never be trusted. You are eaten up by jealousy.

You appear so like the fae, yet are nothing more than animals."

"If I'm so abhorrent, why capture me? That was a high price you paid for me."

"That was nothing. You, my little pet, are bait," he said, bending down farther and stroking Dagstyrr's hair. "The real prize is worth one million ungrateful commoners, or more."

Dagstyrr's heart sank as his suspicions were confirmed. All the while, the foul stink of the Emperor poured into his nostrils as small creatures were born, died, and fell from his cloak and crown. If the Dark Emperor decided to ransom him in exchange for Rella, she'd come. He prayed Viktar and Bernst would be able to restrain her.

Bernst would come to his rescue—he had to, for they were both promise bound to Drago.

If the Dark Emperor knew he was a dragon-talker, who knew what tricks he might employ to lure a dragon here? Dagstyrr must not, under any circumstances, contact Drago. The easiest people to manipulate were those tempted by hope, and Drago's family had survived on hope for years. As appealing as it was to ask Drago for his aid, Dagstyrr would die before he'd help the Dark Emperor capture a dragon.

"What? No smart comeback? You must be hurting more than I intended. Don't worry. I'm not going to kill you—yet. I want her to watch you die. Slowly, very slowly," he said, his cackling laughter ringing across the courtyard. "Then, she'll be mine forever."

Dagstyrr fought to stay calm. If this creature managed to rile him into losing his temper, he was doomed. Yet he couldn't help saying, "She'll never be yours."

There was nothing to stop the Emperor pretending to ransom him, and then killing him slowly in front of Rella anyway. Dagstyrr pushed those thoughts from his head. He needed to assess his situation calmly.

"Oh, but yes, she will. She'll be drawn like a moth to a flame when she sees where the real power lies."

"From what I can see," said Dagstyrr, gazing at the fallen eagle's wing, "you don't have such powerful magic. She'll see through you in a moment and dismiss you for the jumped-up imposter you are."

Dagstyrr saw the Emperor tremble to control his rage.

"Come on, get him to the tower," he ordered his servants. "Strip him naked and hang him up. I will eat now," he said, striding off toward high oak doors to what looked like a traditional hall. Shadows appeared and followed him in. Something about those shadow men made Dagstyrr's flesh crawl like never before.

CHAPTER 23

"**I** should have been told immediately," said Rella, pacing her tent. "You two think you know everything. That doesn't give you the right to interfere in my life. And make no mistake, Dagstyrr is my life. What has happened to him?" she said, turning to face both Viktar and Captain Bernst.

In the dim confines of her tent, Viktar's long legs stuck out just like Dagstyrr's did, and she wanted to kick them out of her way. Bernst sat with his ankles crossed and his head down, only looking up when she addressed him directly.

"Princess, he's dead," said Viktar, quietly standing and coming to her side.

Rella felt the air still around her as if the world had stopped. She struggled to draw breath. "No. No, he is not. I would know if Dagstyrr were dead," she said, feeling the truth of her words tainted with doubt. Was their mating strong enough that she would feel his loss even at this distance?

She could see that Bernst truly thought Dagstyrr was dead. "Pordu was the only one to make it out alive, and only because Dagstyrr drew the ire of the Dark Emperor on himself. Pordu saw him fall..."

"Fall like the others? That makes no sense. Why did he let Pordu live if Dagstyrr was already dead?" A cold rage was growing in her chest. Fingers of ice settled in the spaces of her soul that were his and his alone.

Viktar raised a hand toward Rella. "I'm sorry, my dear, that is what we went to ask the mountain elf."

Rella slapped away the warrior's hand, something she'd never dream of ordinarily, but she was beyond all fear of consequence. He couldn't be dead. She'd know if he died, wouldn't she? Her heart thundered a tattoo in her breast. It echoed in her sensitive ears until she thought her head would burst. "So, what was his excuse?"

Both men sighed. Viktar looked up. "No excuse, Rella. He said he was allowed to escape to tell the tale. After all, how could it hurt us if we didn't know what had happened? How could it hurt you?"

"Eaten alive by crabs in a forest," said Bernst. "A horrible way to die and worthy of the Dark Emperor." Bernst spat on the ground, still too superstitious to speak the Dark One's name without guarding against evil. "He takes delight in such things. There is no doubt he's mad."

"Wait a minute," pounced Rella. "To tell the tale? Were those his exact words?" she said, clinging to hope.

"No. At first they were all going to die, then Dagstyrr persuaded the Dark Emperor to let one of them live. The Emperor chose Pordu. He doesn't know why," said Bernst.

"So, he didn't see Dagstyrr dead. He could still be alive," she said, pouring a cup of wine and drinking it down.

Viktar stood. "No, Rella. Don't deceive yourself like this, please. Pordu said Dagstyrr was the first to fall. He was the Emperor's main target."

"I am not deceiving myself, Viktar. It is Pordu who has deceived you."

"Why would he do that?"

"Why does anyone lie? To enhance their standing, to hide their guilt," she said.

"He was dying. He could not expect any future. As for guilt—what guilt? Besides, I used a truth serum," said Viktar. "He swore Dagstyrr was the first to fall."

"Fall perhaps, but die? I want to talk to the leaders of the newcomers," said Rella, throwing on a cloak and marching out of her tent.

Viktar and Bernst hurried after her. "I know you want to believe he's alive," said Bernst. "I do too, but the chances are that even if he was alive when Pordu escaped, he's dead now. The Emperor hates humans. I'm sorry, Princess, but we have to come to terms with it and decide how we're going to carry on without him."

"I won't live with defeatist attitudes," she said, marching through the encampment toward the newcomer's tents. "If you want to learn the truth, come with me. Otherwise, go back to your ship. You're no use to me."

Viktar and Bernst exchanged glances, then fell in on either side of her.

Dagstyrr opened his eyes slowly and tried to make sense of what he was seeing. Whatever potion they'd forced down his throat was wearing off. He had no idea of how long he'd been unconscious. Shafts of light from high arrow slits pierced the darkness. He was bound tight, unable to move more than his fingers. That would be useful if he were fae like his brothers, but it didn't do him any good.

He discovered he could move his head slightly too. He was upright; his arms stretched out either side of him, his legs splayed and bound to wooden struts. Tensing his muscles, he pulled against his bindings. They only bit deeper, but a strange sensation of floating washed over him. Staring into the dark, he tried to make sense of his surroundings and quickly wished he hadn't.

Dagstyrr hung at least twenty feet from the floor beneath. A complicated system of ropes and pulleys held him suspended, like a giant spider caught in a web of his own making. As the potion cleared, every muscle in his body screamed to move. Until a series of tiny muscle twitches rippled up and down his body, bringing a pain he'd never experienced before. Dagstyrr knew he'd been hanging here for a long time.

He dreaded to think what the Dark Emperor had in store for him, but he knew he'd live until Rella arrived. He was bait. Once more, Dagstyrr thought of Pordu. That lying little snake was going to lie again when he reached the wild fae, of that he was sure. Hopefully, Viktar or Bernst would see through him first and not Rella.

She was the Dark Emperor's target.

Dagstyrr knew Viktar's overall plan included keeping her to the rear of the battle. She'd be high on a rise where she could see the attack and direct her troops. Would Viktar be strong enough to prevent her from coming close to this hellish place? Now he understood why she shivered every time she thought of the Dark Emperor, and now he knew just how brave she was even to consider launching an attack on Thingstyrbol.

Drago. The last thing he wanted was for Drago to know about his predicament. The dragon must not help Dagstyrr this time. If the Dark Emperor found out, he would gladly share such tidings with the vizier, hoping to secure a dragon of his own.

Yet he couldn't help wondering whether Drago's heat could somehow destroy his bindings and set him free. *Mmm, free to fall twenty feet onto a stone floor.* He might survive it, he might not, but he'd not risk leaving Drago's family with no hope of rescue. Besides, he had the uncanny feeling that somewhere in the dark, someone or something was watching him. The fact that Dagstyrr was a dragon-talker must remain a secret.

Movement from below had his senses on high alert. Shadows moved along the walls. Dagstyrr hoped they were figments of his imagination. A scuff of leather on stone told him someone was there all right. They paced back and forth, as if deep in thought, perhaps planning something. Dagstyrr hoped he wouldn't be the recipient of those plans, though he suspected he would be. Then the stink of him drifted upward in the tower to Dagstyrr—it was the Emperor.

"Are you awake yet, human?" said the Emperor, raising his face. "Come now, don't play coy. I know you can hear me."

Dagstyrr said nothing. The more he could convince the Emperor he was incapacitated, the longer he'd be left alone.

"Bring him down."

A flurry of activity sent ropes creaking to signal his descent to the floor. Dagstyrr's feet ached to touch solid ground, but no, they stopped just short of that. The Emperor's servants tied off the pulley ropes, then left.

Dagstyrr let his head roll from side to side, and a moan escaped his lips. When boney fingers grabbed his face, he allowed his eyes to open partially.

"You are a weak specimen, aren't you? Strange, you look

strong enough," said the Emperor, running his hands down Dagstyrr's arm. "Human, that's the problem. Tell me, was your mother very disappointed?"

He'd discarded that foul living cloak and was standing, tall and boney in tight green leggings with a matching shirt. His hat, or crown, or whatever it was, still graced his head, bits falling off whenever he turned too quickly. The thing was growing and dying at an incredible rate, just as his cloak did. Dagstyrr wondered whether they had anything to do with his power.

"Astrid made a big mistake, you know. It doesn't do for fae princesses to whelp humans. Oh, well, time to get some exercise," said the Emperor. "Now, where should I start?" He walked over and started to peruse a rack of whips. They varied in size and design—some with studs of metal, others with knots. There were many choices in length and ferocity.

"As you're human, I will confine my fun to a little one," he said, choosing a short many-tailed whip.

"You do enjoy whipping things, don't you? First the horses and now a human. It's rather perverse, you know," said Dagstyrr with as much aplomb as he could muster. His mouth still felt clumsy from the effects of whatever potion they'd fed him.

"Oh, it talks!" said the Emperor, turning with a smile and swishing the whip through the air.

Dagstyrr felt the breeze as it passed close to his face and automatically flinched.

"No, I think for that, you deserve a bigger one," said the Emperor, replacing the whip and choosing another.

Dagstyrr tried to reason that this was all part of the torture. The Emperor had never intended to use that first one. The second one was much longer with multiple tails, and each tail held barbs along its length. It would flay a man in no time at all.

The first lash drew spots of blood blossoming across his naked chest. Dagstyrr knew he was going to die, slowly and in agony. Ironic that his mother had gifted him protection against magic weapons, yet it was a simple whip that was going to be the death of him.

The Emperor was watching the damage he'd inflicted with an eerie fascination. He came up to Dagstyrr and raised his finger to catch a drop of blood. "What frail creatures you are," he said, watching the bead of blood run down his finger. "But juicy." He raised his finger to his lips and licked.

Then came the second blow, and the third. A barb caught the corner of his eye, and he felt it swelling as blood dimmed his sight. "You can do better than that!" His voice was hoarse. If he could goad the Emperor into using magic instead of that infernal whip, he'd stand a better chance of surviving another day.

"Ah, you want to die? Not yet, dragon-talker."

Dagstyrr's stomach lurched. He knew about Drago. Of course he did. Beatty and his band of sniveling cowards would have sold the Emperor a great tale of Dagstyrr's "special" trait. Determined to keep his mouth shut, Dagstyrr closed his eyes as the whip fell again and again.

He must have passed out, for when he awoke, he was once more suspended twenty feet in the air.

No light fell from the arrow slits, and Dagstyrr shivered in the night air. With one eye swollen shut, he was unable to see the whole room. Thankfully, his other eye was functioning. Dagstyrr assessed the damage.

His lip and cheek were cut, sending rivulets of blood running down his chest. He couldn't count the cuts on his limbs or torso, but so far, everything except one eye was still functioning. It was unfortunate that the Emperor knew about Drago; all he could do was deny it and make damn sure he didn't contact him.

Taking a deep breath, he felt the damp night air caress his bleeding body. As long as Rella stayed away, he stood a chance of tricking this monster into letting him go. He'd managed to manipulate the Emperor into sparing Pordu. Perhaps he could do it a second time. *Stay away, my darling. Stay away.*

CHAPTER 24

The new refugees were sleeping in makeshift tents and under wagons. They'd posted guards. *Someone knew what they were doing,* thought Rella. It spoke of good leadership. She marched straight up to the first guard she saw. "I will speak to your leaders now."

"They're asleep." The man was tall and wide, a seasoned warrior with broad shoulders and dark fae eyes sparkling obsidian in the night. He spoke as if his word were law and not up for debate.

"Do you know who I am?"

He looked her up and down. "A nuisance."

"I am Rella of the wild fae. Get them out here now."

She could see the warring emotions on his face. He looked behind her to Viktar and Bernst, assessing the situation. "I heard there were no light fae among you?"

"It is none of your business. Now, wake your leaders and bring them here."

"We've had a long…"

"…journey. Yes, I know. This is urgent. Wake them, or I will."

"Best do as she says," said Bernst.

"What is it, Barros?" said an older woman emerging from the trees.

The woman was sedate and regal, with more poise than Rella had seen for a long time. This woman could put the courtiers of Casta to shame. Her hair was blue-grey in the moonlight and rippled down her back. She wrapped a multicolored shawl over her shoulders. Rella noted her black eyes and manner denoting she was a dark fae of high pedigree.

"I am Berta, mother to Barros and late of the queen's bedchamber."

"Greetings, Lady Berta. I am Rella, late of Casta and for now, leader of the wild fae."

"It is a pleasure to meet you at last, Princess," she said with a short bow.

"There are no princesses here. Just Rella."

"Then you must call me Berta."

"My mother is Princess Berta," said Barros, moving to stand by her side.

"As Rella says, my son, there are no princesses here. Berta will suit me very well," she said graciously.

"Perhaps, but people should not forget who you are, Mother." He turned to Rella. "She is sister to our last queen. Royalty, as you would call her in Casta."

"Now, now," she said, putting her hand on his forearm. "I think Rella comes with urgent business this night. We must make her welcome. Wake the lesser council—they might be needed—and bring refreshments."

Berta's tent was large and makeshift. The few possessions she carried with her were beautifully crafted and well cared for. Rella surmised this royal princess had known only luxury. It spoke well of her that, in changed circumstances, she managed to retain her poise.

"Please make yourselves comfortable," she said, offering around a tray of cups filled with the best Samish wine.

The men sat awkwardly on small chairs and cushions designed for a lady's bedchamber, not for large warriors. Barros sat opposite Viktar at the table, their long legs knocking clumsily across the short distance.

"You must forgive Barros. He's only ever encountered light fae on the battlefield," said Berta.

"Then he's probably met some of the troops I trained," said Viktar, never taking his eyes from Barros.

"You should have trained them better before sending them against the dark fae if you wanted to see them again," said Barros.

"Enough! If you two can't be civil, there is no place for you in my chambers," said Berta.

They stopped immediately, and Viktar stared at her. It was surely a long time since anyone had dared to chastise the old warrior like that.

Berta looked worried. "Forgive me, Rella of the wild fae. Old habits are hard to change at my age. I should not have spoken to your man like that."

"There is nothing to forgive, Berta of the dark fae." Rella could be a little formal if it made this woman more comfortable.

Berta composed her face as she sat down. "This must be very urgent, to take you from your bed at this time of night. Please, speak your mind."

"I would know the circumstances of your coming here.

What prompted your people to decide to follow the wild fae? It is not easy to live in a tent when you are used to a palace," said Rella.

"It is a long time since any of us have lived in a palace. When my sister died, we were turned out of the palace but confined to the villages surrounding Thingstyrbol. Prisoners of the Dark Emperor." She stopped to sip her wine. "He wants only a few minions surrounding him in Thingstyrbol. He uses spies and treachery so much it leaves him paranoid about letting anyone near him."

"Why do you want to know our history? What can be so urgent?" said Barros, clearly concerned for his mother.

Berta waved her hand to shush him. "Rella of the wild fae should hear this. If she is going up against him, then she needs to know."

"So, your sister was the Dark Queen?" said Rella.

"Yes, for seventy years, Queen Aletha ruled, and peace reigned with the dark and the halflings. War with the light fae was unthinkable." She turned to Viktar, smiling. "You are our cousins."

"If the dark fae are so magnanimous with halflings, light fae, and even humans, tell us why this Dark Emperor wants to war with the light fae and kill all humans on sight?" said Viktar, echoing what Rella was thinking.

Berta bristled. "He is not one of us."

"What do you mean?" said Rella.

"He is not one of us. He is an abomination," said Barros.

"My lady, he is an abomination all right, but you cannot escape the fact he is dark fae," said Bernst, ever the pragmatist.

"I don't care what he is," said Rella. "What prompted him to let you go now? What did you promise him? Whose life bought your freedom?" said Rella, choking back angry tears.

Rella turned her back to the others. She would not break down, not now. After drawing three deep breaths, she realized no one was talking. Turning, she faced Berta. "Well?"

"I'm not proud of what we've done..."

"You sold a man and six mountain elves to this abomination to save your skins," said Rella, her voice colder and harder than it had ever been before. It matched the brittle emptiness growing steadily within her.

"No, you don't understand. The elves made the bargain without our knowing," said Barros. "One thousand dark fae, in exchange for one captured dragon-talker."

Rella felt her spine turn to steel and her body drain of all warmth. She looked at Viktar and Bernst. "Pordu lied with his dying breath, and you two didn't see it."

"Princess," said Viktar standing, "I am..."

"...sorry, yes, I know. That won't bring Dagstyrr back!" screamed Rella, almost losing control altogether.

"It was a decent bargain," said Barros. "We kept to our side of it, but the Dark Emperor didn't. He killed all but one of the elves."

Rella rounded on the big warrior. With the speed of a lightning strike, she pinned Barros's face against the table and his arm high behind his back, about to snap. "It surprises you that this abomination you speak of doesn't keep his word? What kind of fools are you?"

Barros's face was turning bright red as he struggled to maintain his calm. Rella looked up at Berta, whose face was white with shame. Her great age showed clearly on her face, but Rella wasn't going to be ensnared by pity.

Viktar and Bernst came up either side of Rella, ready to

protect her if necessary. She nodded to them, then let the warrior go. "Well?"

"We wanted to believe it was the right thing to do," said Berta. "One thousand lives. Men, women, children, and all we needed to do was lure one human and hand him over to the Dark Emperor." She looked up at Rella, pacing the floor. "What was he to you?"

Rella stared into her black eyes but could find no compassion for Berta. "Everything." Rella thought they must all hear the thunder of her heart in the silence that followed.

"What have I done?" said Berta, sagging in her chair.

"It's not my mother's fault," said Barros. "She didn't know. Beatty said he was a rogue human claiming to be a dragon-talker, and trying to woo the wild fae. Everyone knows there are no dragon-talkers."

"Is that right?" said Bernst. He and Viktar positioned themselves either side of Barros, ready if the big warrior attacked.

"You don't understand the pressures my mother was under. People looked to her to lead them, but she had never been a queen, only a warrior."

Rella approached him slowly, one hand on the hilt of her sword, and with a deadly calm in her voice whispered, "Tell me, I've always wanted to know. What makes one life worth more than another?"

Barros had the decency to look ashamed, which probably saved his life at that moment. For Rella had never been so angry, never more ready to kill. She wasn't just furious, but heartbroken thinking of the degradations the Dark Emperor would put Dagstyrr through before killing him. Still, she refused to believe he could be dead without her feeling his passing.

Turning to the others, she said, "Viktar, take Berta up to your tent and get what information you can from her about Thingstyrbol. I'm sure there is more to learn. She is the one to teach us. Make sure you use truth compulsion. I am not about to believe anything she says."

Barros surged forward at that insult. "You wouldn't dare!"

"Let it be, my son. I would do the same if the circumstances were reversed." Gathering up a fine blue cloak encrusted with bright stones around the hood and hem, she said, "Will you let my people stay? Join the wild fae?"

"No."

"They had nothing to do with the capture of your mate. It was my decision alone."

"It's a bit late to discover a conscience, princess," said Bernst.

"I have over three hundred well-trained troops disguised as farmers among the thousand people I brought with me. They can help you," said Berta.

"I will take your troops," said Rella. "They will fight in the vanguard when we attack Thingstyrbol. Everyone else remains here as prisoners to ensure the loyalty of your troops," said Rella.

A gasp went up. Even Captain Bernst and Viktar were shocked at talk of prisoners.

"It's true what they said about you. You are a hard-nosed bitch," said Barros.

She walked up to him. "Oh, you haven't seen a fraction of what I can do." Poking her finger into his chest, she said, "You will take Dagstyrr's place and lead the attack on the towers."

"No," escaped Berta's lips in horror.

"Don't worry, Mother, I know my way up there better than most," he sneered.

"I'm counting on it," said Rella, leaving the tent and picking up a spear. Then she ran with the spear in one hand and her long legs eating up the spaces. Her light fae magic kicked in automatically, allowing her to cover a great distance. Her feet barely touched the ground. Blinded by tears, she ran as if her life depended on it.

Her heart was breaking, and it hurt so much she thought she might die. Rella tried to push all thought of Dagstyrr from her mind, lest she go mad. She focused on running, one foot in front of the other, while the sharp agony of his loss opened a wound in her chest where her heart had once been. The roar of water filled her ears, the stones under her feet became slick, and Rella knew what she must do. It was time to do what she should have done a long time ago.

CHAPTER 25

Dagstyrr's teeth chattered as he awoke to freezing air, every muscle in his body tight from shivering in his sleep. The morning brought no relief from the cold that had plagued him through the long dark hours. Perhaps it was his wounds making him feel cold, for it wasn't winter.

The sun spilled her warmth through the arrow slits high in the tower, but none reached Dagstyrr hanging in his web. Awake now, he recalled the time he and his father had found themselves becalmed on open water, and the temperature dropped to freezing. He could almost hear his father's voice saying, *Deep breaths, Dagstyrr. Slow deep breathing will warm you quicker, son. Just make sure to keep your mouth closed.*

So, he did as his father had taught him until, at last, he could think clearly. His shivering had stilled. It wasn't cold enough to kill him, just severe enough to make him very uncomfortable. Why? It was not a natural cold. So, what was the Emperor thinking?

Drago!

Of course, it's a test to see if I am a dragon-talker. He must consider me a very petty man if he thinks I would use a dragon to warm myself.

The air inside the tower grew colder, until crystals of moisture floated in the air. As Dagstyrr became lethargic, the cold didn't bother him so much. Moisture from his breath misted in front of his face, crystallized, then fell tinkling to the floor many feet below. *So pretty,* he thought.

Frost tinged his eyelashes—prisms that created rainbow colors everywhere he looked. Shaking his head from side to side, he tried to wake up. Dagstyrr fought the sleep that would bring death with it.

Lifting his eyes to the roof, he roared out his father's battle cry: *"You die today!"* He imagined his sword at the Emperor's neck. Dagstyrr was not ready to give in. Not yet.

The squeak of pulleys sounded in the tower's cavernous space, and Dagstyrr's weight shifted on the ropes. He groaned. What new delights had the Emperor in store for him now?

Rella checked that her spear shaft and shield were sound before strapping on her sword and knives. Her war councilors entered the tent, obedient to her call. Viktar, Bernst, Patrice, and now Barros and Berta arrived without ceremony. "I am going ahead. It will take time for you to muster the army and get to Thingstyrbol. Dagstyrr may not have that time," she said.

Bernst let out a loud sigh as if he'd been holding his breath. "We're with you. I want to find him alive as much as anyone here. I need him there when we attack Hedabar, but it takes time to move an army, even on water."

Viktar's face was set like granite. "I doubt very much that

he's alive. The wild fae need you giving orders, Rella, not dead on the battlements," he said. "It is your banner they have rallied to."

"Don't try and stop me, Viktar. We will meet again at Thingstyrbol," she said, pulling a dark cloak from her trunk. "Somehow, I always knew it would come to this. Just him and me."

"No, Princess, this is our fight, too," said Berta. "You were only the catalyst. The storming of Thingstyrbol was inevitable from the moment that monster defeated the Dark Queen many years ago."

"I'm not here to listen to arguments. I am relying on you all to be there as soon as you can," said Rella. From the concern on their faces, they didn't think she could do it. "I can do this. Dagstyrr is my mate, and he's in danger."

"Very well," said Viktar, understanding what was driving her. "On a forced march, I can have the wild fae warriors outside Thingstyrbol in three days, no sooner."

"I can get the longships there in two or three if we don't run into a storm," said Bernst. "If we do..." He shrugged.

"That is up to you. I am going to kill the Dark Emperor now."

"Alone?" said Viktar. His voice, so like her father's, was filled with concern and yes, with admiration.

"I won't be alone." Dagstyrr was alive. She'd know if he were dead, no matter what Pordu said, but there was no point in telling these people. They believed he was dead, and she was alone.

"He won't kill you quickly," said Berta, huddled in her cloak. Her ominous words echoed like a death knell.

"It doesn't matter. If Dagstyrr is dead when I arrive, then the Emperor will already have done his worst. My death will not matter," said Rella, looking her in the eye.

"Don't despair, Rella," said Jul, who'd just entered the tent with a tray of refreshments.

Rella looked at her. Little Jul, youngest of the war-maiden family, looked like a smaller version of her older sisters. Her dark soulful eyes had not yet lost their innocence, and her hair was a halo of dark whispers around her face.

"I will kill him, Jul."

"That is inevitable, I think," Jul said with a smile. "However, I beg you, don't listen to anything the Dark Emperor says. His words are poison and will not serve you well in battle."

Rella put her arm around Jul's shoulder. "Thank you, I will remember that. I'll leave you now. Until Thingstyrbol," she said, hefting her shield.

"I will go with you," said Barros.

"No! You will lead the vanguard up the two towers as agreed," said Rella. "Stick with the orders I've given you."

"You don't stand a chance," said Barros.

Berta stood tall. "If Rella of the wild fae is victorious, the army will still be needed. There is much to put right at Thingstyrbol, and it will take a lot of magic, disciplined magic."

"Do you think she can defeat the Dark Emperor where you and your sisters failed? Don't be ridiculous," said Barros, turning his back on everyone.

Viktar's hand landed on his shoulder. "If you don't believe he can be defeated, there is no place for you in the wild fae."

Barros turned. "He can be defeated. Of course, he can. I just don't believe *she* can do it," he said, looking down on Rella's slight figure. "Do you? Single-handed? Come on, at least be honest."

"It is important that we all believe in one another," said Jul.

"You are wise, little one," said Berta.

Jul blushed before pushing past Rella and rushing out of the tent.

"Barros, I don't care whether you think I can do this or not," said Rella.

Before he could answer, Berta stood and put her hand on his sleeve. "Let it be, my son."

"I just can't see her on the throne of Thingstyrbol," said Barros with a sneer.

Silence followed Barros's last statement, until Rella burst out laughing, the harsh sound bringing smiles to Patrice, Bernst, and Viktar.

Patrice said, "Rella has no such ambition."

"Is that what she says? You believe her?" said Barros.

"I am Patrice, eldest daughter of the House of Threme, and I say this woman will not sit upon the throne of Thingstyrbol. I say she has no such ambition."

Barros at once bowed his head. "Lady Patrice, forgive me..."

"There are no titles in the wild fae," said Patrice. "Besides, everyone here is a princess, or lady, or lord. Have you not worked that out yet?"

Flustered, Barros bowed again before going to stand by his mother. She whispered in his ear, causing him to bend to her level.

Then Lady Berta stepped forward. "If your mate still lives, he will be imprisoned in one of the two black towers. Choose carefully. Once inside, there is no link between the towers except along the obsidian walkway, which is easily defended. Also..."

"Also?" said Rella.

Barros stepped forward. "When he arrives back at Thingstyrbol, the Emperor sends his troops home. He keeps a few elves for servants, but..."

"We believe he's using shadow men," Berta's voice sounded a cold warning, sending shivers down everyone's spine.

"That changes things," said Bernst, standing and twisting his face to the wall.

"It changes nothing. Ghosts of fallen warriors do not frighten me," said Rella. "Besides, I'm not sure I believe in such things."

"Neither do I, Rella," said Berta. "However, I thought it fair to warn you. Those are the rumors spreading throughout our people."

"And powerful rumors they are," said Viktar. "Spreading fear with each retelling. An army, even just a personal guard of such creatures would be undefeatable—they can kill, but are already dead."

Rella refused to be drawn into their discussion.

Barros stepped forward, his eyes raking Rella with barely disguised contempt. "He was born light fae and chose to turn dark, thinking it would increase his magic energy. When it didn't, he found other ways to boost what power he had."

Rella paused. "Then I might be the perfect foe to defeat him, where the dark fae failed."

"Your arrogance will be the death of you."

"Perhaps, but don't forget, you will lead the assault upon the obsidian wall, shadow men or not."

"I will be there."

Viktar growled his frustration, a warning if ever there was one. "Wait, Rella."

"Goodbye, my friends. I'll see you again at Thingstyrbol," she said, not waiting for a reply as she ran into the night, her easy lope eating up the forest miles.

CHAPTER 26

Rella huddled in the corner of the tavern. Anonymous in her dark hooded cloak, she sat like any other traveler grateful for a hot meal and a bed. After leaving the wild fae, Rella had run herself to the point of exhaustion before realizing that probably wasn't the best idea. She needed to rest; there was no point in arriving feeble and unable to fight. She'd made good ground so far, and tomorrow she'd get within striking distance of Thingstyrbol.

Concentrating all her thoughts on the Dark Emperor, she admitted that her terror had been holding her back. That fear was gone. Only those with something precious to lose fear death. Rella had someone precious to save. Now, she longed to face the Emperor, relished the thought of being in his presence, dreamed of the ways she could kill him. It was what kept her running, one foot in front of the other, and it kept memories of Dagstyrr tamped down in her subconscious, so she could think clearly.

The landlord's name was Themdi, a mountain elf. After

Beatty's betrayal, Rella didn't feel inclined to socialize with mountain elves. If she never saw another one again, it would suit her just fine. However, she needed rest, and this was the only accommodation hereabouts.

Throwing a coin on the table to pay for her meal, she headed upstairs to the room assigned her. When she was halfway up the stairs, Themdi called to her. "Mistress, would you like fresh hot water now, or in the morning?"

"I'm fine," she said, not even breaking her step.

"It's no trouble. My wife can bring it up."

Rella rounded on him, her voice like steel. "I said, no."

Themdi cowered back. She saw him eyeing her sword and shield, the spear in her hand, and her lack of baggage. He wasn't intimidated by her appearance, but he knew what she was. Used to dealing with deadly warriors of all kinds, the elf was naturally cautious. But he was no danger to her, and probably just wanted to charge extra for hot water.

Rella opened the door to her room and was surprised to see a bed built for large beings. So, she was right. He did cater to warriors.

It was a long time since she'd slept in a real bed. Rella started to regret her hasty decision to forgo hot water, but then she stripped off her clothes and fell onto the clean linen sheets. As soon as the covers settled around her, exhaustion claimed her, and she fell fast asleep.

The floor of the Dark Emperor's tower was warm. Dagstyrr could feel the hot air rise to meet him as he hung frozen on the ropes. The blessed heat tingled along his muscles as the pulleys lowered him to his next torture.

He welcomed the heat, yet feared what awaited him

below. Focusing his thoughts, he reminded himself to say nothing of Drago or Rella. No matter what the Emperor had in store for him, he could bear it as long as they were safe. When the pulleys juddered to a stop just shy of the floor, he couldn't help thinking of Rella. He wondered whether he'd ever see her again.

"What have you to smile about?" demanded the Dark Emperor, testing his long, studded whip by flailing the air with it.

"Why don't you just kill me?"

"Oh, you'd like that, would you?"

Yes, thought Dagstyrr, *for then, I can't endanger Rella or Drago's family with anything I might let slip in front of this monster.*

The Dark Emperor was dressed as usual in his green clothes, his living hat dropping small insects as he moved. Then Dagstyrr noticed there was something tied to his wrist. Dagstyrr almost cried out when he saw it—his ribbon. The one saturated with rose and mint that he'd carried with him when he left the camp. He bit his lip to stop an involuntary curse from escaping. The Dark Emperor must know the ribbon was significant. He would sense the spell the old woman had put on it, preventing the scent from ever fading.

"I do like your ribbon. Rella's favorite scent, I believe," said the Emperor, lifting the ribbon to his nose, his eyes never leaving Dagstyrr's. The Emperor's tongue flicked out, pink and wet like a lizard's, tasting the strip of silk.

Dagstyrr stared back, trying not to show how much it hurt. He would not give this creature more ammunition with which to torture him. "It is popular among humans."

"Nice try. I recognized the scent from before, when my future queen came to beg my help."

Dagstyrr laughed; it sounded more like a croak. "Rella never begged in her life."

"Oh, but she did for her brother, and will for you too, I think. I'd like to see her on her knees, begging me."

Dagstyrr refused to let his mind go there. "She will not beg."

"She is going to watch you die. See for herself what sniveling wretches humans are, and what a mistake it was to mate with one."

Dagstyrr felt panic rise in his gorge. Rella would die herself before she'd watch him die. The only way he could save her was to die first. Then she'd be angry, and she'd kill this monster.

"She won't come here alone," he said, praying it was so.

"Don't even bother to lie, human. My informants tell me that she is on her way," he said with a smile. "Even now, she runs like the wind alone and eager to reach me."

Dagstyrr's heart filled with dread. He had no choice but to brave it out. "I don't believe you," he said, watching two extremely old mountain elves push and twist a large bed into the chamber.

The Emperor fell laughing onto the bed piled with cushions. Then waved away his servants, who scuttled away as fast as they could. Dagstyrr wondered what on earth the madman had in mind now. "I tell you what, talk to your tame dragon while I watch, and I'll let you sleep here for the night."

"If I had a tame dragon, you'd be dead," said Dagstyrr.

"My informants say different. Tell me, does it hurt to join with him? Why don't you just teach me to do it, it would be a very useful trick for one such as I, don't you think? I don't know what a puny human expects to gain from it?"

"There hasn't been a dragon-talker in hundreds of years. How would I know anything about it?" said Dagstyrr, forcing a laugh.

The Emperor stood and paced, his temper rising. "Very well, we'll just wait for Rella. I'm sure she can persuade you to be more cooperative."

Stroking his gnarled hand over the silk, the Emperor looked up at Dagstyrr. "Do you think she'll approve of our marriage bed?"

So that was it. The bed was just another goad. "Won't ever happen," croaked Dagstyrr.

"Oh, yes, it will," said the Emperor calmly. "She is on her way to me now. I will take great pleasure knowing you are hanging there when I strip her naked and explore every crevice of her body before claiming it as mine."

"I'll be dead before she gets here," said Dagstyrr.

"No, no, no, I won't allow that. Mind you, if you truly can't talk to dragons, then I suppose it makes little difference whether you are alive or dead. Either way, she will still see you hanging there while I mark her as mine, forever."

Try as he might, Dagstyrr couldn't banish the nightmarish image of Rella, terrified, lying on the bed next to the Emperor. He turned his head to hide a tear of frustration sliding down his cheek. The only possible way he could free himself was to ask Drago for help. The minute he did that, the Emperor would have the means to access a dragon.

He'd threaten to let the vizier know about his relationship with Drago. Then he'd use Dagstyrr to entice a dragon here. The Emperor hadn't given up on his desire to ride a dragon, and who knew, with the rest of the dragon's nest at stake, the poor creature might even allow it.

The Emperor's voice echoed around the tower. "Oh, it is

going to be so much fun," he said, throwing back his head and exposing his scrawny neck. Dagstyrr would dearly love to get his hands around that neck. The Emperor laughed his madman's cackle. The sound sent shivers up Dagstyrr's spine. He would not turn his head to look at the bed.

The heat from the fireside that brought so much welcome warmth a short time ago was now becoming a new torment. As Dagstyrr's cold muscles warmed, the pain set in. Was this the torture set for today, or was he going to use that flail as well? If the Dark Emperor intended to use the whip hanging from his wrist, Dagstyrr would indeed be dead before Rella got here.

Better to let his death be over before she arrived. Let that give her the strength to defeat this monster, not nightmares for the rest of her life from watching him die.

How long must he hang in this tortuous web? Moisture dripped from his hair as the ice melted. The cuts covering his body started to bleed again, and the Emperor stopped laughing.

"I never really believed Beatty's tale of a dragon-talker, but I thought it worth exploring," said the Emperor.

Dagstyrr's shoulders sagged, at last one small victory.

"You're just a puny human, nothing more. So why, I ask myself, would a light fae princess choose you?"

The Emperor stood and walked over to peruse his collection of whips. "Rella comes alone. Soon she will be here, all mine, and you will watch while she welcomes my caresses," he said, pointing at the bed.

Dagstyrr felt the world spin around him. Closing his eyes, he fought to banish such images, repeating a mantra inside his head: *He lies, he's full of tricks, do not give in. He lies, he's full...*

Rella awoke from a deep sleep. She'd dreamed Dagstyrr was beside her on the bed. She'd felt his presence as if he were there. His warmth, his strength, the safe feeling that he brought to her filled her with comfort. She jumped from the bed. Did this mean Dagstyrr *was* dead, and what she'd felt was his spirit close by?

Harsh voices came from the corridor outside her room. Rella listened intently. It was the landlord, Themdi, arguing with a woman. The woman insisted on bringing Rella hot water, while Themdi said it wasn't necessary *this time*. Which was an odd thing to say, for Rella had never been at this inn before.

"We used hot water spells on the human male. They worked well and saved us no end of trouble," argued the woman.

Cold horror danced down Rella's spine.

"Aye, but this one is not so big. Anyway, she's on her way to Thingstyrbol to meet with the Dark Emperor, which is what he wants. So, no need to go to the expense of hot water and costly spells."

"I suppose so. It was different with the big human," conceded the woman.

"Exactly. Thankfully, Beatty insisted on binding him before he handed him over, or he might have done damage to the inn."

"A lot of good that did him," said the woman, snickering as she walked away.

"Wait. You got me thinking," said Themdi. "What if we presented the Dark Emperor with her, all nicely trussed up? He might be more generous with his gold this time."

"You mean, take her to him ourselves?" said the woman.

"Aye, wife. We can say she gave us no end of trouble," said Themdi, failing to suppress a laugh.

"She won't be expecting anything. When she comes downstairs, you grab her hands and keep them down while I truss her up," said Themdi's wife, her feet clomping on the stairs as she left.

These were Beatty's helpers, and now they thought to capture Rella. How many others had they betrayed to the Dark Emperor like this, and for what—gold?

This bed was where Dagstyrr had slept his last night of freedom. Some residual energy belonging to him must remain for it to bring her beloved so vividly to her dreams. Rella ran her hand over the crumpled linen then lifted the sheet to her face, trying to absorb any trace of him—there was none.

She finished dressing then secured her weapons. On silent feet, Rella descended the worn staircase. With every step, her fury grew.

Both Themdi and his wife were in the taproom when she walked in. They were startled by her sudden presence. "It's very quiet down here," she said.

"Yes, mistress. You're the only guest. The others from last night live hereabouts," said the very beautiful petite woman. "What can I get you to break your fast?"

"Nothing," said Rella, to the woman. "So, only your family here?"

"Aye, mistress," said Themdi, cautiously moving to circle behind her while flexing his long fingers.

Rella was ready for him. In a flash, her spear tip was at his throat.

"I have a tip for you, landlord. Light fae have acute hearing. You shouldn't whisper outside our rooms."

He flinched. "But you is dark fae, mistress."

"I am wild fae," said Rella, letting her words sink in. Then she turned her back and exited the inn. Once she'd gone twenty yards from the door, she put down her spear and lifted her arms.

Themdi and his wife came to their door with knives ready. They knew they were in trouble, but not the extent of it. Rella looked across the yard at them and felt no pity. They'd betrayed Dagstyrr and, no doubt, others as well. Sold him for a few coins to the worst monster she could imagine. They deserved no mercy.

First, a bolt of blue energy blasted the inn's roof, sending gobbets of thatch flying through the air. No sooner had the blue bolt landed than a cloud of green battle energy poured from her other hand and raced along the ground toward them.

They ran with all their mountain elf swiftness. He went right, she left. Rella's green battle energy entered through the inn door and blasted the taproom to splinters. She was using her dual battle energy for the first time, and she thrilled to witness the effective destruction it wrought.

Themdi was lying on the ground mouth agape. "Blue *and* green, mistress?"

She ignored him and sent a bolt of blue to bring down the chimney. Bricks flew across the yard into the forest, tearing through tree bark and leaving white wood scars.

Themdi stood and ran toward her, a large kitchen knife in his hand. She sent a dark cloud of green racing across the yard to meet him. As it engulfed him, he froze, not daring to move. The look on his face was one of pure horror. By staying motionless, he was only delaying the inevitable.

"Why, mistress?" pleaded his wife. "What's a human to you?"

"Everything," said Rella quietly.

"Don't kill my husband, please. You're the Dark Queen. You're powerful. Please, release him."

"Too late," said Rella, watching the dark green cloud gather around him, poised to kill.

When it came, the explosion sent Themdi flying back toward his inn. His head hit a wooden beam, blood spurting from his hairline. Themdi fell to the ground, motionless. His wife ran to him and gathered him in her arms. Rella's fury was still not satisfied. She rained bolts of blue and clouds of green battle magic down upon the inn until there was nothing left but a massive hole in the ground.

When the smoke and dust settled, Themdi lay in his wife's arms. Her tears streaked down her dusty face to land on his. "Why?" she kept repeating. "Why'd you have to kill my man?"

Rella walked toward them, her sword pointed straight at the woman's throat. The woman bled from a dozen small wounds caused by flying shards, but she didn't seem to notice. Rella had already demolished her home and business and killed her man, yet the impulse to destroy drove Rella on. The question was: should she let this woman live?

"Why did you kill my man?" she asked again.

Rella put the tip of her sword on the woman's neck.

"You might as well go on and kill me too. I've got nothing left. You've taken it all!" cried the woman, rocking back and forth, nursing her dead husband's head on her lap.

Then Rella saw it, a flicker of the man's eyes. He was alive, and this woman thought to trick her. Themdi's long fingers wrapped around the knife's handle where a moment ago, they'd hung limp. She saw him glance at her middle and start to raise the deadly blade. In a trice, her sword left the woman's throat and pierced her husband's. At which point, the woman jumped up and ran, screaming. "You killed him! You really killed him this time."

"Like you killed my man!" Rella shouted. The woman wasn't worth pursuing.

Then Rella heard through the woman's weeping. "Yours ain't dead, just captured." Rella froze.

CHAPTER 27

L ast night's punishment had been the worst yet. The Emperor had used a flat board to batter Dagstyrr's broken body. Yet that was not what tortured him. Fear of Rella walking into Thingstyrbol alone was eating away at Dagstyrr's sanity.

He tried to move but only succeeded in sending pain screaming through his body. Yesterday's icy frost would be welcome now. It might numb the pain, but no, the sun poured in through the arrow slits and landed hot and heavy on his broken body.

One eye was still swollen closed, and pus encrusting his eyelid prevented him from even trying to open it. Dagstyrr reckoned he'd lost sight in that eye. Lacerations covered his body, and he'd counted at least three broken ribs. *This might be my last day,* he thought, struggling to work out how long he'd been unconscious this time.

In his fevered dreams, he'd found himself tied and broken in the deepest dungeons of Hedabar, held by chains as the Dark Emperor poked at him and the other dragons with a barbed stick. Eventually, he'd roared out his pain and sorrow with fire shooting from his mouth.

In his confused mind, Thingstyrbol and Hedabar were all mixed up together and he was the dragon.

Thirst declared its monstrous need as always when he awoke. It would be many hours before a servant raised a cup of water to his lips. Perhaps the servant who brought it would be kinder than the last, and let him die.

Dagstyrr thought of his father and mother. It had been a long time since he'd seen his parents. Because of his commitment to Drago, he'd avoided spending time at home. They had enough trouble dealing with his addict brothers, without him burdening them all with his promise to Drago. Now it seemed they would bear that burden after all. Unto ten generations had been Drago's demand.

What a terrible legacy to leave your family.

Then he thought of Drago and his family. "One hundred and sixty-eight dragons, not counting hatchlings or eggs," murmured Dagstyrr. Noble creatures of ancient magic, captives of a fiend who bled them daily to intoxicate his light fae prisoners so that he could milk them of their magic. Dagstyrr would likely not be the one to free them.

A vision of his Rella fighting with the speed and grace of a true fae warrior was the last thing he saw before passing out.

Rella ran with hope restored. Like the wind, she flew through the forest glades, skirting towns and villages, a blur of energy. She ran past the deserted villages closer to the Emperor's stronghold until eventually coming to a halt in the forest surrounding Thingstyrbol.

Falling to her knees, exhausted, she stared at the massive black palace ahead of her. Gulping air into her lungs, needing the oxygen to replenish her exhausted muscles and to help her think, she lay still on the soft earth under the trees. Throughout the long day, niggling doubt had pricked at her. Had the woman lied? Was it all some ruse to get her to Thingstyrbol? The mountain elf's wife probably hoped the Dark Emperor would compensate her with gold for ensuring Rella came here.

Yet a flame of hope still flickered. If Dagstyrr was alive and at the mercy of the Dark Emperor, she must get to him. Rella was determined to kill the Dark Emperor for all his atrocities, but most of all—for taking her mate.

Now she lay on her stomach hidden just inside the tree line, absorbing as much energy from the forest floor as she could to replenish her magic. A creak of chains alerted her to the drawbridge lowering. Suddenly, every nerve in her body was ready to run again.

Rella watched and waited, but dared not move in case her movement was detected. No one came out. *Then they must be expecting someone to arrive,* she thought. After some time, the Dark Emperor stepped out onto the drawbridge and looked directly at her position. "Come on, Princess Rella, I know you're there. Let's not waste any time. I have such exquisite fun and games prepared for you and your human. But I don't think he's going to last much longer, so you had better hurry up."

Dagstyrr *was* alive!

The Emperor could be lying, but Rella chose to believe he spoke the truth.

She didn't dare move a muscle, not even to smile. Watching his gaze drift across the tree line, she knew he was bluffing. His tiny creatures would have let him know she was here all right, but he didn't know exactly where.

"Very well," he said. "I'll leave the drawbridge down to make it easy for you."

Rella watched him re-enter the palace, leaving the darkened doorway at the end of the drawbridge lit by flaming torches. In a strange way, it did look inviting. Multicolored vines climbed up and around the door. Blocks of blackened stone made up the outer walls of Thingstyrbol. Except for the one portion that consisted of two stone towers linked by a high black obsidian wall, which was the last place the Dark Emperor would expect her. That was where she'd enter.

Making her way slowly through the forest until she came to the trees directly opposite the towers, Rella hoped she wasn't too late. Then, pushing all thoughts aside, she surveyed the wall.

It was just as Barros and his mother had shown her. There *was* a way up the wall. Dangerous and almost invisible from the ground, nonetheless it was her way into the towers.

The sun began to set at last. With a wave of her hand, she covered herself in a dark mist to appear like a shadow of black on a black wall. After securing her spear and sword to her back, she crouched down and made her way across the open space separating the forest from the wall.

Rella began to climb.

The spaces between handholds were made for larger warriors. She jumped to reach the first notch and grip its icy smoothness. With a steadying breath, she pulled herself up, swung out to grab the next one, and just missed. The black glass sliced the tips of her fingers, stinging. She must be more careful. Up close, she could see the glass wall peppered with shards of knifelike edges, ready to destroy any who failed.

Reluctant to use a healing spell in case the Emperor sensed her whereabouts, she struggled on. The evening was warm this far south, and Rella's hands were soon slick with sweat and blood. Each handhold was positioned just a little too high for her short stature. Swinging back and forth each time before pushing up toward the next notch, she thought of Dagstyrr alive and waiting for her. When she missed, she bled. Ignoring the pain, she kept moving slowly up the wall.

Bloodied and exhausted, she finally reached the battlements and threw herself over onto the deserted walkway linking the two towers. The sun had set, and moonshine tempted her to lie and absorb its magic-giving energy, but she dared not.

Which tower held Dagstyrr?

"Rella." The sound of his own voice croaking in the dark awoke Dagstyrr. Visions of her stubborn face gazing up at him filled his head. She was a law unto herself, never taking no for an answer. Always finding a way.

That's what troubled him.

He'd been unconscious for some time. Night had fallen, and the stars twinkled through the arrow slits. He hoped she was lying beneath those same stars, far, far, away in the safety of the wild fae camp.

He knew she'd come for him, but he hoped she'd have the sense not to come alone.

One of the Emperor's servants was crawling along the thicker rope holding him—another mountain elf. At the elf's waist hung a water bottle and clean towels. Dagstyrr suppressed a laugh. When the man reached his side, Dagstyrr didn't even lift his head. "Don't tell me you're going to wash me?"

"Wake up, son of Halfenhaw."

Dagstyrr ignored him. Whatever this new torture was, he wasn't playing.

"Look at me, boy. It's me, Englesten."

Dagstyrr opened his one good eye. "Sorry, old man. You'll have to look to Bernst to rescue your people."

"That's your job, and you're not getting away with shirking it," said the Ghost King, rubbing fresh water over Dagstyrr's face and neck.

Dagstyrr couldn't resist opening his mouth to the life-giving water Englesten poured into him. Almost immediately, his muddled mind began to clear.

"What are you doing here?"

"I've come for you."

"He'll kill you as soon as he sees you. I'm the one he likes to keep alive to torture."

"Aye, that would be because of your mother."

"What? No, old man. It's because of Rella."

"It started with Astrid. He never got over Princess Astrid choosing a human mate. Her rejection unhinged his already troubled mind, and he turned dark."

Dagstyrr's thoughts reeled. Was it possible the Emperor was once light fae? That he'd turned dark because Dagstyrr's mother spurned his advances all that time ago? If that were true, he'd be going after Dagstyrr's mother. "No, it is Rella he wants."

Englesten continued to wipe Dagstyrr with the damp cloths he'd brought with him. "Her too. Princess Rella also chose a human, rejecting him all over again. You should feel better in a moment."

"I feel better already," said Dagstyrr, and it was true, he did. The water must be healing spelled. "Do you mean the Emperor was once light fae?"

"Yes."

Shocked, Dagstyrr whispered, "That explains his madness. Get away from here. He usually comes in about this time of evening."

Englesten looked about him, his eyes darting along the walls. "Okay, drink some more. Don't be tempted to let him see you're feeling better. It will only encourage him to hurt you more." Like a spider swinging on a web, Englesten disappeared into the shadows of the tower.

Dagstyrr wasn't sure whether magic was to thank for the way he was feeling or whether slaking his thirst made the difference, but his mind was undoubtedly clearer.

While the Emperor tortured Dagstyrr, he probably imagined he was punishing Earl Magnus for marrying Astrid. Desire, rejection, humiliation, and the need for power were all mixed up in the Emperor's twisted mind, and all focused on Rella.

Dagstyrr whispered, "Stay away, my darling."

The stink that accompanied the Dark Emperor permeated the air around her, and suddenly all her senses were alert. Rella lay on the slick surface of the obsidian walkway, trying to catch her breath. Raising herself to her elbows, she searched for any sign of him along the length of the battlements. There was none. The shadows were long and dark against the moonshine on the black volcanic-glass towers.

Jumping to her feet in one smooth motion, she leveled her spear, ready for attack, while sending her green healing magic to restore her cut fingers and legs. A shadow moved accompanied by a whiff of decay. She'd know that foul odor anywhere. The Emperor was hiding in the gloom.

She was about halfway between the two towers. Dagstyrr was in one of them, and the Emperor was close.

But which one held Dagstyrr?

Rella didn't dare choose the wrong one. She could end up trapped in the endless corridors and rooms that made up Thingstyrbol. If that happened, the Emperor could play cat and mouse with her for days.

A shade shimmered to her left. The Emperor had moved, letting moonlight shine on the obsidian where a moment ago it was dull. So, where was he now?

Rella hefted her spear. "Show yourself, coward."

A laugh filled the air, sending shivers up and down Rella's spine. Her skin crawled as if a thousand insects moved over her flesh, and it took some effort to tamp down her natural repugnance. He was only one person. A big one, a mad one, but only one. She could best him.

Rella almost laughed at the ridiculous fears that had stopped her coming after him sooner. "Come on, you crazy madman. You and me. To the death."

He stepped out of the dark, not looking at all afraid. "I am annoyed with you, little Rella. You killed one of my people. I had no idea you had such a temper."

Immediately, she sent her spear flying through the air toward his chest. At the last moment, he lifted his hand and caught it. Without even turning his eyes from her, he threw it over the side of the walkway. He was faster than she'd expected, but that wasn't a problem. "Let's get this over with," said Rella, standing tall and positioning her hands for the real battle. Magic would win this fight, not iron or steel.

The Emperor moved into the alcove in front of the door

to one of the towers, and lit the lamp hanging there. "You mean we don't get to talk about it, first?"

"We have nothing to say to each other. You will die tonight."

"Don't you want to see your human first?"

Rella's heart lurched. "I've come for you," she said, struggling to keep her voice steady.

"Oh, you do flatter me."

"None intended." She wanted to strike him, but he was moving back and forth, his lamp casting shadows and reflections that danced on the obsidian wall, confusing her eyes. She dare not blast the wall so hard the glass would shatter and break the wall asunder. Disconnecting the towers might cut her off from Dagstyrr. She didn't know which tower the Emperor kept him in, and she'd been warned not to choose the wrong one.

Now that she was confronting the Emperor, there was no room for mistakes. Rella imagined she could feel Dagstyrr's energy all around her. With great effort, she pushed that from her mind. If she was to rescue him, she must concentrate on one thing—killing the Emperor.

It was not going to be easy. He stood grinning at her, but then she heard his voice come from behind her. "What fun we are going to have, Rella."

She swung around and there, in front of the door to the second tower, stood the Emperor. He was trying to disarm her by confusing her senses. Not even he could be in two places at once. "Come and get me!" she cried.

Suddenly, multiple images of the Dark Emperor flashed along the length of the walkway, each one looking as real as the last. "Do you like my display?"

He sounded as if the madness was taking control of him, but she dared not forget the power he wielded. It was formidable. She'd felt it the first time they met, when he turned her dark and gave her the mark.

"Smoke and mirrors to scare children," said Rella. "I expected something impressive."

"Well, how about this?"

An image shimmered in the void beyond the wall. An image of Dagstyrr, tied and broken on a web of ropes suspended high above the grassy field below. Rella's heart missed a beat. She forced a laugh. "More false images. Perhaps that's how you'll be remembered, as the Lord of Fakery. Or better still, as a pathetic madman."

"Oh, you think I'm a fraud?" said the Emperor, his temper rising. "I am the same as you, little Rella. That's why we'll make such a perfect bonded pair. We'll show the world what real magic is. Power like ours should not be squandered on petty squabbles. We will rule the light fae and the dark fae. All will bend to our might." A puff of green battle energy swept her off her feet as a blue strike flashed skyward.

The Dark Emperor had both light and dark magic? That meant he was light fae turned dark, like her. "You are mad," said Rella, leaping to her feet, her thoughts reeling.

"Don't say that!"

"I am nothing like you, you crazy bastard." The image of Dagstyrr wavered in the air. She didn't trust anything he showed her, but perhaps she could goad him into stretching his magic too far. The more he concentrated on these ridiculous displays, the less he had to defeat her with.

"Of course you are. We were once light. Now we are dark. We have both blue and green at the tips of our fingers. We are the most powerful beings in the world."

"Power, is that all you think about? You claim your magic is potent, yet all you have to show me are tricks that any fairground con man could conjure," she said, trying to keep track of the many images of the Emperor moving along the black glass walkway. One of them was the real thing. Which one?

Was this madness what lay ahead for her?

She pushed that thought aside. Rella needed all her concentration if she was to fool him into showing himself. "Liar. I don't believe you have green and blue magic. You are the Dark Emperor. Only dark green magic is at your fingertips, and shining blue lights in the sky won't convince me otherwise. In fact, it is rather boring."

"Perhaps you'd enjoy a tussle with my guard instead?" The Emperor waved his hand in a complex pattern, calling something to him.

His black toothy grin sent shivers of disgust down her spine. What now?

She didn't have long to wait. A long arm snaked over the side of the wall, and a deformed shadow of a wounded warrior pulled itself up to sit on the edge. Its eyes were dark holes, but somehow managed to convey a terrible sadness. She could see right through it. However, the weapons it carried were real, glinting silver in the moonlight. Rella had never seen anything like it before, but she knew what it was. A shadow man!

The deadly creature sat close enough that she could make out his uniform—Casta livery from her own royal cohort.

The Emperor had sunk far lower than she had imagined. To manipulate the dead was the worst kind of deviant magic imaginable—stealing souls at the time of death and tying them to their maker's will. The shadow man lifted an arm and pointed at her, then turned his head toward his maker. Rella steeled herself. "Is that all you have? Where are your warriors?"

"I pay them well and send them home after every battle. That way they are always happy to return. My personal guard and some servants are all I need while at Thingstyrbol. You will get used to it, my dear."

"What guard? I see only one shadow man," said Rella, hoping it was so.

"Oh, I have thousands. Every battle brings me more." A smile of triumph accompanied the Emperor's voice.

The thought of more shadow men climbing onto the walkway sent fear dashing through Rella, for these stolen souls could not be killed. Only the death of their maker would set them free.

"Look," said the Emperor. His multiple images pointed down the side of the wall, where a cloud of shadow men swarmed around the base of the palace. "If you're very good, one day you may have your own guard."

Rella choked back her disgust. At the foot of the wall a horde of shadow men swarmed like insects mindlessly milling around. The moon glinted off their weapons clutched hard in their hands. That was the army the wild fae would have to fight to win Thingstyrbol unless she could kill the Emperor now.

"You cannot expect me to admire that!" she said, not hiding her contempt. "I am a light fae princess, or have you forgotten? I want only strong magic. Bright blue battle magic, clean and powerful," she said, trying to make him show his position.

It worked. The tower to Rella's right shimmered with the blue of light fae battle magic for just a second before a bolt flew out and felled a tree in the forest.

It was the clue she was seeking. Instinctively, she ran to

the source of the bolt. Her dark magic poured choking green mist in front of her before rising to surround the Emperor. Rella drew her sword and plunged it into the Emperor's breast. The image crumpled to dust.

"Nice try."

"Coward. You won't face me one on one," said Rella, spinning around only to be surrounded by multiple images of a laughing Dark Emperor. The shadow man on the wall grinned silently as if it retained a sliver of its former self. That annoyed the Emperor. Perhaps he didn't have full control of them after all.

With a wave of his hand, he dismissed the shadow man, who slithered down the wall to his companions.

The Emperor's smell was suddenly stronger. Rella knew he must be close. Twisting, she searched the faces of the images for one that was different, even if just slightly—too late. Iron-cold fingers slid around her throat, and Rella froze.

Fighting back panic, she made one final lunge with her sword at the Emperor whose hand held her captive. His other hand blasted the sword from her grasp. It clattered down the obsidian wall to the earth far below.

"Be careful, my princess," her captor warned. "Just the smallest amount of battle magic spilling from my fingers, and you're dead. That would be such a shame, don't you think?" Rella could feel his deadly energy burgeoning at his fingertips, and knew he spoke the truth. Only the thought of Dagstyrr stopped her from provoking him into releasing that deadly spark. She'd rather die a hero's death than be in thrall to this creature, but while there was a chance Dagstyrr was alive, she'd fight on.

CHAPTER 28

Dagstyrr knew something was different tonight besides Englesten's visit. The Emperor should be here by now, whip in hand. Dagstyrr could think of only one thing that would distract him from torturing his captive—Rella. All his senses came fully alert, all pain dismissed with the help of Englesten's potion. She was walking into the Emperor's lair, and Dagstyrr was the bait.

Even if she knew it was a trap, she would come anyway. But the Emperor had been planning for this encounter for a long time, which meant Rella was rushing headlong into unspeakable danger to save the man she loved. She was definitely the rescuing kind, and he loved her for it but wished just this once she'd let others guide her.

Bernst and Viktar would have tried to persuade her to wait for her army. That, he realized, was wishful thinking. No one could stop her once she made her mind up. Rella would come alone, and he could sense that tonight was the night. Dagstyrr glanced at the floor, his gut twisting at the sight of the bed prepared below—but he would not let that distract him. For once, the shadows that often moved in the corners were nowhere to be seen.

Somehow, he must get down from here. A task he'd put his mind to many times throughout his captivity, but had failed to find a weakness he could exploit. He ran through all the possible scenarios again, frustrated by finding no answer.

Wishing he hadn't sent Englesten away so quickly, he looked around for any sign the Ghost King was still here. The little man was strong and agile, and, as he boasted, very fast. Perhaps together, they could find an answer.

Dagstyrr had been hanging on these ropes for so long now that one or two were starting to fray from the constant strain of his weight working against the pulleys. Unfortunately, none were anywhere near breaking point.

A flash of blue light beyond the arrow slits grabbed his attention. So, his worst fears were realized—Rella *had* come for him. His heart sank. Then the Emperor's crazy laugh shattered the quiet. He was talking to someone, but they were too far away for Dagstyrr to make out what was said. He knew it was now or never. Yet all he could do was hang there. In his frustration, he threw back his head and roared. A tear sprang from his one good eye.

Time dragged as he hung in his web, desperate to know what was happening on the walkway between the two towers. Flashes of light shimmered in the dark beyond the tower. Dagstyrr yanked violently at his bonds, which did nothing to help his broken ribs.

Either Rella or the Emperor would appear victorious in the doorway of the tower. He locked his eyes on the door and waited.

～

"That's better, little one," purred the Emperor in her ear. One deadly hand grasped her neck, preventing her from killing him. She could feel the battle magic pulsing in his fingers ready to fly. If she made a wrong move she'd die.

He led her toward the farther tower. Rella prayed it was where he was keeping Dagstyrr. At the Emperor's prodding, she opened the door to the tower, then waited to allow her eyes time to adjust to its dim interior.

"Look what I have here, human," said the Emperor.

Rella could sense Dagstyrr's presence. His protective energy, though weak, reached out to her. Her heart began to race, and she couldn't stop it, even knowing that the Emperor would feel her quickened pulse.

Where was he?

There was no sign of him. A large bed dressed in silks and satins waited in the middle of what looked like a torture chamber. Along one wall, a rack displayed different whips, some of them still bloody from use. A couple of braziers burnt in the corners with irons heating in the coals. Something moved in the shadows, but it was too small to be Dagstyrr. Rella didn't want to know what plans the Emperor had for her in this room.

The Emperor's fingers twisted harder into her throat, raising her chin to the dark ceiling high above. Something bloody hung in a complicated web of ropes, suspended in the air twenty feet up. At first, she couldn't make out what it was.

Her knees buckled when she recognized Dagstyrr.

His head hung to the side, one eye swollen shut. His breath came short and raspy. With her experience of those wounded in battle, she knew that a rib was broken and had pierced a lung. Covered in cuts from a variety of lashes, he was encrusted with gore. The ropes holding him had dripped blood onto the floor below, leaving brown stains etched between the flagstones. Ignoring her instinct to reach out with her healing magic, she stood tall.

"Ah, how quaint—exactly the reaction I expected," said the Emperor. "So, it's true. You have taken this piece of human excrement as your mate? Why? That's what I don't understand. You're a princess. You deserve so much more."

Rella ignored him. She gazed up at the broken, bloody man hanging in the web. Using her acute hearing, she heard his heart beating under his labored breath. It was strong and steady despite the punishment he'd taken.

"I think he's dead," said Rella. If she could convince the Emperor to lower Dagstyrr to the ground, she stood a better chance of rescuing him.

"Oh, I think not. Not yet, anyway. I've promised him an entertaining evening. Look what I have prepared for us." The Emperor walked her toward the silken bed.

So, that's what he had planned. Well, he was going to be disappointed. She would kill Dagstyrr and herself before she'd give in to this monster. Rella felt both her light and dark magic energies grow steely and strong, manifesting her determination.

"I'm tired. Let's lie down and admire my handiwork."

Rella was forced down to lie at the Emperor's side. His hand never left her throat, not for a second. His fingernails dug into her neck, bringing forth small droplets of blood. She closed her eyes, trying to concentrate on how best to free herself.

"Open your eyes, little Rella. Look, our guest is watching us," said the Emperor, running his other hand down the length of her body.

Determined not to show her fear and disgust, Rella

looked up at Dagstyrr and saw fury glowing from his one good eye, and she took heart. He had fight in him yet.

"Why do you wear such unbecoming clothes, Rella, dear? Once I've crowned you the Dark Queen, you will dress in silks and velvets. Still, I will take such delight in divesting you of each item. I want to see your hair loose, falling down your bare back as you prepare yourself for my attention. You'll like that, won't you?"

"So, you are the one who started the rumor about me becoming the Dark Queen?" said Rella, ignoring the horrific images conjured by the Emperor.

"No rumor, dearest—a prophecy. You will be my queen, and I will be your ever-loving king!"

"It will never happen," said Rella, tearing her eyes from Dagstyrr. How could she get him down from there without killing him?

"Of course it will, and you will enjoy being queen of the dark fae. Just think, once I've defeated your brother we'll rule Casta as well. Won't it be wonderful? Oh, and I'll forgive you for lying to me and making false promises to get what you want. We're just too alike you and I."

Refusing to be goaded, Rella ignored him.

"I'm bored," he announced, then lifted his other hand and sent out a blue bolt that severed three of the ropes in Dagstyrr's web.

Forgetting the danger she was in, Rella sat upright. "Stop it. He'll fall." Luckily, all she suffered were further scratches from the Emperor's nails. If he'd thought she was trying to escape, he'd have killed her, but he was becoming complacent, thinking he had her.

"What fun. I've changed my mind. I won't kill him just yet. Humans are boring, but you, my dear, react so well. It is going to be an entertaining evening."

With one hand, he used his dark magic to persuade a living vine to speed across the floor to the bed. Once there, it started to wind itself around Rella. She struggled to get away from it, but the Emperor raised her head so that she saw only Dagstyrr. "I will kill him now if you wish."

She stilled. The vine continued until her hands were firmly fixed to her sides. Now she couldn't use her magic. Rella lay perfectly still as his hand left her throat and he slid off the bed. He hadn't taken three steps before she threw herself from the bed onto her feet, dragging the vine behind her like a chain.

"I knew it." His voice echoed around them, striking sharply off the walls. "There is nowhere to run, little Rella. I have you now, and your hands are tied." He laughed even louder this time. The high-pitched sound grated on her taut nerves. "There is no saving your human, but I might be persuaded to let him live a little longer if you were to cooperate."

"What do you want?" she asked, her eyes glancing at Dagstyrr high in the web.

"A kiss. I want you to come to me and kiss me." The Emperor's smile revolted Rella. The idea of kissing that disgusting mouth was enough to weaken her strongest resolve. Even as he spoke, foul-smelling spit sprayed across his coat.

She saw Dagstyrr whisper something and strained her ears to hear. *No kiss, cut ropes.*

"Look at me!"

Rella strode a few paces farther away, refusing to look at him. "You disgust me. I will never kiss you," she said, in arrogant, high light fae style, while wondering if Dagstyrr's request to cut his bonds and send him hurtling to the floor might be some kind of suicide attempt. No, she knew him better than that. But he'd never survive such a fall.

"That's better, Princess," the Emperor said delightedly. "I knew the real Rella would surface sooner or later."

"Remove this vine from my hands, immediately," she demanded.

"Ah, no, that won't happen. Not yet, anyway. I need to know I can trust you first," said the Emperor, twisting his long fingers.

"You can't trust me, though. Can you?" said Rella, smiling at his dismay.

In a fit of anger, he fired a bolt of blue energy upward to cut through more of the ropes holding Dagstyrr.

Rella winced.

Dagstyrr smiled.

CHAPTER 29

Dagstyrr felt the web loosen, and he dropped about three feet before pain shot through his body as he jerked to a stop. The fall left one leg hanging loose, no longer attached to the ropes. Muscle spasms continued to race through him as the wooden strut his leg had been tied to crashed to the floor below him. *Good girl.* After seeing Englesten clamber over the web, Dagstyrr felt confident he could too. It had carried his weight all this time, so there was no reason for it to fail once he was free. He gently twisted his fingers around strands of rope, ready to hang on—for whatever came next.

Below him, Rella paced in front of the Dark Emperor, only looking up at Dagstyrr when her back was to the creature. She was magnificent, but the Emperor was becoming more erratic. That strange finger twisting usually presaged one of his more spectacular tantrums. Then he'd become unmanageable.

Dagstyrr must get to Rella before that happened.

A door creaked open below, and one of the Emperor's minions rushed in. Falling to his knees in front of the Dark

Emperor in a panic, he said. "Majesty, we are under attack! We've managed to raise the drawbridge, but..."

"Don't interrupt me now!"

The man paled and backed out of the room. Dagstyrr could hear a commotion. When he saw Rella smiling, he knew he'd welcome whoever they were. Then he heard the Captain's voice in his head. *Hang on, boy. We're coming for you. Only one shipload of warriors, but the wind was with us.*

Dagstyrr was never so glad to hear Bernst's commanding tone. One glance at Rella and he knew she'd heard it too.

"What are you two smiling about? It's only some rabble from the villages."

"Your villages?" said Rella imperiously, still playing the light fae princess. "I thought they were deserted. Don't you have *any* control over your people?"

Dagstyrr knew she was deliberately taunting the Emperor. However, she was playing a very dangerous game.

The Emperor's face turned still and cold—not something Dagstyrr had ever seen before. Instinctively, he knew it didn't bode well. "I control everything. I am the Dark Emperor, king of the dark fae. You've seen my shadow men. They obey my every whim. Soon, I will capture the soul of Astrid's favorite son and gift him to you. His shadow will be the start of your entourage. I control everything," he whispered in her ear, then raised his hand. An arc of battle magic tore across the web.

Dagstyrr fell like a stone, the floor rushing toward him. He reached out to grab a rope, any rope, but it had all happened too quickly.

Rella's scream filled the air.

He tried to remember to crumple and roll as he reached the stone floor, but his muscles wouldn't obey. It was like being hit by a battering ram. Dagstyrr lay in a heap, trying to pull air into his damaged lungs while he looked for Rella.

Without warning, the door to the walkway opened, and a huge dark fae warrior stood there. Was this more trouble? Rella whispered a name, but Dagstyrr missed it.

"No, no, no, no. Out. Get out!" yelled the Emperor, striding across the floor toward the man, blue and green energy sparking dangerously from his fingertips.

"Not this time, Emperor," said the warrior, advancing.

The Dark Emperor's face twitched with anger. "You!"

Dagstyrr knew he was completely out of control now. A perilous situation, but the warrior seemed unfazed by the Emperor's disturbing display.

"Rella, I did as you commanded and led the climb up the wall."

Rella edged toward Dagstyrr. With her hands still bound to her sides, he knew she couldn't use her magic. Dagstyrr dragged himself along the floor toward her. Every bone in his body felt rattled out of position from the impact. One leg was broken for sure, and an arm hung uselessly, probably broken as well. Surprisingly, however, his head was intact, and he still had his wits about him.

The Emperor kept his eyes on the warrior but turned his deadly hand toward Rella. "Don't move, warrior, or she's dead. Rella, stay where you are."

Rella sat down on the floor as close to Dagstyrr as she dared. "You are becoming boring, Emperor. Barros has no loyalty to me," she said.

"Then why did he obey your orders? Tell me that."

"Simple. It was my punishment," said the big warrior, much to Dagstyrr's surprise. Punishment wasn't ever meted out in the wild fae camp as far as he knew.

Dagstyrr continued to drag himself slowly toward Rella.

"I came here to kill you, Emperor. It's that simple," said Barros.

"Barros?" the Emperor repeated. "I know that name. Your aunt ruled here before me, didn't she?"

"Yes, and you killed her. Now, I am going to kill you."

"I mean it when I say I'll kill Rella," said the Emperor, a grin splitting his face.

"I've paid my debt to her. She is nothing to me," said Barros, dropping his sword and preparing his hands to fight the Emperor with magic. It was a brave move against such an accomplished foe. The Emperor might be crazy mad, but his magic was strong.

"No, Barros. Let me deal with him," said Rella.

"I don't take orders from you, Rella of the wild fae. This is dark fae business," said the man before unleashing the darkest green magic Dagstyrr had ever seen. It rushed across the floor at speed, only to stop when it met the barrier of the Emperor's equally strong dark magic.

The Emperor grinned, triumphantly. His magic easily held back that of the warrior.

Just then, Patrice burst through the doorway, sheathed her sword and, lifting her hands, poured her green clouds of battle magic to join with Barros's. "I told you to wait for me," she said. "Those shadow men held me back."

Patrice winced as her battle magic smacked into the full force of the Emperor's defense. Barros nodded to her in recognition. "We need to kill the maker, otherwise they'll just pick up their weapons again and again. They're slow, but invincible."

The two dark fae warriors fell silent as they poured their battle magic against the Emperor. But even the combined battle magic of such powerful fae failed to break through the Emperor's shield. His magic was powerful.

Dagstyrr kept his eye on the Emperor as he continued to crawl toward Rella. As he reached her, she nodded at the knife protruding from her boot. "Quick, get me out of these bindings," she whispered.

He grasped the knife with his one good hand and started to hack at the vine binding her hands to her sides. To his horror, the vine grew back as fast as he could cut into it. He looked up at her, knowing he was defeated.

Rella smiled at him with so much love that it almost broke his heart. Somewhere, deep down inside, he gathered a strength he didn't know he possessed. Determined not to give up, he continued to hack at the sinuous vines, but they grew back again and again.

Together, Patrice and Barros's energy continued to press the Emperor, but they couldn't break through the shield of magic the Emperor held in front of him.

"Patrice," said Rella, "the vine source."

"I can't. Not now," said Patrice, sweat trickling down her face.

"The Emperor is stronger. How do you defeat a stronger enemy?" said Dagstyrr, hoping their battle training had been as thorough as his, and they'd know how to use the Emperor's strength against him.

Lady Patrice nodded and said, "On three."

With wolfish grins, Barros and Patrice withdrew their magic, at the same time they leaped like tumbling acrobats across the floor. The Emperor's green barrage flew across the floor and exploded where the warriors had stood a split second before. The sudden release of pressure from the dark fae warriors caused the Emperor to stagger forward, falling almost to his knees. Before he could recover, Patrice's battle magic surged forward and knocked him to the floor.

Barros was faster on his feet than his bulk would

suggest. He spun in the air, landing to the Emperor's far side, where he sent a wave of green energy flying across the floor toward the vine's long root-stem.

Incensed, the Emperor jumped to his feet lashing out with a blue bolt that shattered the green energy before it reached the vine. Then he turned his attention back to Barros and Patrice. The two warriors were ready for him.

Undeterred, Dagstyrr continued to hack at the vine with one hand. To his surprise, it stayed cut. He glanced at the root-stem and smiled when he saw that the Emperor's blue bolt had severed the vine from its source.

Rella was free.

One quick kiss, and she was up and ready to do battle. Dagstyrr watched in unashamed admiration as Rella stood fearlessly to face the Dark Emperor. Rella, Patrice, and Barros circled him. He could not put the full force of his magic in any one direction without leaving himself vulnerable to the other two.

"Do you hear that, Emperor?" said Rella, as the roar of fighting on the walkway raged just outside the door. "That is the sound of the future. The wild fae have come to Thingstyrbol."

His laughter echoed around the dark chamber. "I am the dark fae *and* the light. I am the future!"

"You're a monster," chorused Patrice and Barros.

"A madman," said Rella, using a little compulsion in her voice.

A twisted, deranged, maniac, thought Dagstyrr as he hugged his useless arm and struggled to pull breath into his damaged lung.

"Don't call me that," said the Emperor. "I've told you before!"

Barros, guided by Rella's clue, added his assessment. "A

madman for sure," he said, nodding to Rella as the Emperor's face twitched in anger, and his hands shook to hold his magic shield in place.

Dagstyrr had no idea who this dark fae warrior was, but he knew what he was doing. Suddenly, the Emperor fisted his hands and summoned an enormous amount of magic before releasing both blue bolts and green clouds of battle energy toward Barros.

Barros sent his dark green battle energy to contain both, but Dagstyrr knew he couldn't hold it for long.

Patrice gasped before moving to use her battle magic to shield Barros.

Knowing this was the most important fight of her life, Rella stood calmly summoning her battle magic. With both hands open and ready, she felt the power surge through her veins. The pressure built as the two forms of magic inside her grew in intensity. Then she raised her hands and, with a deep breath, let it go. It was spectacular. It didn't fly like a bolt or creep along the floor. It grew in long surging tendrils rising from her hands and intertwining. Floating above the fighters below, it moved as if it knew exactly what to do. Rella produced it, but the energy directed itself. It twisted and turned in the high-ceilinged room filling the space with beautiful light.

Dagstyrr had no idea what was happening. Neither, it seemed, did the Emperor. Though locked in a struggle, they all gaped at what was happening above them. Dagstyrr saw it as his one opportunity to strike.

He hefted the knife in his good hand and sent it flying through the air toward the Emperor's chest, where it stuck fast. The Emperor turned to him, astonished, and then, ignoring the protruding blade, he turned his attention back to Patrice and Barros.

It wasn't a deathblow! Desperate, Dagstyrr looked around for another weapon.

Just then, Rella's magic started to descend. It wove a net of blue and green energy that glowed with a golden light. Twinkling flashes sparking off the net only added to its ethereal beauty.

The Emperor appeared mesmerized by it. As it slowly descended toward him, he stopped fighting, allowing Barros and Patrice to step back for a much needed respite. They were exhausted.

When the net of glittering magic came within inches of his head, the Emperor's expression changed. Panic showed in his black eyes, and he pulled Dagstyrr's knife from his chest and slashed at the pretty light show falling around him. Blood poured from his chest wound but didn't stop his high-pitched screaming.

The net of fae energy was somehow preventing the Emperor from using his magic. He held his head as if in the throes of extreme pain. Patrice and Barros, seeing that Rella appeared to have the Emperor under control, looked toward Dagstyrr. This was unlike any fight they'd ever seen before. Patrice drew her sword in readiness. Dagstyrr shook his head. "Stand down. Stand ready," ordered Dagstyrr, every word costing him more pain.

Patrice and Barros had been well trained and understood how to take orders. They backed toward the doorway. After a glance at the fighting on the walkway, they stood ready to defend the door, and then cast their eyes once more toward the light show forming around the Emperor.

Rella stood calm and in control as the net covered the screeching Emperor. It caused no wounds anyone could see, but all the little creatures that made their homes among his clothes deserted him. Scuttling across the floor, the spiders, beetles, mice, moths, and many others escaped the net like a shadow running across the flagstones. The Emperor fell silent as the magic spurting from his hands diminished and went out.

Then he fell to his knees. At first, Dagstyrr thought he was going to vomit, but it was nothing so simple. Black grease oozed from his mouth, nose, eyes, and ears, even from his chest wound. The black gunk gathered in front of him inside the magical net and grew, even as the Emperor appeared to shrink.

Crouched in a heap, his long limbs folded under him, he stared ahead. There was no mistaking his fear. Then, with a horrible slurping sound, the black grease moved over him until he was consumed within it and was no more. All that remained was a large puddle of oozing black tar.

Dagstyrr and the dark fae warriors watched in awe as the black mass writhed on the floor appearing to consume itself until nothing existed inside the net any longer.

He remembered some of the words his mother had spoken about the fate of those light fae who turned dark: *You will be eaten by darkness. Your evil will consume you.*

Was this what she'd meant?

Suddenly, Englesten was by his side. Dagstyrr reached out and gripped his hand. "Show me what's going on outside," he demanded, knowing the elf had the power to show him as he'd shown him a battle a long time ago.

"I don't think..."

"Show me!"

Immediately, Dagstyrr saw the shadow men crawling over the obsidian wall. The wild fae fought bravely. Each time they disarmed a shadow warrior, the wraith walked off and was replaced by another.

The shadow men moved slowly, leering and laughing

each time they lost a weapon. Then they simply retrieved their weapon and carried on. There were too many of them, and they didn't tire.

Bernst lead a sortie on the other tower, his sailors climbed like they were born to it, but inevitably they were beaten back by the sheer numbers of grotesque shadow men. These were warriors whose essence had been stolen at the point of death. They should be feasting in halls of the dead with their ancestors, not fighting on and on like beasts without the ability to reason.

Then it happened. One of the shadow men approaching Bernst disappeared. Then another. A large shadow warrior reached out his hands to the sky, smiling. Dagstyrr saw its shadow self dim and dissipate into the ether. So it was true, now that Rella had defeated the Dark Emperor, his army of shadow men was no more. Dagstyrr watched the wild fae swarm up the wall just as Englesten withdrew his hand.

"I'll see you at Hedabar, dragon-talker."

CHAPTER 30

Rella knew she'd conquered her magic at last, and it thrilled her. This use of two magic energies together must be how magic worked before the light fae and dark fae separated. She pulled her net of blue and green light back into herself, working on instinct alone and trying not to think too much about what she had just done. That time would come, but not now. The energy wove its way through her body, becoming part of her again, and she was complete.

Exhausted, she staggered before looking to Dagstyrr with a small smile of triumph on her lips. "He's gone." Then she turned to Patrice and Barros. "Your people are safe now."

Barros was down on one knee. "I am yours to command, my queen."

"Get up, Barros. I have no intention of being the Dark Queen. It is not my place," she said, making her way to Dagstyrr, whose eyes were ominously closed.

"But..."

Turning to Barros she said, "I know now who started

those rumors. It was the Emperor, he wanted to alienate me from the dark fae. As Patrice told you, it was never my intent. If you want to make yourself useful, seal off this tower while the others round up any servants still loyal to the Emperor. Make sure we're not disturbed." Rella went to Dagstyrr's side.

"I'll have Clar and Nan take care of that," said Patrice going to the door.

The battle noise outside stopped just as Bernst burst through the doorway, brandishing his ax. "Is he alive?"

"Yes, Captain, though only just," said Rella, kneeling on the floor and cradling Dagstyrr's head in her lap. A tear ran down her face as she gazed on his broken body. Putting her hand in his, she urged her healing magic to flow into him. "I wish I hadn't ordered Gimrir to stay behind."

"We don't need him," said Bernst. "You and I can do this."

She glared at him. "He needs real medical magic. It can only be Gimrir."

"And who does our spirit-fae go to when he needs help?"

Dagstyrr's eyes opened, and he gazed up at her. "I feel better already."

"That's because I'm numbing the pain," she said, smiling.

"I'll do that," said Bernst, taking Dagstyrr's head in his hands. "Healing is always more powerful when it comes from love. Go on then. The way Gimrir taught you. Use both light and dark. It's your specialty," he said, grinning encouragement.

"You don't know the half of it," whispered Dagstyrr.

Bernst had been the first person to teach Rella how to use healing magic. He was no physician like Gimrir, but he understood battle wounds and how to heal them.

Rella moved her hands over Dagstyrr, and her energy came strong and purposeful as never before. She saw the way forward, sensing and probing for the severest injuries. "His leg is broken."

"Very well, you know how to knit bones, just not all the way, remember. Leave a little for nature to finish," coached the captain.

"He's broken three ribs, and they've pierced his lung," she said, no longer needing Bernst to guide her.

"So, heal the ribs. Not all the way mind. Then work on the lung." He smiled, encouraging her.

"Aye, all the way," she said, thrilled that it came more naturally to her than ever before.

"Aye, soft tissue scars are not a problem."

"I understand." Rella allowed her tears to fall while she continued to assess the damage. His arm was pulled out of its socket. Most warriors could fix that one, but it would be painful—she could do it painlessly. The myriad weeping cuts would take time. Some were scarring, others needed sealing, and the tissue must be persuaded to knit together again after cleansing. His eye concerned her most. When Rella investigated, she saw to her relief, that the way was obvious—she must clear the pus and reduce the swelling. His sight was intact.

It was going to take a long time to heal each cut individually, but she knew no other way.

Barros stood sentinel by the door as the hours passed.

Eventually, Rella reached a point where she could do no more. Dagstyrr would be in pain for some time yet, but the worst was over. She sat back on her heels and nodded to Captain Bernst, to let him know she was done for now.

Bernst stretched out on the floor. "You did well, Rella."

"I hope it's enough," she said.

Barros approached. "Let me lift him onto that bed for you. You can both rest there."

"Anywhere but that bed," mumbled Dagstyrr.

He awoke the next morning to her scent filling his head. For a moment, he thought he was still tied to the web, and her presence was a dream. Then she murmured in her sleep and stretched her arm over his ribs. It hurt just enough for him to know she was there and not a figment of his imagination.

Pulling her closer, he dropped a kiss on her head. The nightmare was over.

They were in a bright room with gauze curtains billowing in the early morning sunshine. The bed was a living vine, woven to form a nest and filled with a downy mattress and soft pillows.

Dagstyrr had never been so content in his life. *If there truly is an afterlife*, he thought, *then this is how it must feel.* A breeze gently ruffled the leaves of the vine overhead, bringing with it the fresh, salty sea air, which reminded him of home. He had his woman in his arms and was almost free of pain. What more could a warrior ask?

Rella mumbled in her sleep, and he drew her even closer. Looking down, he saw her eyes flutter open. She sat up with a start.

"Whoa. You're safe," said Dagstyrr.

She looked around the room, her eyes wide and startled. "Where are we?"

"I have no idea."

Then she fell back into his arms. "All I remember is Patrice coming in and ordering you carried out of that hell-hole. I was so tired I just followed along and climbed into the bed with you."

"This is not how you described Thingstyrbol," said Dagstyrr, indicating the bright sumptuous room.

"This is not the Thingstyrbol I experienced," she said, gazing around.

A knock on the door sounded, and a bevy of women led by little Jul entered. They carried hot water, towels, and fresh clothes. "Awake at last, and right on time," said Jul, smiling.

Dagstyrr looked puzzled. "How long have we been sleeping?"

"Four days," said Jul with a laugh. "Don't worry, you were under Captain Bernst's wellness spell, and Rella was so exhausted, we put a 'do not disturb' spell on the room. Everyone wants to talk to you. You are celebrities."

"Is everyone here?" said Rella, remembering that Jul was supposed to stay behind with the wild fae.

"Yes. Once we knew Thingstyrbol was ours, we traveled day and night to get here. Some people are still arriving. We've waited a long time for this, and we have you two to thank for it," she said. "We will always be grateful."

When he smelled the fresh water pouring into twin bathing tubs, Dagstyrr understood how badly they must both stink. Then his stomach rumbled, loud enough for all to hear.

He put his hand on it. "My apologies, Lady Jul."

Jul laughed and clapped her hands. "Yes, we know you must be starving. We've brought food."

Rella had lain half-asleep until the smell of eggs and toast entered the room. Then she sat up. "I can't believe it's been four days," she said.

"We'll leave you both to eat and freshen up, and then we request your presence in the great hall," said Jul.

Dagstyrr felt a shiver run through Rella at the mention of the great hall. He frowned and looked at Jul. "Perhaps we could meet somewhere else, my lady?"

"I think you will find the palace much changed since last you saw it, Princess Rella. This," she said, indicating the room, "is what the palace looked like before him. We do not mention his name. I think you will find the hall quite beautiful now."

"How? Who changed it all?" said Rella.

"We did—all of us. The dark fae have been working hard day and night to banish the last vestiges of him. We will soon be finished. What remains is Thingstyrbol as it always was. I think you will like it. Besides, is it not better to allay those fears that haunt our nightmares?"

Rella smiled. "You are wise as always, little Jul. We will be there directly."

"There is no rush. Take your time," she said, clapping her hands. The servants left the room, followed by the diminutive Lady Jul.

"She's a treasure," said Rella. "Once Lady Patrice is crowned, Lady Jul will serve her well."

Dagstyrr lifted an eyebrow questioningly.

"I know. It isn't my choice, but I do hope the dark fae choose Patrice," Rella added earnestly.

"You, my love, are the treasure. I still can't believe what I saw you do," said Dagstyrr, taking her in his arms.

"Neither can I. It baffles me still, yet I know that's how my magic is supposed to work. The two energies acting in unison, like they're talking to each other. I am just a conduit. The magic energies already know what to do and how to do it. I just thought of my intention, and then let it flow. It all felt so right."

"It's like nothing I've ever seen or heard of. Rella, you were magnificent," said Dagstyrr, pulling her close.

"All this time, I've been fighting the change from light to dark magic. Trying to exert my will on it. I've still a lot to learn, but I am confident now. I trust it," she said.

"Rella, what I saw you do is beyond anything I could have imagined, and believe me, some of the stories my brothers told me about how magic worked were wild. Your magic is what myths are made of. It is a wonder."

"Still, I want to keep it between us few. The last thing I want is to be treated like a fairground freak," said Rella.

"We'd make a pair, you and me. A dragon-talker and a fae with dual magic!" He laughed.

"It's not funny, Dag. We'd be hunted down and forced to entertain the courts or worse."

"Yes, there are many who would use us for their own ends, but I have work to do rescuing Drago and his family. You are right. We'll keep it quiet, both my gift and yours." He kissed her lips lightly. "Breakfast?"

"Mmmm. In a moment," she said, pulling his face to hers and claiming his mouth. Dagstyrr succumbed to her desire. They were dirty, smelly, and starving, but she was the only sustenance he couldn't live without.

He slowly stripped away her brown leather tunic and ran his hand down the length of her. Then starting with the mark near her eye, he followed it around her body, dropping kisses until he heard her sigh.

Then he smiled into her laughing eyes and claimed her for his own. They made love slowly and purposefully, relishing each other like never before. A warm breeze wafted across their damp skin, lifting gooseflesh.

Rella wrapped her legs around him, drawing him in and clinging until they were one. He thought he might die of happiness. She was his woman, and always would be. He tucked his hand under her bottom, lifting her even closer. She moaned her pleasure in his ear then bit his lobe.

Laughing, he took both her hands in his and raised them above her head, carefully watching every nuance of emotion passing over her face. They moved together until, with a cry, she climaxed. "I love you," she whispered.

Her words, like a goad, drove him on until he too fell panting on top of her. "I love you too," he said.

"I know," she teased.

Dagstyrr laughed aloud. "I think I died on the web and am now in the afterlife."

"Don't say that. I nearly lost you," she said, suddenly serious.

"But you didn't," he said.

"What is to become of us?"

"We have a job to do, remember?"

"You have a job to do. I don't think Drago will appreciate my presence."

Dagstyrr lay with her in his arms, thinking for a moment. "It's true he doesn't want you there. You came to Hedabar armed with dragon's-blood pellets for your brother. However, this is nonnegotiable. I need you there. Now, more than ever."

"I don't think Drago ever negotiates."

Dagstyrr thought about the task ahead. It was going to take everyone he could muster to rescue Drago and his family. Even then, it was a long shot. It was going to be very dangerous. "I won't take you in there unless he agrees, but I'm sure I can persuade him."

"Now that I think about it, I'm sure he will agree."

"What makes you say that?"

"Word of what happened here will spread like wildfire. He will want someone like me on his side," said Rella, confidently.

"He is proud."

"How proud is his family? One hundred and sixty-eight dragons, not counting hatchlings or eggs?" said Rella, lifting a finely arched eyebrow.

CHAPTER 31

R ella stepped into the sweet-scented water and knew immediately that Lady Jul had infused it with a healing spell. She looked across at Dagstyrr lying in the other bathtub, his damp hair thrown back, his eyes closed. Whether he realized it or not, he was soaking up the healing spell, and a powerful one it was.

Looking around the room, she wondered whether the rest of Thingstyrbol was as pretty. She couldn't help but remember the dark, dank nightmare that was the Emperor's palace, despite Jul's reassurance that all was normal now.

"I suspect much has happened while we've been sleeping," she said.

"If this room is anything to go by, then I hope the restoration is finished."

"I hope so too. The last thing I need is a reminder of that monster. It's hard to believe he's gone," she said, hoping no semblance of the nightmare remained.

Dagstyrr turned and smiled. Then he stretched out his hand for hers. *Somehow,* she thought, *he always knows what*

I'm feeling. She reached for him, their wet fingers entwining. She drew comfort from his touch. "Hungry?"

"Starving," he said

"Then let's eat." She stood and wrapped herself in a large white towel, then used her magic to dry her long fae hair and twist it into a tight braid behind her. Watching Dagstyrr emerge from his bath, she wondered at his capacity to bear the myriad scars covering his poor battered body.

"Let me erase these for you?" she said, running a finger along a puckered raw scar on his shoulder.

He clasped her face in his hand. She saw him war with himself. He'd never allowed her to do so before, but now there were so many, both old and new. "You can erase every scar that madman gave me, except the one you just touched."

Puzzled, Rella couldn't think of a good reason for keeping such an ugly mark. "Why make an exception with that one?"

"A reminder, as a wise man once told me."

"Viktar! But I don't want to remember."

"I do. It is part of me now. I need to understand the lessons learned here, even if I can't fathom them now. There were times I dreamed things as I hung in that space, strange things that I don't comprehend. But that is for another day," he said, bringing his focus back to the present.

"But I can erase the others?" said Rella.

"Only the ones *he* gave me."

"Very well, my love. You are so much braver than me. I'm afraid to open our chamber door to see what lies behind it. I fear this room is some illusion built to lull me into a false sense of safety."

Dagstyrr laughed. "Oh, Rella, you are the bravest person

I know. You came here single-handed and faced your worst nightmare—alone. Nothing is hiding behind that door that you can't deal with. I'd open it to show you, but I suspect once we open that door, the world will claim us, and I'm enjoying being alone with you far too much."

"I hope you are right," she said, not convinced.

"Now, food, before I collapse at your feet."

With a wave of her hand, Rella warmed the eggs and toast and cooled the mead, which they downed hungrily. They were like children, wrapped up in warm towels, bathed, and enjoying a well-earned meal, smiling at each other with mouths full.

As he tucked into a second helping, she quietly sent her magic out to erase his new scars—except for one, as promised. When she had finished, she smiled at her handi-work. Dagstyrr hadn't even felt her working.

A knock on the door surprised them out of their happy indulgence with each other. Dagstyrr rolled his eyes as Rella answered. "Come in."

Barros entered, his arms full of fresh clothes. "These are mine. I think they will fit you well, Dagstyrr of Halfenhaw, if you will do me the honor of wearing them until we can outfit you better."

"You honor me, Lord Barros," said Dagstyrr, standing and reaching out his arm to thank the big warrior. "I owe you my thanks. You acquitted yourself well against the...you know who." It was going to take some practice to not say his name.

"No, lord, your lady did that. I think we both know the truth of it."

Dagstyrr nodded. "Call me Dagstyrr. There are no titles among the wild fae."

"There are among the dark fae, but I hope you will do me the honor of calling me Barros," he replied.

"It will be my pleasure," said Dagstyrr, understanding he and the dark warrior had just claimed each other as friends.

"Tell me, Barros, are all those poor creatures that inhabited...that lived here...are they gone?" asked Rella.

A broad smile split the dark warrior's face. "All gone, my lady. We've discovered the reason for them, and for the strange hat and cloak he favored."

"What was it?" said Dagstyrr.

"He was pulling power from all the little creatures to bolster his magic," said Barros. "The dark fae understand that life is strongest when it is new, so he favored those with short lifespans and many offspring."

"The light fae know that too," said Rella. "A newborn babe is vulnerable, but its energies are powerful."

Dagstyrr frowned. "Before the net of light came down, they all ran away. Do you mean all those insects and small animals on his hideous clothes, constantly being born, dying, and shedding everywhere he went, *that* was where he got his power?"

"Not completely, no," said Barros. "As I explained to Rella, he was born light fae. He chose to turn dark, thinking it would increase his magic. When it didn't, he found other ways to boost what power he had."

Dagstyrr's brow furrowed, and Rella could almost feel his mind working on something. "What is it?"

"It explains why he wanted a dragon. I always wondered about that. He didn't want to ride a dragon into battle, as suggested. Everyone knows that is impossible. He wanted to milk its energy, the same way he did those little creatures."

"The same way the vizier of Hedabar does to the fae he captures," said Rella.

"Exactly. Thankfully, you upset that plan when you rescued the light fae slaves," said Dagstyrr, thinking that perhaps the deaths of all those light fae and Crystal Mountain healers aboard the *Drake* were not in vain, after all.

"I will await you in the great hall," said Barros, turning to leave.

"What is happening in the great hall, Barros?" asked Rella.

Barros's smile lit his dark features again. "It is time to crown the new Dark Queen. I understand the ladies will be here shortly with your trunk. They won't start the ceremony without you, but I am to tell you that there is no rush."

Rella's eyes darted to Dagstyrr. "Then surely we must rush. I would not keep them waiting. Who will be crowned?" she said, and Dagstyrr could hear the trepidation in her voice. After all, this young warrior's aunt had been the last Dark Queen. He may well have a relative with high expectation of being crowned. Perhaps even his mother.

"It is the turn of the House of Threme, my lady."

"You take turns?" said Rella, incredulous. Keeping the excitement out of her voice, she added. "Such a thing would never happen in Casta."

"I know, my lady. We have five great houses. We each take turns unless there is no one suitable. In which case, the next family in line takes the throne. It is a great honor, as well as a great responsibility," Barros said. Then the handsome warrior left, giving them some privacy.

"Threme. That is the Lady Patrice's house!" Rella said with glee, smiling up at Dagstyrr.

～

In honor of the wild fae, Rella chose to wear a green gown, and in honor of Viktar, she decided to wear the gown he'd given her. The one with the white ghost-toadstools adorning the hem and sleeves fit her well and it was her newest.

"How is Viktar coping with being in the Court of the Dark Fae? I'm sure he never thought he'd be a guest here," said Rella.

Jul laughed. "Your Viktar is thoroughly entranced by Thingstyrbol and our ways. I've never seen him more relaxed."

"I don't think I've ever seen him relax either," said Rella. "As the Commander of all Casta troops, he must always appear ready for battle, poor man."

"Well, he is enjoying himself now. Would you like me to do your hair, Rella?" said Jul.

"Thank you, but no. You must get yourself ready; it is an important day for the family of Threme," said Rella.

Jul looked at her with solemn dark eyes. "It is the most important day of my life. You are right. I must prepare. As long as you have everything you need?"

Rella looked at Dagstyrr. "Yes, Jul, I have everything I'll ever need right here."

Jul blushed and turned on her heel. "Then I will see you in the great hall."

"She is very young," said Dagstyrr, after she'd left.

"Yes, but with four older sisters, there isn't much she doesn't know. She may be inexperienced, but she can surprise you with her insight."

"As the youngest of four brothers, I can attest to the truth of that. Younger siblings tend to grow up faster than the older ones."

"It must have been hard for you as the only human in a family with three fae brothers. No wonder your mother sought to protect you," said Rella, using magic to twist a white ribbon through her braid.

"Well, how do I look?" said Dagstyrr, turning slowly in the unfamiliar black leather and velvet clothes.

Rella turned to admire him, and her heart leaped. Seeing him in such flattering clothes made her realize how handsome he was. The black burnished leather shone to match his dark hair, and his blue eyes twinkled at her. A finely wrought courtly sword hung at his waist, the silver scabbard catching the light and setting off the fine filigree details covering his doublet. Yet he seemed most pleased by his long black leather boots, replete with silver ornaments.

Laughing, Rella went to him, put her arms around his neck, and pulled a lock of his hair through her fingers. "You need a haircut."

His arms swiftly encircled her waist. "You always say that."

"It is always true!" She laughed. "Any longer, and I could lend you a ribbon to tie it back."

"Don't exaggerate!"

"Okay, it might take a few weeks yet to reach that stage, but it curls very sexily around your collar, and I don't want to give any of these beautiful dark fae ladies ideas."

Suddenly the amusement in his eyes died. His blue gaze bore into Rella like a storm until she felt he was exposing her very soul. "I love you, Rella. Nothing will ever change that. I may not be light fae, but my family mates for life. You must believe that."

"I do. I love you too, and you will be my one mate until I die."

"I won't hold you to that, Rella. You and I both know you might live hundreds of years, and my life will be very short in comparison."

"I will never want another man."

"That's what my mother says," said Dagstyrr with a sad smile, "but my brothers and I are reconciled that when my father dies, she cannot live the rest of her life alone. It may take her some time, but sooner or later, someone will appear in her life. If she is ready, I will be happy for her, and so will my father."

"How do you know? Does your family talk about such things?"

"We do. It is the only way to make sure there are no misunderstandings later on."

"I want our family to be like that," said Rella, reaching up and kissing his mouth. "Just don't expect me to take another mate—ever!"

Dagstyrr laughed. "Very well, we can argue this at every family gathering, just like my parents do. Are you ready to go?"

She nodded.

"Rella, come here," he said, striding toward the window and pulling back the delicate gauze drapes.

Cautiously, she followed him, not sure what he was thinking.

"Look down there," he said, wrapping his arm about her shoulders.

Rella looked. Thousands of dark fae were crawling over the far side of Thingstyrbol. As they moved their green magic ahead of them, they swept away the foul black, leaving pristine white stone instead.

"They are almost finished. I imagine the great hall would have been high on their list," said Dagstyrr. "Are you ready?"

Rella nodded. Taking a deep breath, she slipped her hand into Dagstyrr's proffered elbow and went to the door.

Just as he opened it, Rella closed her eyes then felt his hand on hers.

"It is beautiful, Rella," he said softly.

And it was. Rella opened her eyes to a wide hallway stretching in either direction, carved of palest stone and festooned with garlands of bright flowers. To the left, a wide stairway with a broad polished banister wound its way down to the lower floors. It bore no resemblance to the black, fetid, palace oozing with small creatures.

As they approached, some happy children were sliding down the banister. Dressed in multicolored gauzes in all the colors of the forest flowers, they giggled and laughed their way down. Then turned and ran back up, skirting around a large figure lolling on the stairway. "Viktar?"

"Come, sit with me. Aren't they delightful? Light fae children would never behave like this, especially at court. I think they should, don't you?" said Viktar, sweeping his long hair away so that a little girl would not trip on it.

In honor of the occasion, Viktar wore his blue-and-white Casta commander's uniform. Rella smiled when she saw a little girl leaning down and plaiting flowers into the back of his hair. He was oblivious to her ministrations.

"I doubt you could convince the court to allow it, don't you?"

"A pity."

Rella and Dagstyrr joined him on the broad stairway. She had never seen her old commander so pensive.

"What's happening, Viktar?" she said.

"Nothing. All this," he said, opening his arms to indicate the happy scene in front of him. Families milled around, and laughing children ran through the pillared hallway. "This is how it used to be in Casta. Now it is all pomp and perfection. I fear the court at Casta has taken things too far recently. It is one thing to control your emotions. Our politicians must argue their points of view without becoming murderous, but that should be the extent of it."

"That's the problem, Viktar. Light fae become dangerous and uncontrollable when they allow their emotions to manifest. Their magic becomes unpredictable, and some even lose control altogether."

"We think ourselves so superior to the dark fae," said Viktar.

Rella fought her instinct to defend her light fae home. No one knew the court's faults better than she did. "I remember learning about the terrible feuds during my great-grandfather's reign. Of how people murdered each other right there in front of the sapphire throne. Casta may not be perfect, but I think it is a lot safer for good manners."

Viktar sighed. "Of course. You are right, Princess, but an old man can dream."

"Look, I hate to disturb your philosophizing, but we have a coronation to attend," said Dagstyrr, getting to his feet.

Rella stood with him and put a hand under Viktar's elbow, insisting he join them. Viktar stood and straightened his uniform. His face automatically resumed its usual countenance as they descended into a passageway leading to the great hall.

Rella couldn't remember being so excited. "Today, my friend will become the Dark Queen, and the war will be truly over."

"I hope it all goes well," said Dagstyrr solemnly.

CHAPTER 32

Flutes and harps played several different tunes from the corners of the vast hall. Somehow, they managed not to clash too severely. Their melodies weaved in and out rather than jarring against each other, leaving the listeners soothed.

The great hall was now showing light-colored stone behind the live trees that grew along the length of the room on either side. Their branches intertwined, creating a bright green canopy. The multicolored floor beneath Rella's feet was a mosaic fashioned from natural river pebbles, glinting and appearing to move in the bright sunlight shafting down from the ceiling.

At one end, a raised dais stood with a second higher platform in its center. This central platform was constructed of a living vine, similar to the bed Rella had shared with Dagstyrr, but grander. The vine stretched up the back, creating a cave-like effect of bright green leaves. The middle was covered in thick swan's down—was that the throne? It looked like an elaborate nest. Four ornate chairs—two either side of the throne—awaited occupants. The whole effect was stunningly beautiful yet regal.

Dagstyrr, Rella, and Viktar slowly made their way through the great hall, awed by the beauty surrounding them. Those who'd arrived earlier made way for them, until Barros appeared and led them to a position to the left of the dais. There, his mother awaited them. She looked majestic in silver-grey silk, yet appeared uncertain when Rella and Dagstyrr drew close. "Mother, you know Rella of the wild fae. May I introduce Dagstyrr of Halfenhaw?"

Dagstyrr stepped forward and touched her proffered hand to his forehead. "It is my privilege, Lady Berta."

The older woman took his hand in both of hers. "I am the privileged one, Dagstyrr of Halfenhaw. I must beg your forgiveness for my actions. Your capture and imprisonment were all my fault, and I truly regret it." Rella saw a small tear threatening to escape her eye while the older woman fought to maintain her dignity.

Dagstyrr looked down at the older woman. "I know the truth of the story, Lady Berta. You were not solely to blame, only a pawn in another's schemes. Your son, Barros, was instrumental in my release, so let us start our acquaintance with a clean slate."

Rella wanted to slap her face, hard. Dagstyrr was far too forgiving. Had he forgotten all those scars so soon?

Yet, the woman's kind eyes spoke of regret and gratitude. Rella thought perhaps she was sincere, which was just as well, because Dagstyrr held her hand as if she were a long-lost relative.

"I hope I have your forgiveness too, Princess Rella?"

"Just Rella. If Dagstyrr is willing to forgive you, so am I," said Rella, knowing in her heart that it would take a lot more for her to trust Lady Berta.

Just then, the music died, and people shuffled to find their places. Apparently, there was some precedence, as everyone knew exactly where to stand, though as with most dark fae rituals, Rella couldn't work out how. She saw Bernst standing across the hall, one hand firmly on Billy's shoulder. She smiled, and Bernst acknowledged her with a nod.

Billy saw her and waved enthusiastically, but thankfully, remained silent and in his place.

Loud drumming approached from outside the doors, and a group of dark fae warriors ran the length of the hall, their boots adding another layer to the rhythmic beat of the drummers following behind. The sound echoed around the stone hall until Rella could feel the vibration in her bones.

Lady Berta stood in front of the dais as if to confront the dark fae warriors stomping their way toward her with swords and shields raised. She lifted her hand, and the drums and menacing warriors stopped.

"Who dares approach the throne of Thingstyrbol?" said Lady Berta in a voice used to addressing large crowds.

Rella, Dagstyrr, and Viktar watched, fascinated. No human or light fae had ever attended this ceremony before. Barros stood behind them, and Rella saw him grin at the flowers in Viktar's hair. He whispered behind them, "Mother is the only one left of her sisters. She will receive the next Dark Queen."

The warriors parted, and Patrice, in full battle gear, approached Lady Berta. "It is I, Patrice, eldest daughter of the House of Threme." Patrice never looked more dangerous.

Lady Berta answered. "Our Dark Queen is dead. Does anyone challenge the right of the House of Threme to ascend the throne?"

Silence.

Three times Lady Berta asked the question, and three times her query was met with silence.

Rella held her breath and slipped her hand into Dagstyrr's. She'd dreamed of this day for so long. Now the nightmare that started when she set off to rescue her brother was finally over.

Her first visit to Thingstyrbol had been to ask a favor from the Dark Emperor, having no knowledge of his madness or the atrocities he'd inflicted on his people. He'd marked her for his own and extracted a price she refused to pay. Now she was witnessing the return of the rule of the Dark Queens. Peace would live here, and the war with her brother, King Calstir, would be over.

"Bring us the new Dark Queen so that all may know her."

To Rella's surprise, Patrice turned on her heel and ran from the hall. The drumming started up again. Then Patrice, Sophy, Clar, and Nan entered, carrying a wooden bier full of swan's down on their shoulders. In the center sat Jul, dressed in a simple gauzy lawn shift.

Rella gasped. Jul? Were they choosing Jul?

Barros leaned forward and said softly, "I should have warned you. It is our way that she comes naked before her people. They will remove her shift to let everyone see her before she is crowned."

"Why?" said Rella stiffly, not liking that little Jul must endure this exposure.

"To show the future queen is who she claims to be. The magic of the head of each family will reach out and touch her gently. From that moment on, everyone will recognize her. The Dark Queen will not be able to disguise herself from her people, and no one will be able to disguise themselves as the Dark Queen."

"But only the head of each family?" asked Dagstyrr.

"Yes, they will pass the knowledge on to their kin," said Barros.

"The knowing."

"That's right!" Barros didn't hide his surprise that a human had such knowledge.

Dagstyrr whispered to Barros, and Rella listened intently: "I thought it would be Patrice. She is the eldest."

Barros's smile sounded in his voice. "No, that's the human way. Not ours. Why do you think everyone kept her in the background, never allowed her to bear arms? I will explain in more detail later on."

The sisters were putting down the bier in front of Lady Berta. With the help of her sisters, Jul stood up calmly.

Rella looked around and saw the men in the hall were closing their eyes. Of course, they only needed to see her with their magic. Rella nudged Dagstyrr's rib with her elbow and whispered, "Close your eyes," which he did immediately.

Nan and Sophy removed her shift, and she turned in a slow circle. "Once, that all might know the Dark Queen. Twice, that all might recognize the Dark Queen. Thrice, that all might pay homage to no other as the Dark Queen," intoned Lady Berta, while Jul turned in three slow circles. She turned, unashamed, exposed in her womanhood for all to see, her eyes cast down demurely.

"This explains why her sisters were always so protective of her. I thought it was just because she was the youngest," whispered Rella. She noticed Viktar frowning hard, not liking this part of the ceremony at all. He had not only closed his eyes but had turned his head away from the ceremony.

Patrice covered Jul with a swan's-feather cape. Then all

her sisters led her up the steps of the dais before lifting her onto the throne. She hugged the cape around her as she looked out across the hall, her dark eyes soulful in her pale face. Her four warrior sisters arranged her hair and cloak to their satisfaction. When they were sure all was in order, they each stood behind one of the chairs. Lady Berta had retreated and was now standing next to Viktar.

"You can open your eyes now," whispered Lady Berta. "I'm afraid this goes on for quite some time, but as it happens so rarely, no one wants to miss it."

One by one, the four older sisters swore their allegiance to Jul. They took the time to promise to protect her, counsel her, and bear children for her to instruct in the ways of the dark fae. Rella turned to Berta. "Won't she have children of her own?"

"No. That is the queen's sacrifice. Her people are her children now," replied Berta.

"It also ensures her children don't take precedence in the next generation," said Viktar wisely, his eyes focused on the ceremony unfolding on the dais.

Always the strategist, thought Rella, smiling again at the flowers disrupting the back of his otherwise perfect light fae mane of golden hair falling below his waist.

Later that night, Dagstyrr still had many questions. They were in Berta's new rooms. Now that she was no long sister to the queen, she'd had to vacate her old ones. Boxes and trunks lay about, spilling her treasures into the room, and giving the place a sense of casual elegance. Barros was attempting to explain why the youngest daughters became queens.

"Ask yourself this, Princess Rella," he said, obviously using her old title on purpose. "What is the most important tool a monarch has?"

Dagstyrr and Viktar were listening intently. She listed them, counting off on her fingers. "A monarch needs people to rule, land to house and feed them, and an army to protect them."

"All these and more," said Barros.

Dagstyrr had been thinking of Calstir and his cold, marble palace filled with formal unsmiling courtiers. It was hard to make a favorable comparison. Then he remembered Calstir's first actions on returning to Casta and turned to answer Barros. "Is it counsel?"

Lady Berta tapped him on the shoulder with her fan. "Well done, young man."

"Jul has always struck me as wise beyond her years," said Rella, remembering Jul's quiet presence during all the critical meetings. How her wisdom was dispensed quickly and quietly without a fuss, and her sisters were always present to support her. *I should have guessed it would be Jul*, thought Rella, taking a sip of wine.

"Her wisdom runs deep in her," said Berta. "When we tested her, she scored high."

"You tested her?" said Rella, shocked.

Viktar's hand rested on her shoulder, "Don't worry, it is not like the Crystal Mountain fae. Simply an indicator of the future."

"How do you know?"

"Barros has been instructing me," he said.

"With her sisters to counsel her, there will be a pearl of formidable wisdom ruling the dark fae," Rella added, beginning to understand.

"The Dark Queen cannot marry, nor bear children. She is married to the people," said Barros.

"Yes, you said. But that seems very unfair." said Rella. "Is she at least allowed a lover?"

"No, indeed, she is not. It has been our way for thousands of years. No pressure was exerted on Lady Jul to accept the position. Indeed, no one would have thought badly of her if she had declined it," said Berta.

"Has anyone ever declined it?" asked Viktar, sounding cynical.

Lady Berta laughed. "Why yes, Viktar. I myself declined that honor in favor of my sister Aletha. You see, I had already met Barros's father, and nothing, not even a crown, would have kept me from him," she said with a loving smile for her son.

"What if she changes her mind?" said Rella. "She might meet someone and fall in love as you did."

"It has happened, but only once that I can recall. Being the Dark Queen is a full-time job, at times a difficult one, and not to be taken lightly. She has the love and affection of all her subjects. Her sisters will marry and give her nieces and nephews to teach and help raise."

"She will be instrumental in raising her nieces and nephews? Again, that is strange to me," said Rella.

Berta smiled. "They will enter her council chambers once they are old enough, and have proved themselves worthy."

"So, Barros, you were part of Queen Aletha's council?" said Dagstyrr.

"No. I was too young, and intent on being an army commander," he said quietly. "My two brothers and three sisters were part of her council. They all died with her when we lost the queen."

"I'm sorry," said Rella, looking at Berta. Perhaps she had judged the older woman harshly after all. Having lost her whole family, Berta sought to save her last child. She'd just gone about it the wrong way.

The door burst open, and the Threme sisters entered, laughing gaily. They were now dressed for feasting. Gone were the stiff uniforms of battle maidens and the swan feathers of the Dark Queen. They wore gowns of silk adorned with live flowers. Yet, Jul still looked like a queen. Her gown was snow white and sparkled with diamonds that looked as if they had fallen from the night sky, and she wore a circlet of swan's down on her head.

Barros leaned in toward Dagstyrr. "You probably think it strange that we don't all feast together in the great hall, as you would?"

"It had crossed my mind," said Dagstyrr.

"Tonight is sacred. Each family group feasts together, separately from the rest. My mother hosts the feast for the incoming queen, as she is the only one of Queen Aletha's sisters left. From now on, this day will be celebrated as a feast day while Queen Jul reigns."

"Queen Jul. It sounds so strange," said Rella with a broad smile. "To think this morning she was offering to fix my hair!"

"I still will. Anytime you like. I enjoy doing hair, and yours is so beautiful," said the Dark Queen, collapsing on a pile of silk cushions. Rella had rarely seen her so animated. She was no longer the quiet youngest sister. Jul was what she had always meant to be, the Dark Queen.

Servants interrupted them with trays of food and glasses of rare sparkling wine. Suddenly, everyone seemed to realize they were hungry and settled down to enjoy the feast without toasts or protocol—like a family.

"Where is Billy? If this is a family occasion, he has none, and I'm not sure Captain Bernst's family will welcome him," said Dagstyrr.

"He is difficult to have around with all his strange ways, but don't worry," said Patrice. "There are only one or two of the Bernst family here, distant cousins I believe. They have taken him into their house, on condition he sails with the captain."

"All Bernst's family are distant cousins, but I understand there are a lot of them," said Rella.

Dagstyrr sat back and relished the normality of the lively scene in front of him. He still ached in places when he moved too fast or twisted awkwardly, but that would soon pass.

Seeing the happy family celebration in front of him sent his thoughts flying to Drago and his family. Tomorrow he must set off to rescue one hundred and sixty-eight dragons, not counting hatchlings or eggs. He had no idea how he was going to muster enough men or ships.

"Englesten!"

"Excuse me?" said Barros.

"What happened to Englesten? He was there. In the tower," said Dagstyrr, remembering gripping the elf's hand and seeing the end of the battle, but nothing else.

Barros laughed. "Why do you think we call him the Ghost King? He comes and goes as he pleases."

CHAPTER 33

T he sun threatened to rise through the windows of
Thingstyrbol, gracing their bedroom with its eerie
predawn light. Restless, Dagstyrr stood by the
open window, sipping the remnants of the sparkling wine
he and Rella had enjoyed earlier.

Nightmares of Drago had invaded Dagstyrr's sleep, and
not even Rella's presence could banish them. Half remembered dreams of when he was strapped to the Emperor's
web mixed with his fears for Drago's family and created new
terrors. Once more, he'd dreamt that *he* was the dragon
spouting fire and bringing death to everyone in sight. Then
he'd awoken with a terrible thirst and a heavy sense of
danger.

He could feel Drago's presence there in the background
of his mind. He need only reach out, and the dragon would
come roaring to the fore.

It was time to attack Hedabar.

He would speak to Captain Bernst. Dagstyrr hadn't seen
him since the tower, except for one brief moment in the hall
before the ceremony. Still, he couldn't begrudge the captain

celebrating with his family. Who knew when he'd see them again?

Today he and Rella would leave this idyllic place with Bernst and Viktar. Dagstyrr knew he was in for the fight of his life and was glad to have Bernst with him. The citadel would not fall easily. Bernst's unique ability to mind-speak could mean the difference between victory and failure.

The sparkling liquid slipped down his throat, cooling and sweet. He twirled the glass between his fingers, remembering Rella's delight last night when she first sipped the rare wine. Was he wrong to take her with him against Drago's wishes?

He looked over at his woman sleeping soundly in their bed. No nightmares had troubled her this night. Watching Rella in repose, he thought of how much he loved her, and how much he liked the flower mark gracing her face. The one she hated so much that he dared not tell her without risking her ire.

He sighed. If he didn't take her with him, she'd only follow, which would be far more dangerous. Dagstyrr wondered how many dark fae warriors from the wild fae camp would still want to fight for the dragons. He knew most would have returned to their families now that the Emperor was dead and it was safe to do so. Would they return to sail with him?

Only Dagstyrr, Bernst, and the crew of the *Mermaid* were promise bound. He also had the *Viper* and the *Knucker*. But he needed far more ships and men to stand a chance of success.

"Where are you?" mumbled Rella from deep in the covers.

"I'm here," he said, gazing out the window.

The swish of sheets alerted him to her leaving the bed.

Wrapped in a cocoon of cotton, she came to him. He opened his arms and held her close. "Are you sure you don't want to stay with the wild fae?"

"Quite sure," she mumbled sleepily. "Anyway, Fedric and Reckless will manage fine. There will be very few left in the camp. Most will have returned to their homes."

"Can you trust them?"

"They're both young and ambitious."

"Bound to make mistakes then," said Dagstyrr, grinning.

"I'm hoping Reckless will help Fedric come to terms with being dark fae, and Fedric has all the training needed to lead a small army."

"So, do you want to return to the wild fae when this is over?"

"Where else? I know Queen Jul would make us welcome here, but this is not our home. Neither is Casta or Halfen-haw. I like living free with the wild fae."

"I rather like it too."

"Good, then you won't mind living there. Wherever *there* happens to be."

Dagstyrr remembered the nomadic life of the wild fae. "Have you thought about what happens when we have children?"

"Children!"

"It is normal," he said, dropping a kiss on her head.

"Not for some time, I hope. We have dragons to save first," said Rella, wide awake now.

"Yes. One hundred and sixty-eight dragons, not counting hatchlings or eggs," they chorused.

A knock at the door interrupted them. "Come in," answered Rella before he could stop her. He must remember to talk to her about that.

A servant stumbled in, followed by a large warrior with

bright red hair who strode into the chamber and brought
the fresh ozone of the sea with him.

"Father!"

"Earl Magnus," said Rella.

"Dag, why didn't you tell me?"

Feeling like a boy again, he said, "Tell you what, Father?"

"About the dragon," he growled.

Both Rella and Dagstyrr groaned. "Who told you? Erik?"
said Dagstyrr.

"No. Some Crystal Mountain healers stopped at the
castle looking for a ship they'd lost. They told us. I should
have heard it from you." His steely gaze pierced the distance
between them. Then he looked away, confusion surfacing
on his face. "I think I may have made a mistake."

This was some confession from the great Earl Magnus.
"What do you mean?" said Dagstyrr, ice running up his
spine.

"Get dressed. We need to get you both out of here, now."

"Why?"

"I brought the Crystal Mountain healers with me."

Rella groaned, then hurried behind a screen to dress in
fresh leathers. Using her magic, she took no time at all.

"They tricked me. They don't care about the *Drake*. I
found out yesterday that what they really want, is to test
Rella," Magnus roared, fury in every syllable.

"Test her?"

"Aye. Get your boots on, Dagstyrr. We must leave. They
are in the great hall, demanding the Dark Queen hand her
over."

Just then, Barros and Lady Patrice burst into the room.
"Are you ready to go?"

"They want me to submit to their tests to see whether I
am mad or not," said Rella.

"Aye," said Bernst, running in. "Trouble is, no one has ever survived those tests."

"How do you know this?"

"I hear a lot of things. Turning dark isn't as rare as everyone pretends. There are new cases every year, but once the Crystal Mountain healers get a hold of them, well, that's the last we hear of them," said Bernst.

"We leave now," said Dagstyrr, strapping on his sword belt and secreting his knives. No one was taking her from him!

"I've alerted the ships," said Bernst.

"Aye, and mine are ready to leave, too," said Magnus.

"This is not how I envisioned leaving Thingstyrbol," said Dagstyrr checking his weapons and thinking of all the dark fae warriors he was leaving behind. It couldn't be helped. Rella's safety was more important.

Rella pushed her way into his arms. "It is time to go, my love. I have kept you from Drago long enough."

He looked into her dark eyes so full of love and adventure. "You're right. It is time to rescue some dragons."

In the deepest recesses of his mind he felt Drago's laugh.

The End

ACKNOWLEDGMENTS

Although writing is a solitary occupation, no book exists without the help and guidance of those who have gone before. I have been exceptionally gifted with the wisdom of so many—too many to mention here. I owe a special thanks to my critique group, Naomi, Shereen, and Solveig whose unending patience keeps me on the straight and narrow. Kathleen and Nancy who are so very generous with their knowledge and advice. To Jacqui and Taryn for their expertise, and last, but by no mean least, Lynsey G. for her editing skills.

Any mistakes in this book are mine alone. I hate typos, but sometimes they slip through. Please send any errors to **jane@janearmor.com**. I am very grateful to any eagle-eyed readers who take the time to contact me.

FROM THE AUTHOR

Hi,

Thank you for taking the time to read my book. I hope you have enjoyed reading Rella and Dagstyrr's story as much as I enjoyed writing it. I am always happy to hear from my readers and you can reach me easily at JaneArmor.com. If you have the time, I would love to read your review of *Wild Fae* on Amazon, Goodreads, or just tell your friends. It would mean a lot to me.

I am working hard on launching the third book in this series, *Dragon Fae,* and am beyond excited to see Dagstyrr come face to face with Drago

You can find an excerpt from *Dragon Fae* on the next few pages. I hope you enjoy it.

Yours truly,
Jane

Review *Wild Fae* on
Amazon, Goodreads, and BookBub

DRAGON FAE – EXCERPT

CHAPTER 1

Rella of the wild-fae crouched next to Dagstyrr inside an alcove in the Palace of Thingstyrbol. Despite the cool stone of her surroundings, a bead of sweat dripped slowly down her spine. Rella slipped her hand into his, not ashamed to take comfort from her mate's protective presence. "Ready?" she whispered.

His eyes sparkled in anticipation of their adventure. "Ready."

Seeing the corridor leading to the grand staircase was deserted, Dagstyrr led their small party of warriors silently through the upper corridors of the palace.

Today, their quest to rescue the dragons began. They should be leaving the Dark Queen's domain with fanfares and celebration. Instead, they were sneaking out of the palace like thieves to avoid the newly arrived Crystal Mountain healers. The threat they posed to Rella was too great.

Not understanding the danger, Earl Magnus had brought them to his daughter-in-law Rella's very door. Now, he was helping the couple escape the powerful clutches of the healers.

It was the second day of Queen Jul's reign, and the last thing Rella wanted was to bring chaos to her palace. Which was bound to happen if the healers found her, because she would not let them take her without a fight.

Suddenly, the palace of Thingstyrbol rang with the sound of marching feet. Rella tensed as they all drew back into the shadows.

The new Dark Queen prepared to enter the great hall to receive the Crystal Mountain healers. Rella saw her glance up as she passed below, and was relieved to see Queen Jul wink at her. Jul would keep them busy with unnecessary pomp in the great hall to give her friends time to escape, but how long could she delay them? As soon as the doors closed and the palace guards were on duty outside, Rella, Dagstyrr, and the others would make a run for the ships waiting at the docks.

This would be Queen Jul's first test of diplomacy. Word of Rella's dual magic had spread, leaving her status too controversial for the Queen to openly favor her friend. However, the newly crowned Dark Queen was under no obligation to help the Crystal Mountain healers. On the other hand, she certainly didn't want to make enemies of these influential fae so early in her reign.

Crouching down, Rella's party moved off following Lord Barros and Lady Patrice, both of whom knew the palace well. Earl Magnus, the light fae commander Viktar, and Captain Bernst followed close behind.

My ships are ready to go. Earl Magnus's longships have just tied up, so it won't take long to turn their oars around, Captain Bernst's voice sounded in everyone's mind, which came as no surprise to anyone, except Earl Magnus. The big human warrior stumbled when he heard it, and he shot a look of concern toward his son.

Dagstyrr put his hand on his father's shoulder and nodded to let him know all was well. Earl Magnus frowned and shook his head. Despite being married to a light fae princess, Earl Magnus wasn't used to the diverse gifts of the dark fae. When dark fae sailed with humans, they kept quiet about what they were.

As far as Rella knew, Bernst's gift of telepathy was

unusual even among dark fae. He was undoubtedly a very rare man, and she treasured his friendship and wisdom. He'd steered her thought difficult times before.

Queen Jul will keep them talking an hour if we're lucky, certainly no longer. We must hurry, said Bernst. As if anyone needed telling.

Rella hated fleeing from anyone. She'd rather face them, but she dare not submit to the Crystal Mountain healers' testing. There was always the chance they'd pronounce her mad, then plot to kill her. The possibility of madness was something that troubled Rella in her darkest moments. She knew the lore as well as any other light fae, having had it drummed into her since childhood.

Those who turn dark,
Will be eaten by darkness.
First, you will kill,
Then you will enjoy it,
Then comes madness,
Only then, will your evil consume you.

She had turned dark. She'd killed. She'd experienced the Dark Emperor's madness first hand, and then witnessed his evil pour black and foul from his body before consuming him. Was that the fate awaiting her?

An involuntary shudder tore through her. Shaking off morbid thoughts, she huddled closer to her mate, taking comfort from Dagstyrr's protective energy.

The tall doors of the great hall slammed shut, and Bernst nodded. *Time to go,* his voice whispered in their heads.

They took the stairs two at a time. Music playing in the

great hall dulled the noise their boots made on the stone steps. Rella and Viktar, who were extremely light on their feet, winced as the dark-fae and humans among them clattered to a halt at the foot of the stone stairs.

The young human boy, Billy, came running down a hallway toward them. "Where are you going?" he said, aiming straight for Captain Bernst. The captain lifted him in one hand and clamped his other over Billy's mouth. Together they ran for the gate, Billy squirming like a bag of eels in Bernst's arms.

All the way down to the wharf, they could hear Bernst in their heads entreating Billy to stop squirming. *We're leaving now, Billy. Time to rescue some dragons, like we promised. Remember?*

At that, the boy struggled harder.

I have to take you with me, boy. It ain't safe for you here.

Rella and Dagstyrr glanced at each other, both mirroring the other's concern for the boy. Billy had been traumatized more than once. Now he went about telling everyone he was dark fae while waiting for the magic to appear from his one hand. It was never going to happen.

Bernst was his best chance of a semi-normal life, but for some reason, Billy had taken against him. One thing for sure, it would be far too dangerous to leave him at the palace of the Dark Queen. The wild fae had ignored his strange antics in respect for Rella, but too many dark fae at the palace took offense at a human boy, spouting the ridiculous things he did about dark magic.

Rella looked at the ships gracing the harbor. "I didn't realize you'd brought your whole fleet, Earl Magnus," she shouted in delight as they raced along the pier.

Besides the *Viper* and the *Knucker* belonging to Captain

Bernst, and the *Spider* on loan from Lady Patrice, six other longships bristled with warriors.

And of course, the sentient *Mermaid* had changed her shape to a longship in order to navigate the shallow waters around Thingstyrbol. Rella's heart lifted when she saw her. She tightened her grip on Dagstyrr's hand and shot him a smile. His grin told her he shared her joy. Together, they were going to fulfill his promise to the dragons—at last.

People were stepping aside to let them pass. They probably guessed what was happening. Word of the Crystal Mountain healers visiting Thingstyrbol would have spread quickly. One or two wished them 'safe journey,' others frowned, not sure what to make of it all.

Earl Magnus shouted orders to his captains, his bright red hair standing out like a beacon in the sun. For the first time, Rella recognized what a target Earl Magnus would be in battle. It was something she'd never had to consider before. Only humans sported that strange hair color, and even then, rarely.

Earl Magnus's captains relayed his orders, and his men obeyed without question. They might be disappointed at not getting shore leave at such an exotic port, but they followed orders to a man. These warriors were well disciplined.

Laughing, Dagstyrr picked up Rella and ran with her up the gangplank of the *Mermaid* before depositing her on the deck, and with a swift kiss farewell; he leapt across to the *Viper*.

When he turned to glance back, Rella rolled her eyes, but then she laughed too. She hated him picking her up, and he knew it. Rella may have been brought up a princess, but as a warrior and a very powerful fae, she didn't need his assistance walking up a gangplank.

The ships were ready to leave on the quest to rescue one hundred and sixty-eight dragons, not counting hatchlings or eggs from the dungeons in the citadel of Hedabar.

Rella watched Dagstyrr signal his father to pull his ships out of the harbor first. But the *Mermaid* couldn't leave without her captain, and Bernst still struggled on the pier with Billy who continued to shout his frustration. Lord Barros and Lady Patrice lifted ropes from bollards to free the last few ships from the quay.

Rella watched, as without warning, Billy reached for the knife at Bernst's belt. Sun glinted off the lethal blade in Billy's hand before he drove the knife into the captain's gut. Bernst stilled, staring at the boy dumbfounded.

"Barros!" screamed Rella, as she watched the bloody knife in Billy's hand ready for another assault.

Billy stabbed his mentor again, and then with a quick flick of his wrist pulled it out, only to thrust it into Bernst's belly over and over. As Rella's anguish grew her magic energies pulsed through her veins threatening to burst from her fingers. She had to focus hard on reining it in, because the distance and angle of the *Mermaid* meant any battle magic she used was as likely to injure Bernst as save him. And it was impossible to heal from this distance—all she could do was watch as the *Mermaid* drifted out of the harbor.

Horrified, Rella could do nothing as Billy continued to twist the knife in Bernst's abdomen, pulling it out then thrusting it in—exactly the way Bernst had taught him. Patrice and Barros raced to Bernst's side, but not before Billy had inflicted lethal damage.

Blood gushed over the wooden quay as Lady Patrice bound the hysterical boy in dark-fae ropes of magic. Barros knelt, holding the dying captain. Bernst's deep voice sounded softly in their heads. *Do not punish the boy.*

Rella, you must captain the Mermaid. *Dagstyrr, make sure you free all those blasted dragons. I don't want to die, leaving my family promise bound to Drago.* Everyone heard him but was too stunned to say anything amid the unnatural silence that had descended on the wharf. The bright sun shone, warming the onlookers. The only sound was the cry of a lone gull searching for its next meal.

With his head tilted to the side, Billy stood staring at what he'd done, a quizzical look on his face. Lady Patrice took the knife from his hand and held his shoulder firmly.

Lord Barros cradled the dying captain in his arms. Rella saw the big warrior wave a puff of dark green magic over Bernst's head and she knew it was to relieve the pain. "Are they not even going to try and heal him?" she shouted from the bow, refusing to believe what had just happened.

She hadn't heard Dagstyrr come aboard until he placed his hands on her shoulders. "He is a dead man Rella, not even you and Gimrir together could put right that kind of damage," he said gently, as they watched Lord Barros lift the captain into his arms. "Nooo!" Rella's anguished cry echoed in the hearts of all who heard it.

~

Dagstyrr knew how much Rella loved Captain Bernst. He'd been her mentor, guide, and protector since she first turned dark. "I'm so sorry, Rella."

She turned to face him. "The Crystal Mountain healers!" she exclaimed, her eyes bright with unshed tears. "They can help him," she said, her voice rising in desperation as the *Mermaid* drifted further from the quay.

"No Rella, they won't work with dark fae or humans,"

said Dagstyrr. The spellbound crew stood like statues, staring at the tragedy unfolding in front of them. "Lift the oars," he commanded. If the crew were too stupefied to row, at least the could save the oars from splintering against the quay or another ship.

The men obeyed without taking their eyes off the bloody scene in front of them.

"I can make them heal him," she said, determined. "I have to try." Her words sent warnings dancing up Dagstyrr's spine.

"What do you mean?"

"Those crystal fae want me. I want Bernst healed. We'll strike a bargain. I will pay the price," her commanding voice sounded a brisk staccato in the salt air.

Dagstyrr pulled her tight against his chest. "Don't even think about it," he said.

The *Mermaid* was drifting back toward her dock. He had no idea whether by tide or magic or by whose magic, Rella's or the *Mermaid's*?

"Rella, stop it. We need to escape these crystal fae, not bargain with them," said Dagstyrr, knowing as he spoke that if she was determined, there was nothing he could do to stop her.

"They will bargain with me," her eyes were set on the scene being enacted on the wharf.

He pulled her close so that all she could see was his face. "Don't do this, Rella," he pleaded, his voice rough with emotion.

"I must," she said, her hand soft against his face.

He could drown in those eyes, yet he knew he couldn't make her change her mind once it was made up. Especially when she was about to launch a rescue mission for her friend and mentor. Rella never gave up on anyone, it was one of the many reasons he loved her, but this was one sacrifice too many.

He saw the crew staring at them. They had heard her proclamation to save their captain, and now they stared at her expectantly, waiting for her to follow through.

"You understand?" she whispered.

Dagstyrr wrapped her in his arms and kissed her letting all his anguish and love pour into her. Her arms came fiercely around his neck as she clung to him and he knew for certain that she was going to try and save her friend.

CHAPTER 2

Rella didn't wait for the gangplank. She jumped from the ship's rail to the wooden quay. Behind her, Dagstyrr's feet pounded after her, but he couldn't match her fae speed. Kneeling beside Lord Barros, she reached out felt the flickering pulse at Bernst's neck.

"I have given him the warrior's last balm," said Lord Barros, his deep, steady voice told Rella it wasn't the first time Lord Barros had administered this rite for dying comrades.

"He's not dead," said Rella, trying to hide the panic in her voice.

"No, the balm is to ease the pain of passing to the next life," said Barros.

"Come, Rella, there is nothing we can do here," said Dagstyrr, going on one knee at her side. "Captain Bernst would not want to be the reason those healers get their hands on you."

"What do you mean?" said Lady Patrice.

"Rella wants to bargain with the Crystal Mountain healers—Bernst's life for hers," said Dagstyrr.

Patrice knelt beside Rella, "My friend, they do not treat our kind. You will be sacrificing yourself for nothing."

Neither Patrice's concern nor Dagstyrr's determination could sway her. "Dagstyrr, Bernst has never asked me for anything. He has always been there for me, for us. Without him, I would never have transitioned so easily to dark fae. I would probably have died in the streets of Hedabar."

"I know he is your friend. He's mine too. We both owe him so much," said Dagstyrr, his blue eyes dark with emotion.

Rella turned to Dagstyrr. "He taught me how to heal. Please understand, I cannot desert him now."

"Drago," whispered Dagstyrr. Rella felt the name pulled from him in a sigh of anguish and understood the depths of his pain. She knew the dragon's family suffered in the dungeons of Hedabar. Dagstyrr could feel their agony like no other. He was a dragon-talker.

He stood, pulling her up and into his arms. "I will be right by your side when you speak to them in the great hall, but no matter the outcome. Promise me. We will sail free from here today."

Patrice stood, pity in her dark soulful eyes. "They won't let you. Once you are in their power, they will never let you go," she said.

"I must do this," she said, "and quickly."

"I will not be parted from you again, Rella. Do you understand?" Dagstyrr's words of warning sent relief coursing through her. She was not nearly as brave as she sounded.

Unable to hide her gratitude, she smiled. "I never doubted you."

"I mean it Rella. Remember Casta? I will do the same here if I have to," he said.

"Very well. You must carry Bernst. I will take Billy. Lord Barros and Lady Patrice should not be part of this," said Rella, taking Billy's hand.

"Of course we are part of this," said Patrice, her shoulders squaring ready for a fight.

"You are the Queen's sister. Who knows what is about to happen? You dare not be part of this."

"You don't seriously expect me to allow you to walk in there alone?"

"I am not alone," she said, looking at Dagstyrr. "Lord Barros, I beg of you, talk some sense into my friend," said Rella walking a stunned Billy toward the palace of Thingstyrbol.

Rella saw Dagstyrr's face become a grim mask as he carried the unconscious captain into the palace. Bernst's torn body dripped a path of bloody gore behind them. If only Dagstyrr knew, it was his presence that gave her the courage to do what she must.

As he strode into the hall, Dagstyrr looked around with the practiced eye of a warrior. She had no doubt he'd call on Drago for assistance if he had to, but the last thing she wanted was to destroy Queen Jul's palace. It had only just been restored to the dark fae.

At their approach, a hush descended on the dark fae courtiers. They carried their unconscious friend toward Queen Jul's throne and the Crystal Mountain healers. The healers were imploring her to bring Rella to them. "Ah, there it is," said one of them at her approach. The relief on their self-satisfied faces was nauseating. They stood very tall and thin, their white beards and hair hung to their knees, giving their youth a solemn appearance.

"It? I am *it* now?" said Rella, her voice pitched to bounce along the hall's length. She saw Queen Jul's stunned expression quickly replaced by her more usual calm concern.

Rella marched Billy right up to the foot of the throne dais and gave a warrior's bow on one knee. "Your Majesty, there has been an accident. We need the help of your guests."

Queen Jul stood and stared sadly at the open wounds spilling foul-smelling gore from Bernst's belly. "An accident?"

Addressing herself to Queen Jul, Rella pleaded in true courtly style. "I ask that these crystal healers, use their skills to mend Captain Bernst's wounds. A more worthy man there never was." Out of the corner of her eye, she could see the crystal fae shudder and step back.

"I heard you had some skill. Is this too difficult for you?" said Dagstyrr, not even trying to hide his hostility.

"We only treat our own kind," said their leader, distinguished by his belt of red miridion crystals.

"You mean you only treat *light* fae?" said Queen Jul. "How dare you come to my court, seeking my assistance."

"Your majesty. It has always been so."

"You dare to come here asking to test Rella of the dark fae, yet will not heal one of ours," said the Queen, cold anger in every word sending an icy wave through her court. A murmuring of dissatisfaction hummed through the hall.

"*It* is different. *It* started life as light fae, then turned," said one of the crystal fae with undisguised revulsion.

"If you call Rella, *it* again, I will kill you," said Dagstyrr, his voice calm and dangerously low. The last thing Rella wanted was a fight. She needed an arrangement with the healers. Then she must leave—quickly.

The Crystal Mountain healers frowned and talked

among themselves as if no one else was there. It appeared that in their eyes, a human was even less than a light fae turned dark.

"If he doesn't kill you, I will," said Patrice, appearing from behind the throne, her hand resting on her sword hilt. That got their attention. As the eldest sister to the Dark Queen, Patrice would not be ignored.

"Enough," said Rella. "My apologies, your majesty, but Captain Bernst needs attention now." She turned to the leader of the crystal fae healers. "I will come to you and be tested after we have saved the dragons. In exchange, you will heal, Captain Bernst. If you fail, I will not subject myself to your tests, and you will no longer pursue me." Rella felt every word leaving her mouth bind her like a chain.

"Why should we let you go? You are here now. We have you," he said, lifting his hand and spinning a rope of bright white light that reached out for her, but not before Dagstyrr reached her side.

She sensed the strong magic in those ropes was hungry to hold her. When the white snaking light reached Dagstyrr's protective field, they suddenly stopped and fell to the ground, useless. "Do we have a deal?" she said.

Shocked, the crystal fae stepped back from her. "What are you?" shouted one at Rella. Not realizing it was Dagstyrr, a human, who had stopped their energy ropes.

Rella squared her shoulders, "I am Rella of the wild fae. Now, are you going to heal Captain Bernst, or not?" She knew the captain's time was running out.

Once more, they huddled together, talking very fast, arguing. Two of them wanted to leave, but their leader was adamant.

"I will accept your proposal, only if you swear on Queen Jul's throne that you will return to us and be tested," their leader said with a smug grin. Oh, he wanted her under his control very badly that much was evident to everyone. Rella had never seen such blatant craving on the face of any light fae.

"No," gasped Queen Jul, rising to her feet. Everyone here knew that by swearing on the throne, all dark fae would then be bound by oath to make sure Rella fulfilled her promise.

"Agreed." Rella's agreement brought a collective gasp from the dark fae gathered in the hall.

The leader of the crystal fae looked smug, his companions less so. One of them had an expression so frozen only Rella, who had once been light fae, could recognize it—fury.

"We will keep the human boy as a hostage. You appear to be rather fond of him, and your reputation for not paying the agreed price goes before you. The last time you started a war and killed thousands."

These men knew how to puncture a person's vulnerability. Rella squared her shoulders and ignored their taunts despite the guilt coursing through her. There was nothing they could say that she hadn't said to herself a thousand times. She kept hold of Billy's one hand as he stood relaxed by her side, staring ahead but seeing nothing.

"On one condition," said Rella. "You have to cure Billy as well as hold him hostage. Plus, he must have access to Captain Bernst as soon as the captain feels well enough."

Once more, the crystal fae laughed at her. "Even we cannot re-grow limbs, my dear."

"Perhaps not, but you can cure his mind. It is his mind that is sick."

Their leader rolled his eyes, "Such a simple mind should be easy enough."

"It is not just his mind," said Dagstyrr, stepping forward.

"He suffers from the warrior's sickness. His spirit is infected."

"That is more difficult, but not impossible."

A moan escaped Bernst's lips. The pain-killing magic given by Lord Barros was wearing off.

Two of the crystal fae came forward, "This is not simple healing. The patient's guts are...."

"Slippery and confusing, I know," said Rella. "If a spirit fae and I can heal such a wound on the battlefield, I'm sure you can."

"Spirit fae?" they chorused with disgust.

"Aye, Gimrir, of the wild fae," said Rella, relying on how much the Crystal Mountain healers thought themselves superior to the humble, but gifted, spirit fae.

"I doubt he could do any such thing, " their leader said.

"I saw it done," said Queen Jul her word law in this place. "The youth's name was Fedric, son of Viktar of Casta."

Those names on the lips of the Dark Queen had the desired effect. "I see. Then I have no doubt we will manage easily enough," said their leader.

Rella had never seen crystal fae so twitchy. It might have been because they were in the Dark Queen's hall, but she suspected it was because they couldn't wait to get their hands on her, and now they would have to wait. If those white ropes were a sample of their power, she hated to imagine what tortures they could inflict.

"Nobody said it was going to be easy," growled Dagstyrr.

"When both are healed and the dragons are free, I will return," said Rella, placing her right hand on Queen Jul's slippered foot. The enormity of her sworn promise was dawning on her. To them, she was a thing to be experimented on and tested. Rella fought down a shudder. She would not give them the satisfaction of seeing her fear.

Check JaneArmor.com for release dates.

ALSO BY JANE ARMOR

The Fae Series

Dark Fae - Book 1

Wild Fae - Book 2

Dragon Fae - Book 3

Contact Jane at her website: JaneArmor.com

Made in the USA
Coppell, TX
18 September 2021